The Devil's in Texas

THE DEVIL'S IN TEXAS

T. LIGHT SYLVAN

ALIEN/ROBOT
PRESS

A SPECULATIVE LIBRARY

Paperback ISBN: 978-0-9860954-3-6
Hardcover ISBN: 978-0-9860954-4-3
Ebook ISBN: 978-0-9860954-2-9

Alien/Robot Press

www.tlightsylvan.com

I'm a monster.
Yes, you are a monster.
We are monsters.
And monsters never die.

Lady Gaga

Author's Note

Please be aware this story contains themes and depictions of violence, blood and gore, explicit sexual content, vorarephilia and necrophagia (which involve characters being consumed or consuming others, including dead or decaying bodies, both in and out of sexual contexts). Read at your own discretion.

The Devil's in Texas

Book 1 of The Last Angel

Chapter 1

A

BREATHIN' HURT LIKE HELL. Always did—from the minute he'd opened his eyes in Alexander's desolate bed all them years ago—but this was different. Sudden, explosive. An inferno where there'd only ever been flames.

Soon as he stepped out from the woods, he doubled over in pain. He coughed so hard that thick, dark blood splashed across the dirt, the grass, and the backs of his weathered hands. The dirt below was baked hard from the sun even while the tall grasses swallowed him right up.

This goddamned pain was such a distraction. Always annoyin' and always clawin' for his attention, and now it was just burnin' through everything. He couldn't even think past it. Couldn't seem to forget, the way he could always forget, that the pain was there—diggin' at him and drainin' him away.

It always came back to this. Thirst, hunger, and pain: a well inside he never knew how to fill.

The thirst left him all lean and tough, with brown leathery skin. The hunger left him 'specially weak, but it wasn't like he ever knew what strength was in the first place. He just existed, floatin' through the pain of daily life, and had actually got pretty good at it over the years. This, though—this sudden drop was the worst by far. Like a tree'd fallen on him.

"The hell...?" he choked out.

What was goin' on? He came out to this neck of the woods all the time and nothin' like this blindin' pain'd ever come up before.

Suddenly—a low flutter of sound.

Ba-bump.

Soft yet clear.

The slow beat of a heart.

An explosion of pain boiled up in him again, climbin' his throat 'til he choked some more. He barely managed to keep on his feet.

A *heartbeat.*

Had his...?

No. No, that just wasn't possible. His heart'd went missin' ages ago.

He'd never heard nothin' else like it, though—the sound of a single heartbeat. His own was dead silent. Alexander's always stuttered. This one, this lonely one, only beat once. And yet, it bounced quietly 'round and 'round in his head.

A phantom heartbeat.

The pain started settlin' soon. Quick as it came on, it petered out the same way. He held his breath, straightened up, and tried to listen for another *ba-bump.* A warm, fragile smell met him, like the breeze 'round a single bluebonnet, but the silence stretched on and on. No beatin' hearts answered, just crows and cicadas.

"Maybe Alexander'd know," he said, weighin' his options. Alexander would be at home. He bit the corner of his lip at the thought. Drew blood.

When's the last time he'd visited home? He was out here in the first place tryin' to steer clear of that house. Of Alexander. The deranged doctor. The failed father. Alexander ain't have too many uses left, given all that, these days just keepin' the house for company. But Alexander could still answer his questions, still help him make sense of things. Maybe it'd be worth a trip home, for this.

He turned back 'round in the tall grass and immediately tripped.

"The fuck...?!"

How sway? Did the goddamned wildflowers and strawberry bushes trip him or what? He'd barely even taken a step.

He glanced up from the ground toward where he'd come from for a better look.

There, sprawled lifeless in the tall grass now, lay a corpse.

He darted back.

"Where the hell'd this thing come from?" And still—how could he've tripped over it without even realizin'?

He shielded his face from the endless curls that always escaped his hair tie, closed his eyes, and took in a slow, meaningful breath. That same fragile smell from before surrounded him. More than a single flower, now the scent overpowered the meadow 'round him. Even if he somehow overlooked the corpse on the way here, there was just no way he could've missed this smell.

Sun-hot petals and stems. As dreamy as the corpse's placid face.

Most of its features were plain and neutral, with some slighter slopes, some steeper angles, deep brown skin, and everything below the neck wrapped up tight in formal black. A cloud of silver curls matched the eyebrows and lashes. Cold, glitterin' contrast.

For a while, he just stared at it, movin' slowly closer. But he couldn't be more sure—both the soft smell and the quiet heartbeat he'd heard earlier belonged to this corpse.

Somehow.

'Cause if that really was true, that heartbeat had to've been its last. In fact, he could almost convince himself he'd imagined it.

"Hey..." he said, just in case, crawlin' to its side.

When there was no answer, he put a hand on the shoulder and eyed the corpse from head to foot. And it absolutely was a *corpse*, but if he didn't know no better, he'd say it was somethin' more, too. Somethin' else. Somethin' greater. It'd be too plain to call it just a corpse. He'd been 'round corpses before, sleepin' in cemeteries. But he'd never felt this bizarre, gut-deep pull.

And he'd never seen a corpse look like this, either.

"Like a star," he said.

That's what it reminded him of—a distant shootin' star that'd fallen to spend the rest of its life sleepin' with the bluebonnets.

Somethin' 'bout this mysterious corpse, this fallen star, called out to him. Lured him in.

Each of his breaths started burnin' like hell again. Lanced through his lungs. More, more, more. Overpowerin', like before. More blood inched from his throat. Copper-muddled roses. Strong as the smell became, so did the pain and the hunger—and somethin' else, too.

An urge to eat.

"Eat."

He said it without even thinkin' 'bout it, but for the first time, his sudden, explosive hunger seemed to make sense.

He needed to eat to live.

He just didn't need food like everyone else. His teeth always ached. Once or twice, maybe, he'd tried eatin' from Alexander's dinner plate. Hated it. Purged everything. Alexander'd just called him a freak and quit sharin'.

Now, his whole body said only one thing.

Eat.

He was supposed to eat this heart that'd reached out to him. He didn't need food for energy. He needed—this. More of this. To live.

Eat...

He yanked the fallen star's collar down to their chest. Leaned in close to the exposed skin. It wasn't warm, but the sun must've kept it from growin' cold, too. The delicate flowerlike scent deepened. Incense smoke, ozone.

"Perfect," he mumbled, gums throbbin'. He moved almost automatically.

Eat!

He opened his mouth, slid his tongue over his lips, and pressed them to the fallen star's throat. It started off a bit like a kiss, but it didn't end up like any kiss he'd ever had before. He ripped right through the skin. The smell hit him first—burnt leaves.

"Mmh..."

Then a splash of hot blood. Warm, wet meat introduced to his tongue. He drank and ate, and drank and ate, and ate, and ate, and ate some more. Everything he swallowed poured into all the scorched corners inside him. Nothin' else in his life'd ever felt so right as this one moment. Tissue, and fat, and water from every organ filled him the way he'd never been filled and calmed him the way he'd never been calmed. The corpse was wine and butter. Minerals, oils. Electricity.

Slowly, the fire inside sputtered out. The well shrank. For once.

As he crunched down on more bone than blood, he found himself movin' on. Searchin', gulpin', and devourin' wide swaths of the body as he did. He wasn't even payin' attention anymore. For the first time since he could remember, he didn't have to. He could just let go—indulge in this wretched, painless peace. And it was so peaceful, here, where nothin' hurt. Not breathin', drinkin', or eatin'. Not a single moment of pain.

Just... peace and quiet.

The kind that could only come from followin' his instincts, instead of fightin' them all the damn time.

It was difficult to tell, at first, but as he fed his hunger, he began to find his strength. His body started to solidify, to center itself—like all the blood and grub he drank down rushed to fill the gaps in his veins. Like it was settin' right an ancient, unknown wrong inside him.

With each mouthful, his mind stretched wider, pullin' in the essence of the fallen star. Fragmented echoes of its past seeped into him: the steady assurance of certainty, the searin' agony of betrayal, and the unyieldin' war zone between them both. All of it kick-started his senses and flooded him with impossible colors.

It felt like wakin' up for the very first time.

He belonged here. Right here. He needed to do this. It was *him*. It was right.

It filled that deep, empty need inside.

He couldn't stop and couldn't let go.

Wait.

Fuck.

He really couldn't let go—he was caged in place.

The fallen star had both of their strong arms locked 'round him, each finger planted deep enough to dig into his skin. It didn't hurt, but he couldn't break free. The grip was steel. He froze in surprise, unable to draw a breath, and coughed up a mouthful of bloody fat and muscle as he struggled.

"Let... me... go..." he sneered.

Instead, the fallen star struck like a snake and bit him back.

Pain blasted down half of his whole body. It almost knocked him out, as drunk and confused as he was. He'd been more than sure that the fallen star was dead, and he'd never experienced pain that wasn't his own. It was so big. So much bigger than him. His body went slack.

He'd thought it was so right to follow his instincts, but now he was trapped.

And worse, his instincts shifted as the fallen star clung to him, drainin' him. Killin' him.

Now, instead of *eat*, he felt the same, soul-deep pull to *die*.

To let the fallen star eat him up just as he'd done to the fallen star.

To end his new life just as quickly as it'd started without even so much as a fight. He deserved no less for turnin' himself into a weapon like he had. No more pain. No more aimless questions. No more constant hunger.

Just let it end.

Die!

"All right—!"

A red light flashed.

It flickered in the corner of his mind—an impression like a half-forgotten memory, or somethin' seen only in a dream, but it was there. A flash of fierce red light.

Then nothin'. Just the fallen star's teeth deep in the side of his neck—its arms frozen solid 'round his shoulders. As if woken from death only for a second to drag him under, too.

When he tried to fight, his body didn't even respond anymore. He could only keep still exactly the way he was. Could only sink into the growin' abyss that unfurled in his mind and threatened to drain the lil bit of life he had left...

Another flicker of red light.

Still small, but warmer, that same glow flashed again in the corner of his mind. Like a gold ring, glossy with fresh, red blood.

A ring of blood.

Gradually, the red light burned bright crimson, and a beautiful calm deadened all the noise and unease inside him. Only the warm, red light remained. It was nothin' at all like the aura of dead flowers that emanated from the fallen star. It shone from some indistinct place inside him and filled his head with a soft, sunny voice.

Wake up, it said.

The command crashed through him.

An unseen force ripped him away from the fallen star. His back slammed into the hard, packed dirt, but he didn't feel it one bit. He only saw black. The city of Houston disappeared.

In its place, a second later, huge, jagged mountains and boilin' rivers sprung up all 'round him. Dozens of broken, war-torn bodies littered the ground, soaked in gore and stretchin' as far into the horizon as he could see. Burnt earth seared his lungs. Above, a few bright blue collisions of lightnin' hit so close that he almost withered from the heat.

His eyes were opened, but his sight was someone else's. Someone who'd lived through hell.

Wake up, the voice said again. Bright. Distant.

And just like before, he obeyed without even thinkin'.

Sat up in the grass and clutched his head as he fought off the vertigo of returnin' to reality. Sun-shimmerin', tree-shaded Houston lowed in the distance.

The fallen star'd collapsed next to him, motionless. Half of its mouth was black with blood while the other half—chewed off earlier—exposed a pair of long twin fangs. Their nails, too, dripped with blood from diggin' into his back. He gulped down another spike of nausea. It was impossible to focus. Everything inside him raced, like it'd only ever crawled before. He was so full of blood, of new knowledge and organic upgrades. If he tried to get up, he'd probably just topple right back into those hellish visions.

"Wake up..." he repeated aloud.

What exactly'd woken him up?

The sky was clear overhead. Sunlight bleached all the blue. It burned a blurry red stain onto his mind. Just like that red light from before.

Slowly, breath by breath, it seemed to calm him down again. The smell of ash cloyed in his throat, turned to metal. He steeled himself and cast a glare back at the fallen star.

Or what remained of it, anyhow.

He'd devoured a good portion of the face, shoulder, and chest, but even on the parts of their body that he never got to touch, the skin and muscle'd started to rot and fade away. Like some sick kinda advanced decay spread out from where he'd bit into it.

His throat tightened up. He couldn't let it go. This fuckin' thing left him with more questions than answers.

And it tasted incredible.

He dove on top of it even as it continued rapidly crumblin' to damp ash. His hand landed in a dark gooey puddle, and before he'd even shoved it into his mouth, the nausea hit again, once and for all. Everything in his gut came up in a thick, odorless purge. The discolored vomit covered the fallen star's fadin' ashes. Soon, though, just like the corpse he'd eaten, the vomit started to disappear, too. He was left alone, always alone, in the overgrown fields and woods outside the city, fightin' the endless hunger that burned away inside.

An empty well again. Not a man; just a void.

Chapter 2

A

H E SPRINTED BACK TO Alexander. Couldn't get there fast enough. Found his way back to the trees he called home, then booked it out the other end, and hit the freeway without even stumblin'.

Downtown Houston's illustrious reach ain't come quite this far outside of town, but there were still lots of its traces out this way. He had a good rear-view of Space City's huge, mirrored towers lined with vertical gardens, green roofs, and hydroponic farms. Buildings like that stretched all the way from downtown to the burbs. Further out, followin' 59 South 'til wide, flat plains flanked him like wings, the towers gave way to sprawl. The land rolled with thick green shrubs, acres of solar and wind farms, and tall trees on either side of long, windin' roads.

This place was the only *real* home he'd ever known. The wild woods 'round here always seemed to shelter him when Alexander didn't feel like doin' it anymore. He preferred the air outside to the crowded walls of Alexander's house, anyway. Though, it probably had less to do with the empty house than with Alexander. He hadn't stayed in that house at the same time as Alexander in years.

Ideally, he'd keep it that way. It'd taken a decade to escape.

But he had to know what Alexander could tell him 'bout this fallen star.

And this new life of his.

Everything whizzed by in a second as he tested out his new strength. Somehow, in a thousand ways he couldn't name, he moved differently now. It was clear in his joints and nerves that his movements were looser, less restricted. He ran like he'd been born to do it.

In moments rather than hours, the farms started to thin out, replaced with huge, isolated ranch-style homes that branched way off the freeway. He spotted the wide circle driveway of Alexander's ranch house sooner than he was expectin' and almost ran smack dab into the honkin' white F-150 there.

Ding. Welcome home, A.

That was his only name. A. He refused anything else. The front door pivoted open as he approached it.

Alexander stood, doe-eyed, on the other side: a tall Black man with an effortless smile and locs that fell in long, dark lines down his chest. His smile was gone, though. Missin' in action. And his shirt and tie sat on him haphazardly, like he'd spent the past few nights in them. Again.

"Alex?" he blurted. "What're you doing here?"

A—*not* Alex—took a reflexive step back. That name always set him on edge. Narcissistic ass Alexander'd had the nerve to name A after himself, take him home, make a pet of him, then just dropped him like a brick one day. Took a trip outta town and ain't come back for two years, once. Then did come back, pathetic and bruised, swearin' to never hurt A again. Too late. A refused to accept the name after that. It was the name of someone who'd promise him a pretty life just to use him up for everything he was worth. Far as he was concerned, he really didn't need a name.

How could he, really, anyway? He ate half a fuckin' corpse-thing in the woods out there and still had no idea who—or what—he was. A name was the least of his concerns.

"Quit callin' me that," he barked, his teeth grindin' together. "Not in the mood."

That's right. On top of everything else, the empty well inside started to groan and stretch again, make him bear down. It was mild, for now. Normal, for now. Pain that he could force himself to forget. This was how it usually went—not the growin' blaze that'd arrested him earlier. Even the memory of it made him clutch at his chest, short of sympathetic breath.

"Whatever." Alexander grimaced as he stepped aside and pulled A into the house by the arm. "Fine, then. What're you doing here, *creature*? You look like you spent the last week rolling around at the bottom of some old grave."

As A caught his breath, his hair slipped the tie and fell across his face. It clung to thin, sticky swaths he hadn't noticed before on his cheeks, neck, and chest. Patches of dirt—or the ashes of the fallen star—smeared his skin and clothes blackish. Alexander's eyes flickered over him, first with disdain, then somethin' sharper, piecin' together what could've brought on all this mess.

Pinpricks of heat crept up the back of A's neck. It wasn't shame, not exactly. Maybe exhaustion, or frustration, or the uncomfortable sensation of bein' seen at his lowest when he was barely holdin' it together. His fingers curled against the filthy fabric of his shirt. He wiped the front of it with a slow, deliberate motion, liftin' his eyes to meet Alexander's.

His voice came jagged, low. "Maybe."

"Really? You expect me to believe that?" Alexander grabbed A's arm again and slammed him against the wall. The floor-to-ceilin' windows that lined the foyer shifted to frost, hidin' the domestic dispute as Alexander stabbed at A's chest with his free hand. "The only way you're getting out of this, now or ever, is when I turn you over to State Troopers. So stop with the lies, and tell me what in the fuck I'm looking at, Alex, or I swear to heaven and hell, I will march you downtown quicker than greased lightning."

A rolled his eyes and knocked Alexander's hands away. It was a lil thing he did all the time.

Something'd changed, though.

Alexander collided with the opposite wall, and the lights of the foyer blinked twice. *Warning: material damage.*

A paused at the tinny voice. The casual display of such strength. It'd been too easy—alien strength.

Then he cracked a thin smirk.

"Don't you put your fuckin' hands on me again. Now you know better," he said with a scoff. He'd have killed to be able to shove Alexander like a few years ago. Too bad he hadn't found the fallen star sooner. "Turn me over to State Troopers, huh? They'll lock you up before me, and you know it. Only reason they haven't yet is 'cause your husband's your shield."

"I damn well—!" Alexander heaved and huffed, and clutched at the back of his head with a lost look in his eye. Slowly, the steam poured out of him, like an old pressure valve'd cracked open, and he sank to the polished hempcrete floor. "Yeah... Jack is my shield. That's true. But if Jack's the shield, what does that make me? Huh? No, I get it. Do me a solid and quit reminding me about shit like that. I was horrible. I'll never live it down. It was just a giant mistake, I already told you. Stay here as long as you want, come and go as you please, use my credit anytime. Just don't keep throwing it in my face. Please. I can't take it."

A usually let Alexander's morose pity parties roll right off him. Nothin' ever really bothered him. Nothin' ever could, with all the pain and distress takin' up his capacity to feel anything else.

But now, after his evolution away from all-consumin' hunger, the stupid shit dribblin' from Alexander's mouth made heat race up A's face in a way he'd never felt before. He braced himself against the wall. His chest tightened to a pinpoint.

"Can't take it? What's to take, Alexander? Havin' to look me in the face after you fucked me half to death?"

"I—" Alexander started, then stopped, starin' blankly at A as if he couldn't figure out what he was lookin' at. "You know what, Alex? Touché. Let's just stick to the old arrangement. Don't ruin my night any more, and I won't ruin yours. You win. Please, just go wash up before I lose it. Speaking of looking half-dead."

A bit back his laugh. It shook off some of his tension, but, somehow, he got the impression it didn't do the same for Alexander.

"Now, listen here." The man creaked as he clambered up from the floor, a teeterin' marionette on drunk strings. "There better not be no State Troopers at my door in the middle of the night because of this. I really will turn you over to them first chance I get if you give me reason. Jack's been itching for it for years. Just cut it out with this—this zombie shit. Christ almighty."

A laughed outright this time. It was rare—the sound came out rusted, toneless, and brief—but what the fuck. *Christ almighty.* Two words he'd never heard Alexander put together before. Maybe the man's mind was as useless as the rest of him now. All those years spent under his husband's wing, worshippin' at the feet of his own cruelty, and where'd it leave him? Fumblin' in a neglected house, cursin' like a relic of a man. Maybe this was just what happened to assholes who loved monsters. Maybe it was the natural progression of a sycophant, left aimless without their perfect, passive pet to grind down into the dirt. Either way, Alexander paid for *somethin'*—with his spine, his will, and, apparently, his brilliant mind.

"Zombie?" A said, wipin' the laugh from his mouth. "S'that the best you could do with that big brain of yours, Doc?"

"Oh, without a doubt. I'm surprised I didn't think of it sooner, to be honest with you. I think I'm finally seeing clearly. You got to be a zombie 'cause you sure as shit can't be human."

Huh.

Not human, at all.

Now there was a thought A'd never considered.

He'd never been able to find out much 'bout who, or what, he was before he met Alexander. Was he a zombie? Could that be the answer? Could it really've been the fatty brains he munched on that quieted the need inside him? He'd barely reached the fallen star's skull, though; searchin' more for blood, for meat. For life.

"Maybe," he said. He could live with maybe. He'd lived with worse 'til now. "Maybe not."

"What in the hell is that supposed to mean?" Alexander swung his hand out, but caught himself from listin' sideways by pressin' it back to his head. His eyes sharpened to a glare. "Listen. Cut out the disgusting jokes. That shit makes me sick. My life is hard enough without you making a mess of every single thing you touch. Do you even know why I'm home right now? I had to leave the hospital early today. Boom—full-blown relapse before lunch. Now they want to pinch my PTO. 'No more mental health days,' they said.

"'Well, then, I guess I'll just have to take some *unpaid* leave,' I said, and so here I am." He paused, his glare deepenin'. "Right. Here I am. Stuck in this fuckin' house with you."

"Welcome," A said flatly. Disasters couldn't get him to comfort Alexander.

"You know, I brought you here because I thought I could love you. I kept trying, even after I figured out I couldn't. I had no idea yet that monsters can walk among us. Monsters and nightmares, like you. *Damn it*, I'm so tired." Alexander rubbed his eyes with forefinger and thumb.

A snapped his molars together so quick that his temples throbbed as he kicked off the wall. "Oh, fuck off. Can't listen to this shit anymore. You could've left me to the authorities or turned me over any time you wanted. Instead, you trapped me here and used me, just to have someone other than yourself to hurt. Been here twenty years, Doc. I know you. You don't change. Got over it a long time ago. You should, too. It's gettin' pathetic."

"Pathetic." Without much defense, Alexander deflated and hung his head. "I'm so goddamned pathetic. You're right."

A ain't said nothin' but the truth. Alexander'd pawed at him so much in the first few years that A just rolled over and took it.

He'd thought he wanted to, or at least, *should* want to fuck a man who so clearly wanted him first. He was pathetic, too. Ignorant.

It was hilarious how ignorant he'd been back then. Even now, he could fill oceans with his questions. All he knew was this house and the Houston woods. Way beyond the plains of Texas, what was the world even like? What'd the distant past been like before the world united? He only knew that which Alexander taught him to look for answers to.

And so, A'd stayed. Through everything, he'd stayed. Graspin' at the bars he'd built on his own cage.

None of Alexander's drunk, sloppy gropin' mattered, compared to that. The answers to his questions—to his constant, incessant hunger—were worth everything. He sacrificed his body everyday to pain; at least, this way, he got to choose what his sufferin' would be for.

"Like I said, let it go, Doc. I'll just shower and jet, get on out your hair. Sun's fixin' to set, anyway."

"Wait, really? But you just got here. Will you come back soon?" Alexander asked, with big, shameful eyes. His whole body shifted with each change in mood. Every few weeks, he seemed to sink further into his own mania in this way. He looked so sad. Depleted.

A didn't care. Memories of Alexander's skin and teeth on him made sure of it. "If I need somethin', yeah."

"If?"

"If."

As he said it, A grinned to himself. He and Dr. Alexander Esmeralda were done. They'd probably been done for years by now. If anything, maybe they'd never really started in the first place. Maybe it was always just coincidence and desperation tyin' them together. He'd never loved Alexander. Never loved anyone. Never even wanted to. At least Alexander'd tried.

"You fixin' to join me in the shower or what? Otherwise, I'ma head out."

For a second, Alexander actually looked as if he was considerin' A's offer, but after another second, he caught onto the rib. "Goodnight," he hissed, and turned to disappear up the underlit staircase. The bedroom door pivoted quietly shut behind him.

Tonight was just effervescent with mirth. A let out another small, rusty laugh as he paced lazily down the first hallway. It might be the last time he ever saw these busy walls again. He wouldn't miss the cracked vines that curled underfoot. Not even a lil bit. Big as the place was, Alexander's creepin' mania filled up most of the space inside, turnin' the walls and rooms into features of claustrophobia. Dilapidated stereolithographs, potpourri, burnt incense, lopsided bookcases, towers of old, glass candles, and broken tablets covered in last fall's crunchy brown leaves littered every flat surface. Beneath, the dim inlaids in the baseboards cut on, synced to his preference for low light, so they barely lit the way.

Yeah, the man that Alexander'd once been was steadily fadin' away, replaced with this spiralin' fella who couldn't even tell A why the sky was blue anymore, much less what set him apart from humanity. Wasn't worth the trouble even askin'.

It was clear A'd never understand himself or the world the way that Alexander saw it now. He'd have to find another way. His own way.

The bathroom door pivoted open as he approached. Warm lights, white tiles, black grout, and soft steam.

Ding. Evening, A.

The gentle scent of herbs and oils rose with the staccato sound of water from the tall faucet. He stripped quickly out of his clothes and stepped into the large walk-in shower. More slick white tile and rollin' steam. Under the downpour, his mind cleared.

The bullshit with Alexander, the State Troopers, even the fallen star—all of it washed away.

Everything except...

Wake up.

There'd been that voice that said, *Wake up.*

While he was trapped and bein' drained to death in the fallen star's grip, that voice'd come from somewhere so faraway. Somewhere warmer and calmer than the fallen star. Maybe, from the ring of light that'd—what? Saved him? Warned him? Snapped him out of it, at least.

What was that ring of red light, anyway?

If not from himself. If not from the fallen star.

And why'd it lure him to live?

Still so many questions. What a waste of fuckin' time it'd been to come back here.

Cleansin' water pounded on his head, soakin' the length of the small black curls that lay over his shoulders. Silver strands, and skin, and meat disappeared into the drain. A full minute passed before the water ran clear again. Black, red, pink; clean.

Chapter 3

ERO

"FINALLY!" ERO WHOOPED AS he sank into the disorienting abyss of the Bridges of Chaos, a wide grin etched on his face. He couldn't help it. The Empyrean Spheres he left behind him had become so stifling lately; he never thought he'd get the chance to leave.

But now, he was on his way to Lesser Earth.

Finally.

First, he had to calm down and navigate the Bridges of Chaos. A thousand crosswinds stole the smile right off his face.

"All right, focus."

It quickly became difficult to breathe, much less speak. Ero closed his eyes, slowed his pulse, and tried to settle his nerves as he kept hurtling through space. As much as he'd prepared for this moment, the Bridges of Chaos still demanded every bit of his concentration to navigate. This inky, interstitial space separating the material and immaterial worlds lacked so many definitions he was used to—light, gravity, and time among them. There were periods he'd done without one or the other back home in the Empyrean Spheres, but never all of them at once. It was chaos, indeed.

Clear head, clear heart. Clear head, clear heart.

Cerviel's advice filtered into Ero. Clear his head, so he could clear his heart. If he ever lost himself—be it in the throes of the Bridges of Chaos, or in pursuit of his mission—he could always rely on her guidance. Like a mother's advice, he had needed it often.

More often than he should need it, if he asked anyone back home.

Heat caught on his shoulder, erupting into an invisible flame. "Shit!"

He had to focus. If he didn't get his head straight, he'd be consumed before he landed.

"Come on, clear heart..." he urged himself through grit teeth.

He couldn't help the doubt, though. The invisible flame at his shoulder slowly spread down his arm as his mind whirled and whirled. Save the effigy and save the world—that was all he had to do to prove himself once and for all. The faith of all the Empyrean Spheres hinged on his efforts here. This mission was the last thing that prevented him from earning it. Then, no one could question him anymore. Everyone back home would have to respect him—some would probably even trust him.

And yet, the flame reached farther back to brush his wing. It licked across feathers and cartilage. A shock of pain stabbed him deep inside. Gasping, he tried to scream, but no sound came out.

Pain meant nothing. He wasn't afraid. He just had to clear his head—

A second later, he slipped and drowned in the darkness.

Water was the first thing he remembered—it had shattered against his impact like a bullet through glass and swallowed him whole. In the water, everything was warm.

Now, only the cold remained.

Ero shuddered, fully waking up as he did, and sprang to his feet. His wings clattered against something behind him, so he spun around to inspect the damage, only to end up creating more confusion and chaos. Glass vases and pale pinkladies clattered to a rug on the floor. Just what on earth...?

"Oh, right," he said.

Exactly that—Lesser Earth.

The world that remained after the last apocalypse.

Distinct from the Infernal fires of hell or the celestial Empyrean Spheres, the Original Earth used to be a perfectly safe cocoon for mortal life. Nature evolved here with effortless balance. Then the angels fell, new civilizations rose, and humans were left on their own. In the end, the Original Earth surrendered to one apocalypse after another, leaving behind fresh, new copies—other Earths. Lesser Earth was one of many realities.

Ero shook his head.

How had he managed to forget his lovely trip through the Bridges of Chaos to get here? The struggle still seemed so clear now that he remembered it. The doubt, the fear, the fire, and the pain that followed still stung. Cerviel would stroke his face to console him, if she knew. Ireul would strike it.

He forced himself to ground. Clear head, clear heart.

Where was he now?

He scanned the room: baby blue walls, a spiral staircase in the far corner, and a small collection of furniture crammed into every available space. Beside him sat the large couch he'd been asleep on a minute ago. His long jacket still lay there, rumpled, dripping wet, and missing huge, tattered patches. Panicked for a second, he clutched at the edge of his wing where the doubt and fear had dug into him before. There was no lasting damage from the flame, thank goodness. Just the same gaping holes in his shirt that matched his jacket.

"Enough," he said with a harsh sigh. So much for grounding.

He couldn't keep thinking of Ireul and insignificant failures. It was these racing, pacing doubts that Cerviel always warned Ero against—being his own worst enemy. She would also warn him that he didn't have to be perfect.

He just had to start.

First, he had to deal with the person who'd brought him here. "Where are you?" he murmured, engaging the eclipse matrix in his mind as he lifted his eyes to the ceiling. "Ah, there you are..."

His unique gift, the eclipse matrix, enhanced many of his un-conscious strengths. His senses multiplied until he could reach through the ceiling to sense the woman above. All the information that he needed to know about her answered him—the smell of shea, the color of lavender, and a warm ocean breeze. That was her, Dr. Lios Grey Hartsend.

She tip-toed down the stairs, eyes on the steps, until she stopped before the landing. "Oh!" she said, hesitating once her gaze met Ero's. "I guess all that noise woke you up, too?" She had shoulder-length curls pulled up into a top knot, and deep brown eyes that hid behind square glasses. A curious Black woman with a careful nature, she reminded him of Lesser Earth. They were both fragile and full of ruins that whispered of past failures. He would have to be careful with her. Most of the others back home might not care, but he couldn't help it. Her caution made him want to cover her. Lios was the first human he had ever met. Who knew if he'd ever meet another?

The least he could do was thank her properly before he started his mission. Right—he had to keep his mind on the mission. Clear head, Ero.

"Yes," he said, forcing a smile. "It was me. Sorry about that. I just came to. Thanks for helping me out back there."

Lios didn't say anything. She didn't seem to know what to say, even though she parted her mouth as if she wanted to ask a heavy, wordless question.

Ero tried again. It'd be characterless to leave her with such a damaged impression of him. He was better than that. He had to be.

"Your name's Lios. Right? Mine is Cerviel, but you can just call me Ero. Pleased to meetcha." He stretched out his hand.

Lios cleared her throat and adjusted her glasses, turning her eyes away. "Excuse me if I don't shake your hand. I did bring you here and all, but it's like you said, I fished you right out the Gulf. The currents brought in a ton of sediment last night. You're a bit filthy."

Ero grinned as he took his hand back to flip a few salt-crusted curls over his shoulder. "And yet, you brought me home. I slept on your couch." He nodded back at it. "Right here."

Lios let out a startled breath. Hot needles of embarrassment pierced through her and settled like sediment in Ero's gut.

He rubbed at his stomach through his clothes. Was this what guilt felt like?

"Sorry. I'm being rude. I can wash up, no problem."

"No, you're right. I'm the one who brought you here. I couldn't help but drag you out of the water. There was somethin' about you... You got to understand, I lecture over at A&M, and I was just on my usual walk to the park-and-ride this morning when I saw you out there, all of a sudden. You looked so peaceful, like you were taking a nap, and I almost left you well enough alone at first glance. Funny, huh? But something drew me to you, and it was like I *had* to bring you home. I even took a sick day. Don't ask me why. I just couldn't let you out of my sight. You were light as a feather when I carried you here on my back. None of it makes a lick of sense."

As she stopped talking, Lios looked to Ero. Her eyes were wide behind her glasses, and her aura—the energy field around all living beings which reflected their inner self—was full of murky confusion.

"You have wings," she finished.

Ero's heart squeezed. Ghosts, like him, often had that effect on humans.

He took pity on her with another smile. "Yes, I do. I guess, from where you're standing, it really doesn't make any sense. Let me start over."

He waited until she thawed—until the needles dispersed in her belly—then extended a hand for her to take again.

"I'm Ero."

"Lios." She accepted the handshake warily.

As soon as their skin touched, Lios' unease dissolved. Ero's aura overtook hers and calmed down all the worries, fears, and anxieties that muddled its color. A faint, mysterious purple peeked through, telegraphing her sensitive demeanor; as lavender as the smell of her charming little home.

"Amazing," he whispered. He'd never felt anything like it.

This was the first time he had ever touched the heart of a human. It filled him with warmth and purpose that he'd ever known—despite his entire existence revolving around both.

Ero's job was to protect humans, like Lios, but it almost came secondary to his life mission. In his wildest imagination, he couldn't have predicted how spectacular it felt just to fulfill his most basic of functions. He'd spent his whole life surrounded by other ghosts and never cared about one of them as much as he did Lios.

Why? Was there something special about Lios? Or something wrong with Ero?

Lios didn't hear him. Now that she was more comfortable under his influence, she pulled an arm from behind her back, which revealed a set of dry clothes that she had fished from her wardrobe earlier. "Well, if you're not going to answer me, you can at least put these on. They probably won't fit too well, not for a while, anyway, but you won't have to stand there drippin' wet in half-burnt clothes while the fit adjusts. Go on," she said, and used both hands to press the clothes to Ero's chest.

He grabbed them. Dry, warm, and snug, everything was black, the way Ero's own singed clothes were. They would be tight for a while—Lios only stood at about five-five. Still, he craved the kindness that came so naturally to her. Ghosts never had time for kindness. Cerviel's training sessions were as close as he'd ever gotten.

"Thank you, Lios," he said, gushing, and set the clothes along the arm of the couch. It was the only dry patch left.

"Y-you can wash up before you change if you like..."

"Of course. It'll just take a second."

Ero flashed a smile, brushed his frizzy, rosy curls behind his shoulders, and tucked his wings in tight against his back. Lios had done a poor job of ignoring them, her gaze eager to trace their shape and long, sleek white lines. He peeled off the remains of his old outfit without disturbing a single feather and swiftly changed into his new clothes. The remnants of the old pair vanished when they hit the floor.

"You're beautiful," Lios said. The words seemed to escape her, like water from a boiling pot.

Ero held back a pained smile. "Oh."

He shouldn't have been surprised. He couldn't blame her for not being able to see all the fine, invisible scars that stretched across his body from his intense training. Back home, it was often the only part of himself he felt others could see—like all his tender, battered guts were on display whenever others looked his way—but Lios was human. All she would see was someone solid, statuesque, and flawless. Someone invincible and incredible.

"Am I?" Ero mumbled.

Lios caught herself by shaking her head. "Sorry, I mean, your wings—your wings are so beautiful. They're not real, right, but why's it seem like they are? I..."

Her eyes glazed over until she trailed off again and, as if hypnotized, reached a hand up to brush against Ero's wing.

Ero caught her by the wrist. "Doctor, you really shouldn't do that," he said, sliding his hand firmly into hers. "I wouldn't want you to hurt yourself."

His wings might have looked gentle and ethereal, but, like himself, their glamor gilded razor edges.

"How could something so beautiful hurt?" Lios blinked with consideration. "Shit, I'm sorry. It's just that they're so..."

"To you, they're beautiful. To me, they're weapons." Ero flashed another assuring smile.

Lios nodded, even if only to acknowledge her persistent confusion, slowly clearing a path in the fog of her aura. "You're dangerous."

"In some contexts." Ero snapped to attention, arms at his sides, and then half-bowed to her. "In this one, I'm just an angel."

"Angel? You're an angel?"

"Yes. At your service." He straightened up, watching her closely.

Confusion passed like a shadow over Lios' face for a long while before her eyes lit up. A kaleidoscope of curious colors melted into her aura. It formed a light that peeked out from inside her, so bright that it overpowered her earlier nervousness. Her sleeping passion, prodded awake.

"You are... an angel?" Lios tried again. "That's why you're so beautiful and dangerous?"

"In some contexts." Ero laughed gently.

"I don't think I understand. Why would there be an angel on Earth?"

"Don't worry about all of that. Seriously, even if I gave you all the answers, you wouldn't be able to understand them. It's the human condition. In fact, forget I'm even an angel. Just think of me as a ghost. You know what ghosts are."

As an immaterial entity—or ghost—angels had sometimes been understood best in this way. The ghosts of millions of humans who'd lived and died crossed into the material realm everyday. Most humans knew that offhand.

Ero was a non-human ghost, though.

He'd never lived. He'd never died. Like all non-human ghosts, his body was immortal, and his life was eternal. He was the perfect protector. If angels healed, helped, and loved, then Ero excelled at all of that and more.

He couldn't really say too much more than that about his role, task, or life—Lios didn't have anything to do with it, anyway. He had no reason to burden her with such knowledge. He shouldn't have told her anything. He shouldn't have been here in the first place.

But in the same subconscious way that something in him had compelled Lios to Ero, something similar compelled Ero to Lios. He had so much on his shoulders, and yet, all he wanted was to take a seat right next to her on the couch and learn about the world through her eyes. Forever.

Maybe he could spare just a few more moments. Even angels like Ero weren't totally omniscient, and there could always be a hidden reason for this abrupt detour that he shouldn't ignore.

"Ghosts aren't supposed to be real, though," Lios said after another beat. "You are real. I know you are because I carried you home."

"Right, Lios. Ghosts aren't real, and I'm not standing in front of you right now." Ero passed a hand over his hair, finally cleaning and drying it in an instant.

A long silence followed as Lios digested all that she could. Then, with a quick breath, she said, "I guess that explains your red eyes, too!" She belted out a deep belly laugh for a solid minute.

Ero's aura gleamed under the shower of her laughter. It tickled, but it also smarted. It reminded him of everything he wasn't supposed to be—free, flawed, human. Still, it was gorgeous.

"Course! Of fuckin' course! Absolutely, it explains everything! Here, I'd been thinking of all the students I see around campus sometimes, always casually wearing the most outlandish things. A couple of my kids in my class show up dressed kind of similar. Imagine my face, haha. I mean, it *is* technically harmless, so I can't really advise them otherwise in good conscience, but damn." She wiped a tear away as she composed herself again. "As for the wings, I actually have a colleague on campus who built a prototype that looks a lot like yours, so it's not like I'm unfamiliar there, either. Oh, my goodness. I can't believe how eager I was to dismiss all that."

Lios dismally tapped her palm to her forehead.

"Hey." Ero reached across the couch to massage her shoulder. "Lios, don't be too hard on yourself. This would be a lot for anyone. Honestly, I owe you another apology. I'm so sorry that I made myself your problem today. It's my fault that I ended up in the ocean, but it's not like my life was in any danger. You shouldn't have had to get involved."

The words leaving his mouth didn't seem like his own. He heard his voice in his ears, of course, but on top of it, he also heard Ireul's.

Just look at you. Lollygagging with a human when the effigy is still out there, killing. You're useless.

He was useless.

"Problem? What problem?" Lios asked. "I don't recall ever having called you a problem. No matter whose fault it is, I'm glad our paths crossed today. You changed my life."

"Stop that."

"No, I'm serious. Listen. I may not have saved your life out there, but I think you saved mine. I'll never see that spot on the beach with the same eyes. Just what in the hell were you doing that landed you unconscious on the business side of the seawall?"

Ah, right. The Galveston Seawall.

The shoreline appeared in his mind directly from Lios' memories. It dazzled under the early morning dawn when the tides were calm and clear, and the seawall gleamed the same soft way. Why did he end up there, instead of at the effigy's side as he should've?

"Accidents happen." Ero lifted the shattered vases from the floor where Lios had simply stepped over them as if she was used to it. Lots of the cracks had been previously plastered. "Like this. Right? I took a wrong turn, or a spill."

Fortunately. Who knew where else he could've ended up, with the way his thoughts had spiraled toward the end? The Bridges of Chaos were notorious for luring lesser angels all the way to hell.

"Sure," Lios said, perplexed enough as it was. "Let's just go with that for now. Accident-prone angel. So then, you're not from around here, and you're not supposed to be here. Where are you supposed to be, then?"

Ero swallowed. This was the part he'd been kind of dreading. He had to face his mission sooner or later. "Where am I supposed to be...?" he echoed. For a moment, he couldn't differentiate between the knot in his own throat and hers. He tried to center himself by covering the vase in hands with a gold-white light that united all of its broken pieces like new. The pinkladies perched undisturbed inside.

"Let's find out."

Again, he accessed his eclipse matrix and closed his eyes, trying to increase his focus.

This was the first step of his mission—to concentrate on the effigy of evil that plagued this planet, which Ero had been sent here to find.

For a long while—too long of a while—there was no answer. He reached, and searched, and stretched far for anything that would lead him to the effigy of evil, but nothing surfaced.

Nothing except for an empty shadow.

The vase almost tilted out of Ero's grasp. His eyes snapped open as he gripped it around the neck.

Lios barely noticed. "What do you mean, 'find out'? How can you leave if you don't know where you're going?"

A smile blossomed onto Ero's face. It was a reflex—the last thing he wanted to do.

He wanted to dig in, grow roots if he had to, and find out why he couldn't sense the effigy. He wanted to know how it was possible that he could've already failed. For the first time in his existence, he had no idea what to do.

"I'm not going anywhere," he said, distantly. "Not just yet."

He couldn't. The void where the effigy should be gnawed at him—a weight more suffocating than the Bridges of Chaos had been. This time, he couldn't choke. He wouldn't.

He was better than that. He had to be.

Chapter 4

A

"SMELLS LIKE RAIN," A muttered to himself, shielded under a network of pine and oak branches.

He'd spent the whole day tryin' to find the fallen star again, but it wasn't no use. He'd just wound up in the back of the woods by the San Jacinto, fifty-some miles north from home. No matter how long he searched, he couldn't even suss out a faint, crumbled impression of its body in the long grasses. He'd mashed his face in the dirt and still couldn't find a single trace of it.

The fallen star'd withered away.

"Shit."

And his hunger was burnin' again. Without the fallen star, it crawled in his organs, chewed on his veins. He shivered, once, from the strain.

Thunder groaned in the distance, rollin' across the inky sky behind dark grey clouds and droppin' down thick pellets of rain. A didn't even budge at first as the cracked dirt under him thickened up into mud.

For a while, he just sat sinkin' into the rain-soaked ground.

He wanted to sleep—to collapse onto his side and pray for a flash flood to sweep up over him. South Texas thunderstorms were known for doin' worse to better folk. But he couldn't even get himself to relax, much less sleep.

The fallen star'd given him a chance to die. His *only* chance.

For some reason, he had a feelin' he'd never get another. His burnin' appetite didn't drain him anymore, deep as it could be. No, he was too strong and sharp to suffer now. Too different.

Altered by that fallen star.

What else had it passed on to him, huh? Aside from this insomnia and those visions of blood-drenched rings. He'd already seen smoother skin and sharper teeth, too. Caught them in the mirror after showerin'.

His senses had never been clearer, either—he couldn't face his reflection. All those dots and lines somehow came together to form "him." It didn't make any kinda sense. Even the night sky he'd known his whole life, right here over the city he'd always called home, seemed so foreign. This familiar hour was usually black with shadows, not so starlit. It turned everything light, bright blue, glitter-white, and midnight. Deeper colors than he'd never seen—but noticed, now, with a nostalgia that didn't belong to him. It belonged to the fallen star. Everything belonged to the fallen star.

Everything exceptin' the answers he needed.

"Why'm I so fuckin' hungry all the time...?"

Every new reminder made him more and more miserable. The sting of his long-forgotten emptiness soared with regret now. He *needed* more. If only he'd been able to hold onto his fuckin' meal earlier.

A finally stood up in the rain.

What else could he do?

Empty and irritated, he just went home.

Walked. On autopilot, maybe, followin' unconscious pathways. Doin' what he always did.

All he knew was that one moment, he was starvin' in the middle of the storm, and the next moment, he'd stopped in his tracks right outside Alexander's front door.

All the lights in the house were on. Alexander never cut the lights on when he stayed home by himself.

His husband, Sgt. Jack Esmeralda, must've returned from assignment.

A stared through the large pivot door, considerin' the lights inside. He almost turned on his heel and retreated back into the rainy woods, slept in the sodden grass somewhere. Wouldn't be the first time—he'd even take the bank of a bayou over Sgt. Esmeralda.

A Ranger with the Texas State Troopers and a right bastard with pale blue eyes and an entitled grin that charmed the pants off most folks. The kinda person who stuck out like a sore thumb these days, flauntin' that standard issue star, spurs, and Stetson all 'round the state like it meant somethin'. Maybe it used to. Nowadays, it just pissed people off.

And A needed to eat soon. Leather and metal wouldn't cut it.

Suddenly, two dark figures flickered past the frosted front door. One shadow, followed by another, they were the same height and build, like the silhouettes of twins. Only difference were the long locs of one versus the short crop of the other.

Sgt. Esmeralda was definitely home. They disappeared out of eyeshot together.

Well, they moved behind a wall together—so they should've disappeared—but they didn't.

"Oh...?" A hummed.

Both Sgt. Esmeralda and Alexander were too far past the wall to see anymore—usually. Now, with all his heightened senses and the bits of knowledge he'd been able to digest from the fallen star, A clearly saw—or smelled, or sensed, *somethin'*—past the barriers between them. Like the walls'd turned transparent.

Like the married reunion was a show just for him to watch.

"Ha," he whispered quietly.

That goddamned fallen star. That perfect corpse, that strange burden.

It'd changed A in more ways than he'd even realized. Takin' him from the comfort of livin' alone in his head, and forcin' him to feel, or experience, or think of all this shit he never would've done before. He lapsed into a kinda trance, watchin' the couple with a line of curiosity that edged out over his need for a change.

He asked a new set of questions, shit he'd never stopped to wonder even once before:

What *was* Alexander like with someone else? Someone he loved? Was he different? Was he kind or warm at all? Did he still gaze at Sgt. Esmeralda with dead eyes when they fucked? Sgt. Esmeralda'd had the same high-and-tight every time A met them—moments counted on one hand. A couldn't imagine a single scenario where Alexander's cold chaos was welcome there.

But he got his answer pretty quickly.

Alexander finally disappeared somewhat behind a couch as he laid down without takin' his eyes off his husband. The two were so damp from sweat and stuck together that A could breathe it in. Hundreds of sleazy sounds, vibrations, and firin' synapses rose like a soundtrack to the sight on the other side of the wall: A's head was a sudden daze of input. Rosehip, sucrose, tea tree. Please, Yes, No. The stretch of cloth against bare skin, and hot, damp air. It was so close—

Ding. Welcome home, A.

The front door opened. One barrier removed. The vision became a lil clearer.

A crept inside.

Alexander and Sgt. Esmeralda were half-naked now, laid out on a blanket that covered the brittle leaves on the floor. And neither of them'd noticed A. Even Alexander, on the blanket, was too wrapped up in his own lil world, and it all revolved 'round Sgt. Esmeralda's rare weapon of a smile. He pressed their hips together 'til his cock disappeared inside and rocked so smoothly that the heat from their bodies stretched all the way across the room. A was drawn to the friction like a moth to open flame.

He marched closer without thinkin', steeped in the sharp tang of their sweat as he reached his hand out—

"Aaahhhh! What the fuck just touched me?!" Sgt. Esmeralda flinched and scrambled from on top of Alexander, hands barred over their stutterin' heart.

Alexander stood, too, less concerned than confused. "Whoa, something touched you? What? Jack? What happened?"

"Your creepy goddamned rent boy—that's what the fuck happened!" Sgt. Esmeralda jabbed a knife-hand at A's chest. "This son of a bitch just snuck up on me."

"Alex? What are you doing here?" Alexander—finally—seemed to notice A's presence.

A couldn't blame him for not doin' so sooner. Aside from his interruption, he'd always had a habit of makin' himself seem smaller and quieter than he naturally was, and the blood of the fallen star seemed to've enhanced that. Like everything else.

He didn't answer, though. What would he even say? "Home for dinner"?

"Hey, punk!" Sgt. Esmeralda didn't even bother gettin' decent before goin' in on A, black uniform shirt still unbuttoned. "Don't you ever answer a thing anyone says to you? Instead of just standin' there like a hump on a log with that goddamned glare on your face."

Alexander's voice cut in with a weight A'd never heard before. "You don't need to worry about him. He speaks when he wants. It's just that there's nothing important to say. Isn't that right, Alex?" he prompted, and turned to face A with a pained, cracked grin.

A met his eyes. Slowly, he stretched his lips to reflect the fake smile right back.

"Yeah," he said, displayin' the long, sharp tips of his canine teeth.

His favorite gift/curse from the fallen star—so far—four sleek fangs in the top row of teeth, and four smaller fangs in the bottom row.

Alexander's face fell. "Holy shit."

Sgt. Esmeralda shrank back with disgust and a split-second of fear crackin' the facade before they snatched their clothes from their floor. "You goddamned fuckin' sonofabitch ass freak. Them teeth—I always knew there was somethin' wrong with you. Sideways as a snake, and can't even hide it anymore, can you? Are you really not gonna tell anyone what the fuck is wrong with you? I already know what you do while you're out hauntin' the town. Don't you know who I am? Don't you get it? I'm Sergeant Jack Esmeralda of the goddamned Texas State Highway Patrol. I know everything about your little ass."

"Enough, Jack," Alexander said as he shouldered into his wrinkled shirt. The weight'd lifted from his voice, agitated again. "Come on, man. I'm the one who brought him here to live with me. Or don't you trust my decision-making skills even that far, anymore? Is that what you're trying to say? I can't be left in control of my own living situation, including who I choose to bring home? I only tell you all that stuff about *him* because *he's* the only one I ever spend any time with anymore. There's nothing else to talk about with you!"

Somehow, it both did and didn't surprise A to learn that Alexander and Sgt. Esmeralda discussed him. Frequently. He'd gotten the impression that they didn't keep in contact while they were apart, but apparently, he didn't know the first thing about a marriage like theirs.

Sgt. Esmeralda scoffed. "Don't defend your attachment to this creep to my face, like I'm not the one who's always puttin' you back together after he done triggered one of your relapses. I'm not the one who's wrong here. It's *him*. He's a monster."

The final word hovered above everyone in the room.

Monster.

A smiled again. Naturally, this time. Small.

Monster, zombie, or otherwise, he was startin' to get really fuckin' hungry and really fuckin' sick of Sgt. Esmeralda's voice. They'd never had a single civil thing to say 'bout A. And now, A saw it plainer, deeper, and better than ever—right there in Sgt. Esmeralda's face—that they never would.

"Monster?" Alexander echoed, balkin', as if he hadn't accused A of the same thing just last night. "What makes you say that?"

"Huh? You kiddin', sweetheart? I left you to your own devices for a few months, and just look at the state I got you back in. You know how much I miss you when I'm away. Who knows what would've happened if I hadn't've come home sooner? You're not safe here as long as he's around. You"—Sgt. Esmeralda turned to glare at A—"Alex, or whatever your name is, I think it's time for you to leave."

"Mh," A said.

Funny. Really. Rusted laugh and all.

There was nothin' Sgt. Esmeralda could do to intimidate him, aside from tote 'round that damn State Trooper title, but that seemed just plumb stupid now.

Ya know, considerin' A was a monster, or whatever.

"Now don't you make me repeat myself." Sgt. Esmeralda wiped a bead of sweat from their face. "I will arrest you in a heartbeat if you test me, you freak. Leave, before I haul you downtown in my just-been-fucked clothes. I don't give a shit. Either way, you're out of my goddamn marriage once and for all."

"Jack, hey, c'mon," said Alexander. "It shouldn't have to come to that. You know how hard I worked to keep him and me clear of the system with this whole situation. He's still missing from the Network, and you know that. It's not fair to either of us if you turn him in just because I made a mistake. Don't blame our problems on him. He's a symptom, not a cause."

Wow. Alexander had somethin' of a heart.

A kept his surprise to himself, though. The boilin' thirst in his blood was startin' to make him dizzy. He leaned against the closest wall while Sgt. Esmeralda sneered at Alexander.

"Not a cause? How's this gnarly ass stray *not* a cause? Everything was fine before you took him in just because you were high, low, *and* horny one night. And to top it all off, you hide him away in this house like some kinda idiot child. Missin' in the Global Identification Network, I couldn't give less of a shit about. Millions of motherfuckers escape registration every year. None of that is what does it for me, Alexander. What fucks me up most is that you refuse to even admit what he means for you."

Alexander cowered back. "And what's that?"

"You're sick! Alexander, it's that you're sick! You can't hide from it forever, and it's ruinin' everything 'cause you try so hard to. I can't put my life on hold to take care of you just because you refuse to take care of yourself anymore. If you wanna be my partner, you'll step aside and let me do this my way. Your way sure as shit ain't workin'. Move aside, sweetheart. I'm puttin' an end to this once and for all, for both of us," Sgt. Esmeralda said, reachin' toward their loosened utility belt.

"I wouldn't," A said in warnin'. He'd been tryin' to keep himself together.

Tryin' and failin'.

The pain found a way to reach deeper than before. He couldn't ignore the hunger for long. It was stronger now, just as he was stronger. The best he could do was do nothin' at all.

"Watch me," Sgt. Esmeralda said. "Go on and put your hands where I can see them. I'm through playin' games. I hereby place you under arrest—"

It was the last excuse A needed. Soon as Sgt. Esmeralda took a step toward him, he moved, too.

A reached out, swift as a scorpion's tail, to grab Sgt. Esmeralda right 'round the throat. He only pushed gently away, but the unconscious strength behind it slammed Sgt. Esmeralda against the nearby wall.

"No."

Ding. Warning: structural damage. Please contact the County Central Appraisal District right away.

"Jack?!" Alexander cried.

"Nghhh..." Sgt. Esmeralda cast dazed looks at the walls and batted at their throat with tremblin' fingers. Delicate streams of blood trickled from their scalp, a streak of red over their blue eye. "What happened? Where are the lights? My head..."

A didn't hear the morose ramble. His heart was thunderin' in his chest, rattlin' rib bones. Never racin', but deep—and loud. A slow, powerful pulse he'd never had before.

Sgt. Esmeralda's blood almost glittered as he stared at it. Just like earlier, when he'd been watchin' Sgt. Esmeralda and Alexander fuck on the livin' room floor, A was drawn to it without thought. Reached out to it without realizin'.

And slowly, yet suddenly, he licked a stripe of blood from the leakin' wound.

"What're you doin' to me?" Sgt. Esmeralda struggled away but couldn't get far. The concussion took care of that. Words slurred.

Alexander finally managed to stumble over. He appeared at Sgt. Esmeralda's side after, as slow to process everything as he was to cross the room, and clamped his hands 'round A's arm.

"Hey, get your hands off Jack!"

"Shut up." A tightened his grip on Sgt. Esmeralda and shoved Alexander away with his free hand. "You got one chance, you hear me? Get outta here or somethin'. Can't see I'm tryin' to spare you?"

Alexander stumbled back, tripped on a stack of books, scrambled to Sgt. Esmeralda's side again. "Not without Jack. I can't live without Jack. I won't. Let them go already. Please!"

It really was pointless.

A'd already made up his mind for tonight. Bein' threatened made everything easy. And Alexander made his own choice.

"I said no." A squeezed down on Sgt. Esmeralda's neck and twisted 'til they started to gurgle, face blue from fightin' the lack of oxygen.

"What are you doing?! Alex, hey, stop! Alex! Stop!"

With his target in place, A struck.

He flashed his long, sharpened fangs for a second before sinkin' them into the meat of Sgt. Esmeralda's throat.

This time, unlike with the fallen star, he knew exactly where to bite—an imaginary, or just faint, dark line that ran down the center of the neck: the jugular.

It opened and released a flood of thick, rich blood into A's mouth. Creamy as crushed roses. He slurped it down with gratitude, windin' himself 'round Sgt. Esmeralda so he could get more. More, more, always so much more...

As he ate, the life in the blood showered over him. Sgt. Esmeralda's life. Their childhood growin' up down south by the Mexican border, where their family'd been for centuries, their meet-cute with Alexander in undergrad, and the opportunity they saw in hitchin' themself to a promisin' young physician. After that, a blur of depression, desperation, and anxiety. And the State Troopers—the only glimmer of hope in Sgt. Esmeralda's aimless life. The only thing worth chasin'. The only thing worth livin' for anymore.

Then, the end.

Sgt. Esmeralda convulsed for another minute before finally goin' still, limbs limp at their side.

Shhlp... Shhlp...

The deep, meaty suckin' sounds echoed in the house. A ate and drank, deep as he dared, holdin' on tighter and tighter as the mess unfolded. His eyes locked with Alexander's.

Neither of them moved while Sgt. Esmeralda died.

Finally, the hunger inside simmered down. An imperfect victory—this person didn't compare one bit to the fallen star. Satisfyin', but insignificant. Still, better than starvin'.

Alexander shuddered. The force of it almost knocked him off balance. "W-what just happened?" he asked tonelessly.

A kept his grip 'round Sgt. Esmeralda's neck as he pulled back. Half of the throat sat gouged open, ripped raw, frothin' up gurgles of dark blood. Their head sat at an angle on their shoulders.

A almost opened his mouth to go back for more, it smelled so good. Earthen and still somehow sweet.

Alexander's damp, glossy face under the livin' room lights suddenly made him sick, though.

"Doc—"

"What?" Alexander said again. "What the fuck just happened? Did you just kill Jack? Jack? Aren't you going to say anything?" He plodded up with heavy feet, like lead lined his shoes. "Jack, baby, please come back to me."

Normally, A would let the scene play out on its own. Just step aside, and let the chips fall. But with Alexander's eyes rapidly growin' wilder and more fearful, it didn't seem the scene would move on without his input.

He sighed and shifted away. "Alexander—"

"What did you do?" Alexander clasped his arms 'round Sgt. Esmeralda's body as if to snatch it away.

A let him. His twisted peace offerin'.

"Ya welcome, Doc. This sonofabitch was a terror to us both. G'night."

He only just stopped himself from tackin' on, *Plus, I was so fuckin' hungry...*

Alexander acted like he didn't hear a word. He wrapped his arms 'round Sgt. Esmeralda's back, dampenin' his temper as he held the body close. Cradled it. Tears filled his eyes.

A didn't know what to do. He was full—or at least, not so starvin' anymore—and there really wasn't much else to do here if Alexander wasn't gonna say nothin' to him. Slowly, he turned to leave.

Alexander stopped him.

"You bastard," he spat.

A looked him dead in the eye. They were round and red. Restless.

"How dare you do this? After all this time... Jack just... and now..." Alexander cried. Cried, and cried, and folded in on himself as he cried some more.

For the first time, A wondered, what'd he just do?

He never questioned himself, and never doubted himself, 'cause he only ever really had himself to count on. But seein' the distress that took ahold of Alexander now that Sgt. Esmeralda'd started turnin' grey...

He didn't know what else to do exceptin' leave again.

Alexander suddenly shot out his hands to ring 'round A's throat. Sgt. Esmeralda's body hit the floor with a thud, and he stepped right over it to get a better grip on A. It was as if all grief he felt for Sgt. Esmeralda transformed into sharp, red rage, aimed solely at A.

"You!" he seethed, teeth bared, drippin' spit. "You ruin everything. You *keep ruining* everything. My home. My health. My entire life!"

A couldn't breathe. His hands rose up to cover Alexander's, but he didn't pull them away. For some reason, he still didn't want to hurt Alexander. Not right now, and not over this. There were so many reasons over the years that A'd had to kill Alexander. This wasn't one.

Least, not yet, it wasn't.

'Cause he was okay.

Maybe it was the blood he'd taken from Sgt. Esmeralda that made him feel invincible—maybe he really just was invincible—but he was okay. He wasn't dyin'. Not in any sorta significant way. This was somethin' he knew with a wisdom that surpassed him—he could suffocate, choke under the pressure, and cut the circulation to his brain, but in this body, filled with so much mystical blood and electricity, those things didn't lead to death. They led to discomfort; inconvenience, at most.

He didn't struggle 'cause he didn't need to.

Alexander fumed and dug his fingers in more, more, more, pantin' and breathless as a red glaze crystallized over his eyes. "I've had enough of you. I've had enough of everything...! Die already! Die, and take me with you! When I first laid eyes on you, I saw that you'd been neglected by the world, and so I took pity on you, and look at where it's got me. I'm ruined because of you. You really want to know why you don't have any memories? I've told you before, and Jack saw it, too! It's because you're not human. What you are"—he squeezed tighter, tighter—"is pure pestilence! You're a *plague!*"

A's shoulders shuddered as Alexander shoved him against the wall. His vision went dim 'round the edges, so sensations started dullin' to distant knocks in faraway corners of his head. He didn't know what was happenin', couldn't feel much of it, neither, with Alexander's hands so firm 'round his neck.

All he felt... was somethin' that stretched and grew inside him, strong enough to tear through his back and dent the wall behind him.

A quick bolt of pain lanced through his spine as it ripped free, stretchin' his skin to its limits. The sound was wet, like shearin' fabric, and the air filled with the scent of charred flesh.

Shocked, Alexander's grip finally slipped. The rancid air made its way back into A's body, and he stumbled back against the wall as he fell to the floor—

But landed against somethin' else.

The weight on his back: tall twin arches that rose up over his shoulders, large enough to cast silhouettes in Alexander's eyes.

They were wings. Veined, leathery, grey-black wings, with a dim, lunar-like limn.

"Holy hell," said Alexander.

A adjusted to gettin' his breath back first. The wings stretched and flexed behind him. Violently as they'd emerged, he barely felt them at all—only their weight, heavy and strange, like carryin' a second body.

"Alex—you're—"

"Get back. And don't call me that," A barked. "Ain't exactly got control of this shit."

"What...?" Alexander stumbled closer, hand outstretched without hearin' a thing.

"I said, get the fuck back, Alexander!" A's wings fussed in protest. The curtains billowed like livin' ghosts. They swayed in the draft of his wings as he staggered a step.

Alexander reached to catch him.

He shouldn't't've.

A's huge dark wings shivered one last time then snapped to a standstill.

"Gughh!"

He slammed his eyes shut—a hot, syrupy spray hit him square in the face. It all happened so fast. He forced himself to face the mess. Didn't even lick his lips first.

A glanced down to find Alexander speared straight through the middle—by the tip of his new wing. He may as well have shoved his arm straight through Alexander's ribs.

"Blegggh…" Alexander coughed, eyes wide, spillin' out a mouthful of vomited blood.

A blinked it away. Alexander's shudderin' heart burned through the last of its fuel in seconds. He focused on it, instead of the stains on the cracked rib bones peekin' through Alexander's torso.

All the blood and fat from Sgt. Esmeralda still sat heavy in the pit of his stomach. He'd never had an opportunity to overindulge before, and it put him right back on edge. No urge to eat or fire to calm, and yet, he could *eat*.

Still wanted to, too.

"Shit, Alexander," he sighed.

Was he nothin' more than a livin' weapon now or what? Was that what the fallen star'd ultimately wanted with him, a new victim? He'd have to find a way to get better control of these goddamned wings. Hide them. Bind them. Somethin'. Quickly.

Although, losin' Alexander probably wasn't so bad, in the end. By his own admission, he wouldn't've lasted long without Sgt. Esmeralda, anyway.

A didn't envy that sorta co-dependence not one bit. If that's what love and marriage was, he saw no benefit.

In fact, he'd been fixin' to leave Alexander himself. Now, he didn't have to. He was free.

He tentatively tried wrappin' his other wing 'round Alexander's limp body for support, then tucked in and took a wide, deep bite.

New knowledge rearranged the electrical wirin' and chemical messagin' of his brain and body right away. It enhanced everything that he was, gave meanin' and distinction to concepts he hadn't understood before. Alexander's hidden answers and darkest corners, his sparklin' dreams, and the dust that piled up 'round them long before he ever laid eyes on A.

Yeah... A got all his answers now.

Alexander and Sgt. Esmeralda'd called him "monster" 'cause that was the only explanation they had. The only thing that made sense. The only way that they could cope with the mountains of fruitless research they'd tried to do behind A's back to find out what made him so damned different...

A was underwhelmed.

Still, as Alexander crumpled to the floor, a faint pang echoed in his chest. Not guilt—never guilt—but somethin' sharper, emptier. Satisfaction? Regret? The man'd taken him in, cleaned him up, and taught him English, after all. There might be a place inside him that valued that much, at least. Maybe.

It didn't take long for the wounds on Alexander's body to start rottin'. A picked at the mess, a bit blankly. Shards in some places, goo in others, everything was a dark, heartless red that turned black as it grew. Fat, dark flowers bloomin' on skin, devourin' everything in its path. The bones beneath the rottin' meat started turnin' to black dust, too.

Much faster than the fallen star.

If he waited long enough, the Texas Rangers would come lookin', no doubt. Sgt. Esmeralda's work buddies would jump at the chance to investigate the disappearance, hunt down the presumed murderer. The warrant for A's arrest'd be widespread for darin' to kill someone, much less two people, so respected in Houston society. Even if he wanted to, he couldn't stay here.

And he couldn't leave a trail, either.

He walked outside into yawnin' daylight. The sun'd started risin' on the other side of the horizon. Early mornin' dew, owls, and dragonflies, too. The whole world was waitin'.

His wings arched up above him, sprawlin' and dark, twin shadows that blocked the blushin' light of the sleepy sun. They were alien limbs on his back, but they weren't goin' anywhere. Just like the blood on his hands.

Chapter 5

ERO

E RO DIDN'T MEAN TO sleep. He'd been trying to meditate, actually. Since he couldn't find the effigy on his own, he figured a visit to higher realms would get him some much-needed help. He could clear his head.

But as soon as he closed his eyes, it was like he just drifted off, and then the nightmares began.

They weren't the nightmares he expected. Nightmares were barely a class of devil who preyed on unconscious human fears. Low-level devils, more monster than intellectual, they would've been easy for Ero to overpower.

These nightmares were something else entirely—they were vast and hollow, pulling at the threads of his very essence. It was like staring into an abyss that stared back, only this abyss was inside him, coiling tighter with each passing moment.

Nightmares drenched in fear.

"...!"

Ero awoke on Dr. Lios' couch again, gasping for breath as if it had been stolen by his dreadful dreams.

Why?

Why was he so scared all of a sudden?

And why was he dreaming about it? Ghosts had no use for dreams, neither angel nor devil.

"Clear head," Ero said, and took a breath. He didn't have much time to spare dwelling on problems like these. He had to get going somehow.

He glanced around the room. It was empty except for long lines of moonlight that striped the floors. Lios had disappeared back upstairs earlier, still fast asleep. For a long, grateful moment, he took the opportunity to square himself away.

"Clear heart."

So, then.

No help from higher, for now, at least. The Nightmares were unusually adept at keeping him away.

If he couldn't get any guidance from higher, and he couldn't seem to find the effigy on his own yet, maybe he was overlooking something else. An explanation that required him to be *here*.

Anything that made sense of his failures so far to find the effigy.

Maybe he was supposed to find Lios, first.

Yeah. That was it... probably.

"All right," he sighed as he stood from the couch. "Let's get this show on the road."

He must've been out for hours. The light outside had disappeared, replaced with indoor LEDs that underlit everything—wall photos of mutated DNA strands, framed lists of mathematical formulas, certificates, and awards, and all manner of recognition from different institutes and organizations. All the details of Lios' house were outlined in dim inlaid light. He dragged his fingertips across floating bookshelves until he reached the aluminum spiral stairs.

They led to the loft, Lios' room. He rose.

It was plainer upstairs than the rest of the home, but no less busy. Lios lay on her back in the middle of the floor with a duvet curled around her. The mattress it belonged to sat next to the bathroom door in the back. An old standing lamp framed the other side, with an alarm clock embedded, reading 3:16 A.M. in dim blue lines. Several monitors, tablets, and printers dominated the rest of the room from on top of a desk that spanned the opposite wall. Storage savers half-packed with old tech like non-adaptive clothes crowded beneath it. Ero sighed, somehow surprised at the mess. How could humans even think in rooms like these?

Lios stirred suddenly from the floor. "Angel?"

He froze. "Caught me."

"Are you in my room?" she asked groggily, rubbing her eyes. The slow rise of her anxiety ran the room hot in an instant.

"Yeah, sorry, sorry. Don't get the wrong idea, please. I just woke up, too. I should've left as soon as I did. In fact, I'll go now," Ero said. Spikes of heat stung his skin as Lios' emotions woke up along with her. If he disrupted her peace so much, he'd rather get out of her hair. Honestly. Something about her made him want to set aside his entire life according to her whims.

He was already halfway down the stairs when Lios called out.

"Hey, Angel! Wait up!"

Again, Ero froze.

"Angel...?" he said to himself.

Whatever happened to calling him by name?

Lios came stumbling to the top of the stairs, wrapped in a single sheet. "You don't gotta run just yet. If you're not in a rush, that is. It's just... Do you got a minute? I wanna show you somethin'. Let me wash up, and I can meet you downstairs. Won't be too long. Okay?"

Ero almost laughed.

This must've been the reason he'd landed here and met her. It had to be.

And to think he almost missed it.

He rested his hand on the rail, marking his position in the middle of the winding staircase as he grinned up at Lios. "Sure. I got all the time in the world for you."

Ero waited outside Lios' cramped stilt house. It was one of many that decorated the beaches of the island and hugged the Gulf coast. Relatively isolated, its weathered grey sidings blended harmoniously with the beachfront. A sprawling porch adorned the front, ideal for watching the waves even in the dead of night, but Ero preferred the fiber cement beams below that broke the coastal winds and whisked the waves and sand into an orchestra around the pilings. He listened closely to rushing, like an extraneous pulse.

"Okay, Angel. I'm all set. Here, take this, will you," Lios said, trotting down the floating porch stairs.

She hit the sand, stuffed Ero's wings into one of her long white lab coats, and then herded him into her Audi A9. It was a spacious, autonomous ride with specialized nav systems. The headlights shone like small beacons across the long driveway. While they pulled into the neighborhood on autopilot, Lios handed Ero an apple to snack on.

"And this, so you don't pass out on me again. Hope you like Granny Smith."

Ero didn't have the heart to tell her he had no need to eat food. His body was built for other things than digestion.

These were the last moments he would probably ever get with her, though, so he accepted.

"Thanks, Lios."

He gently took the apple and a sip of water. Everything in his mouth tasted like chalk and stone, but he chewed and swallowed contentedly. He had put up with worse sensations for lesser reasons.

Besides, through Lios' beaming, joy-filled aura, he found a way to step vicariously into her experience.

Apples were sweet and tart, the water liquid silk, to her.

"Mm, it's good," Ero said, still munching.

Lios pushed his water bottle back up to his lips. "You're welcome. Now quit talking with your mouth all full. I know you weren't raised in no barn."

Ero swallowed. "Sorry."

"You're good, sugar. Just a little Southern hospitality."

"I mean, sorry about passing out earlier. That wasn't supposed to happen. The past two days have just been a series of things that weren't supposed to happen."

"Haha! Welcome to the human world, Angel. It seems like she's embraced you like the rest of us poor shits," Lios said, barely able to prevent her sarcasm from sounding sincere.

Ero tried not to take that to heart. He'd heard he was a lot like humans from other angels before. It was strange to hear it from a human, too.

"So what was supposed to happen?" she continued.

"Hmm?"

"Instead of racking out in my living room. What was supposed to happen? Did you find what you were looking for?"

Ero took another chalky swig of water. "I think so."

"I see, I see. So you know where you need to go now, right?" Lios' purple aura started clouding over with concern.

"I know more than I did before. I'll leave it at that."

Soon enough, the greater Galveston shoreline appeared beside him like a great expanse of churning glitter. As they approached the granite seawall, a majestic view rose against the backdrop of the sparkling horizon. He studied the sandy waters that crashed against the seawall's salt-encrusted barrier. The rhythmic cadence of the waves lulled him.

"Here," Lios said. They seamlessly parked on the boulevard beside the seawall, and she reached over to unbuckle his seatbelt. "C'mon. You can just follow me."

"Lead the way."

Ero climbed out of the A9 and adjusted the fit of the lab coat over his shoulders as he stood. He hadn't had the heart to tell her didn't need it in order to hide his wings, either.

It was a cute coat. He straightened out the collar around his neck.

"Right down here," Lios said.

She found a gritty set of stairs and meandered down to the sand, Ero not far behind. Together, they looked out toward the horizon as they walked. In the distance, blue-black waves rippled across the ocean, while closer to the base of the seawall where they stood, the occasional tide pool nestled and swirled. Its granite surface melded seamlessly with the salt and sand of the beach. The crash of waves echoed in the still night air, carrying the faint scent of brine and seaweed. So much seaweed. Every step felt alive, the beach humming with energy.

"This is where I found you," said Lios.

Ero took it all in.

It wasn't the scenery that made his chest tight, though. As always, it was Lios' simple humanity. For him, this gesture meant nothing—a droplet of rain on the far horizon—but he existed far outside of Lios' finite, material world. For her, and humans like her, extending so much effort to help a stranger was no guarantee. Her aura wasn't just bright—it was steady, unyielding, like a beacon in the storm. He envied that stability, even as it drew him closer.

"Thank you again for taking me home with you. I still can't believe you did that," he said, smiling warmly.

"I can't, either, honestly. I mean, I jog this route three times a week, but look at you. You're huge," Lios said with a laugh. It trailed off abruptly. "I'm glad I did it, though. I wanted to make sure I showed you this place at least once before you burned off. Right. So, if I never see or hear from you again, I—I just wanted you to know about this spot. If you're lost, it might help you find where you're going now. I'll understand. You're free to go."

Ero's heart dropped out of his chest. The only thing he could feel on his skin was the wind—cool from crashing waves. The air shifted, carrying a chill that pricked his skin. Something was coming, not just the rain—he could feel it, like a distant drumbeat growing closer, a pulse matching his racing heart.

"I guess you saw right through me," he said.

Lios' glasses flashed, catching the murky night sky in her eyes. "Angel, you're the only mind-reader here. Not me. Let me tell you something. History teaches humans lesson after lesson after lesson. I'd always be sitting through lecture, learning those lessons, and I'd think to myself, 'If I ever get the chance to prove that we can learn from each other's mistakes and not have to repeat the same pointless cycles, then golly, I'll jump right at it.' We have it so good these days, so easy compared to ancient societies and even those not far removed from our own, you know? I feel like it's all too easy to forget—to not pay attention to anything outside of yourself 'til it's too late." She lifted her chin. "So I'm jumping. I know there's no more reason for you to stay here. I'm not simple. I won't make my ancestors' mistakes."

Goddamn it.

Ero hated breaking Lios' heart like this. She was right: He couldn't stay, and she wouldn't let him. If only he could live life like any other angel—if only he weren't The Last Angel—he could spend every waking hour here and protect Lios for the rest of her life.

Into the next life, if she wanted.

As if in response to his thoughts, a little inner light started to emanate from Lios. The same one that shone earlier, when he told her who and what he was.

"I just wish I was more help," she finished.

Ero stayed quiet a long while, listening to the breeze, and weighing his options. He could just leave Lios right now and never look back. She had already given him the out. He'd understood earlier that this moment must've been the reason he'd found her before anyone or anything else.

He just wished it weren't true.

Finally, he said, "Give me your hand."

Lios obeyed in an instant. "Sure. Why you ask?"

"I have something I want to show you, too."

Ero took a deep breath, touched his eclipse matrix, and cupped her hand between both of his own.

"What are you trying to show me, Angel? I don't see anything," she said, glancing around the dark, empty shore.

"This, Lios. I wanted to show you this. Look close."

Ero revealed a light in the center of Lios' palm—a pale lavender glow that flickered like a flame. The whole beach glimmered softly, as if painted with bright bioluminescent strokes.

"Whoa! It's so beautiful."

"It is, isn't it?" He smiled. "This is what I see when you look at me, surrounding you like a big fluffy cloud."

Lios had no idea where to look. The midnight waves stirred nearby, cast in lifelike glow from the lavender light in her hands. "This is... how you see me?"

"This *is* you. It's your aura, the essence that defines you in this life. Some people are able to sense auras on their own, but I wanted to help you to see yours. You feel it, too, right? How it's warm and full? Don't lose that. Protect it, please. It's precious."

Lios laughed, but her words came out trembling. "What's precious?"

"You are, Lios. I don't want you to ever forget that."

As usual, Ero wanted to say so much more. He was both unsurprised and taken aback by how connected he felt to Lios. The Last Angel, like any angel, was supposed to protect, guide, and shepherd lost human souls.

Simply put, though, he wasn't like any other angel. He didn't expect his love for her to be so strong.

Predictably, the heat in the air around them climbed to the pitch of Lios' nerves. She stayed quiet for a while longer, staring at the pale mirage-like light.

"I have so many questions," she said. "I don't even know where to start."

"Got all night," Ero reminded her. A thundercloud lowed in the distance.

"Okay, then. In that case... why do I feel like I've known you my whole life? I think that's what led me to grab you from the water in the first place. I spent all day thinking about it while you were 'sleep. It's hard to put into words, but it's a feeling like I've loved you as long as I've known you. I actually don't know what it's like to have siblings, but I think I'd feel this way about them if I did."

Ero laughed loudly. "That's somehow not at all what I was expecting you to say."

She was such a refreshing surprise in every way.

In their hands, Lios' mini aura warped into a dark purple that almost blended into the humid night.

"Ah!" She dropped her hands to shake off the embarrassment. The light they were holding vanished. "Mind your business, Angel. It's beautiful and all, but a little telling, don't you think? The second my mood changed, so did the light. Does it always do that?"

Ero barred his arm over his gut to help stop the laughing. "I'm sorry, I'm sorry. That's why I don't want to show you too much." As his laughter trailed off, his smile faded, too. "Hey, Lios. I love you, too, by the way."

Hot, hot, hot—Ero's chest, throat, and cheeks burned from the steam coming off Lios. "You're a bit of a menace," she said, turning her face into the muggy wind to cool off.

"Am I?"

"Thanks for saying so, though. You don't think it's strange that I care so much about you? I hardly know you."

"Oh, no, it's totally strange. But that's why I want you to protect that part of yourself. It's not unique, per se, but it's not as common as you'd think. You know what," Ero said, hand on his elbow. "I'm glad I'm getting the chance to tell you this. Lios, I think you are an extraordinary example of the humanity that I was created to save. Meeting you makes my job easy."

"I'm fixing to faint," Lios said miserably. She took a few aimless steps away from the water.

"I wouldn't let you."

"Oh, I appreciate it, but you have got to do something about that mouth of yours. When you say point-blank what you're feeling like that, it can be a little disarming. We're not all that used to straight-talkers down south." Lios smoothed her hair away from her face and sighed. As she fell silent, she turned to face Ero again, eyeing the distance between them. She seemed as wary of it as a crumbling bridge. "Tell me one last thing before you go?"

Even through the wind and waves, Ero heard clearly.

He said, "Anything."

"What is it that you're looking for?"

"Wow, that's the 60 billion dollar question, isn't it?" He let out a deep, long sigh. "But I'm in search of another ghost."

"Another ghost," Lios echoed, making connections. "You mean someone like you?"

"Not someone like me, no." Ero tried not to balk at the notion. "I'm not looking for an angel. The ghost I'm looking for is a devil known as the effigy of evil."

"An evil ghost?" Lios repeated with sympathetic wonder.

As if in omen, lightning struck in the middle of the ocean. She gasped, gazing at it, and Ero turned toward it, too, almost on instinct.

It wasn't regular lightning. The coming storm wasn't close enough—or strong enough.

This was mystical.

This was mastery—the spiritual energy of another powerful ghost.

And it dragged Ero out into the black ocean water before he could even say goodbye. He had run out of time.

Chapter 6

ERO

Ero let himself plummet to the depths of the sea, cradled by his emerging wings. He knew exactly what was happening and saw no point in trying to resist anyway. It wouldn't do him any good.

That lightning strike hadn't come from out of nowhere.

It had come from home—from the Nine Empyrean Spheres of Sanctuary—and whoever had come with it was no mere Angel.

He surrendered. There was nothing else for it. He couldn't resist anyway, so he took the chance to relax and go limp in the water.

The power of the endless sea set Ero at ease. He didn't feel the weight of worry, or nightmares, or emptiness for a moment. He didn't feel lonely or lost. He didn't feel his mission burden. He didn't feel anything.

Totally calm, he pulled his wings in and sank into the far reaches of the ocean. The cool, dark water grew colder as he sank, the weight pressing against his chest like a heavy hand. The darkness closed in, even while the faint glow of bioluminescent creatures flickered around him, curious and nonchalant alike.

Suddenly, a giant inky shadow turned the ocean an impenetrable black around him.

Like a vision, an angel with a sea-green aura appeared from its depths.

The Angel of Prayer.

Tzelathiel.

He was a vision in the deep, decked out in matte armor. His iridescent lime green eyes flashed underwater, and his long black curls flared loosely around him, floating between his large, looming wings. A flat line pulled his lips taut in a grimace as he roared, "Goddamn you!" One of his strong, armored hands banded around Ero's throat. "I ought to kick your ass, Angel!"

They started sinking into deeper water again, so fast that Ero's back hit the floor, and a cloud of shimmering sediment erupted into the shadows around him.

"I've missed you, too, Tsais," Ero said, nonplussed.

Because that was how Ero knew him—as Tsais—not by the daunting full name and title, *Tzelathiel, Angel of Prayer*. Although, this angel was being way more aggressive than the Tsais Ero knew. He could act annoyed, sure, but never this absolute anger. In fact, like the calm, dark green of his aura, he could be infuriatingly flat. This wasn't like him one bit.

"Are you being watched or something?" Ero continued. "What's with you?"

"Don't fuck with me right now, Angel," Tsais said, his grip squeezing tight.

Ero had no trouble maintaining his composure. If it was anyone other than Tsais, then he might've been nervous. But as things stood, he even cracked a grin. "Oh, I get it now. You need to be seen putting me in my place, right? Pervert."

Tsais barely acknowledged the rib. "What the hell are you still doing here? No, fuck that—what are you even doing here in the first place? Go accomplish your goddamned mission before you get yourself locked up."

Ero's smile dimmed. He slid his hands up Tsais' arm, if they were going to be holding each other so tightly. "I've been *trying* to find the effigy," he huffed. "Why don't you help me out if you're so worried about me? Instead of letting me paw around down here blindfolded. I swear, it's like I'm actively being blocked or something."

Tsais flashed his short angel fangs as if to intimidate Ero, even as his hand relaxed around Ero's throat. It was a moot point and frankly hilarious coming from him. "Don't be ridiculous. This is more than just your chance to prove yourself, Angel. There's a lost legacy resting on the outcome of your actions here. You know I would never take that away from you. You've been waiting for this for so long. That's why I'm surprised you're still fucking here. You think you're blocked, who cares? Weren't you made to find the effigy? Weren't you created to serve this exact purpose? Find a way. Come on. I know you can."

Ero sighed. "Yeah, yeah. The fate of the Angels rests on my halo. Trust me, *I'm* The Last Angel. I know that better than anyone. I wouldn't be allowed to come to the human world in the first place if not for that."

"No, I bet you would still be sent here for the effigy," Tsais said deftly. "We'd find a way to use you. You're too rare of an opportunity for us to pass up."

"Let me go. I hate when you start talking like everyone back home. I must've been gone for too long already." Ero wrenched himself away and made some space between them in the dark ocean. "I swear, I leave you alone with your sister for years, and you're fine, but if I leave you both alone with anyone else for 20 seconds, you turn into another mindless machine, just like the rest of them. I was convinced you grabbed me up like that because you were putting on a front for everyone else. Now I see you weren't fronting at all, just being a bastard."

Finally, dampened by Ero's admonishment, Tsais backed up, too, and schooled his expression. His eyes were cool from the deep water. "Tsk. You spend too much time thinking about others. Worry about yourself for a change. What's with your little friendship with that human, anyway? You're sure taking your sweet ass time fooling around with her. Who is she supposed to be to you? Was she helping you to find the effigy, or what?"

"Now you're the one who's being ridiculous. You know a human can't possibly help me on my mission. Are you going to help me find the effigy or not? Or at least help me find out why I can't find him on my own?"

For the first time, it seemed, Tsais heard what Ero was saying. "What do you even mean, you can't find him? It's your purpose. Just focus on whatever mark is his, and go to it. Don't you have your eclipse matrix engaged?"

"Of course I do. What do you even know about it? It's not like you use one. None of you do. I'm the only one who's mastered using it since the War."

"And how impressive it was that you have where no one else has. Now, use it to find your mark, maybe. He'll show up at your summon soon enough. No one can resist you, Angel."

Ero wasn't as invulnerable to snide remarks as Tsais. His face started to burn, even as he followed Tsais' advice and concentrated on the effigy.

"Don't try to save yourself by flattering me now. It's too late, I already think you're an ass. And stop calling me that. It's Ero to you. Remember?"

"Oh, I remember. Now concentrate, Angel."

"*Ass.*"

Ero knew that the same thing would happen this time as had happened last time when he closed his eyes and reached out for his mission mark. He did it again anyway—for Tsais. There was no change.

Just the slightest bit, he was relieved, but swallowed it to mask his jogging pulse.

"See? No dice. Not even a name, much less a mark."

"That's impossible. Every ghost has a mark. It's inherent to our mastery. Listen, we know he's here somewhere. You wouldn't have been sent here if he wasn't. Try again."

"What? I just did. You watched me do it."

"Do it again. I wasn't paying close enough attention."

What the...? Why was Tsais needling him so much? Were they actually being watched, for real?

Tsais wouldn't reveal to him if they were.

Not now. Not here.

With an exaggerated huff, Ero closed his eyes and meditated, searching again for the effigy while Tsais watched.

Searching. Searching.

He came up empty, as usual.

Ero sighed as he broke his concentration.

"Not even a name," Tsais murmured.

"Did you not believe me? Too busy being jealous of a random human woman," Ero said.

"Wait a minute. That's right, the woman who brought you home with her. You paid more attention to her troubles than your own—I see it now. It's the nightmares, you idiot."

"Huh?"

Ero's nightmares? The ones that hammered loneliness and emptiness straight into his heart? What did they have to do with—Oh...

"The nightmares are being channeled through the effigy," Ero and Tsais said together.

"You started having some pretty terrible visions once you got here, huh?" Tsais said, seriously. He studied Ero, like a new problem to pity, and started to drift back toward him. "That's a bit fucked up. Angels don't have dreams. No ghost does."

"You think that's why I should follow the feelings they give me."

"Damn straight." Tsais came right up to Ero. He was taller and leaner, and spoke with a softer kind of calm, almost parental. "Ero, it's your best bet, your first clue, and your only chance, all at the same time. As soon as you left the Bridges of Chaos and entered the human world, you should've been able to sense him. Just like I was able to sense you when I entered." His eyes flashed underwater, as if to emphasize something he had said.

Ero's heart raced. "So you're saying I'm right? I'm being blocked?"

"Yeah, looks like it, or at least close enough to it. If you follow the nightmares that are being channeled to you through the effigy, it should lead you to him. Don't give anyone any reason to doubt you. Stay on track. There's always a way."

Ero pumped his arm in the water. "Sublime!" He dove lightly into Tsais' ready arms. "I knew you couldn't refuse me in my time of need!"

In a surprisingly tender move, Tsais wrapped one of his wings around Ero as he held him. "I could never refuse you, Ero."

Oh.

Now Ero didn't know what to say. Leave it to Tsais to kill the momentum of a conversation with his flat, serious demeanor.

On the surface, those words didn't mean much. Tsais usually said the most sincere things without even flinching. But when he said them like this, underwater, in his cool, reassuring voice, while he crushed Ero against the armor on his chest...

Ero felt strange.

He hadn't missed this ineffable strangeness that plagued him back home; the sort that spoke to how incongruently he always fit into his life there.

Here he was, one angel embraced by another, with no sense of comfort or connection between them.

At least, nothing close to how he had felt while getting to know Lios.

"I'm never going to see her again, am I?" he asked softly.

Maybe he was trying to minimize how much the answer mattered by keeping the words just between their chests.

Tsais hugged him a little tighter. "Another world. Another time."

Ero didn't say a word. He didn't know what to say.

Please?

Angels never heard the pleas of their own.

"Now get out of here, Angel. Follow the nightmares, just make sure you're careful. We'll keep a close watch," Tsais added, gently, then stepped away and vanished.

Ero was left alone at the bottom of the ocean.

He took a second to collect himself, to shake off the strange feeling from Tsais' embrace.

The next second, his body lifted from the sea floor and catapulted through the surface, into the open Galveston air.

His wings glistened with water as it cascaded around him. He cut a path through the droplets and levitated high above the waves, looking up.

Thunderclouds darkened the skies. Big, fat raindrops pelted his face. Even now, he was tempted to find Lios, wherever she had gone, and tell her, "Storm's coming. Let's head home."

He said his goodbyes to the island before the rest of the rain moved in.

The moon hung high in the velvet night sky, cast a soft but intense glow over everything below. Here he finally was, at the precipice of his quest.

Tsais had given him the answer he was looking for, but it still wasn't going to be easy.

Ero closed his eyes and allowed his senses to expand. His mind reached out, probing the darkness, seeking the faintest hint of the effigy's mark left by his lingering nightmares. He meditated for days, or years, or maybe only a few moments, trying to find the dank nightmares that had initially plagued him.

For a long, long time, poised inside the space of his own mind, he didn't sleep at all.

But eventually, he did.

And the darkness returned.

The same empty, listless darkness that stuck to the bottom of his thoughts like chewed up gum.

Instinct and intuition guided him soundly through. Not that he could explain it, but something had led him here. Something always led him somewhere. All he needed was time, these nightmares, and this void feeling of confusion and fear that accompanied them. He wasn't supposed to have such disturbing visions and emotions—these dull, almost painful aches of dread—but at least it had a purpose. At least there was a reason for the pain he suffered through.

The feeling clung to him like dusk to the horizon as Ero slept, meditating, searching, seeking.

He continued, on and on and on, until the shadows in his mind sharpened into silhouettes: the height of thousands of trees, heavy with leaves, covering a mountainside. There were so many mountains, rolling in deep fog, gleaming in shades of black that mimicked its real-life greens and golds.

The Appalachians. Just a little further east from where Ero was now.

The ancient mountain range was bold and unshaken, its rounded peaks holding a deep, steady quiet in his mind. He felt their heft as he meditated on them; their presence radiated as though the earth itself was reaching back into him. It was a place of roots, a place swallowed whole by stillness. Galveston's shores were so different—so open, restless, and endlessly fluid. Its waves crashed with relentless rhythm, sand clung to his boots, and the salty wind tugged at him like a lesser, second tide. The total opposite of the crowded mountains.

Ero almost cut his meditation short then and there—just like Tsais said, he'd followed the nightmares and finally found the effigy. He couldn't wait to take flight and *go there right now*. His skin buzzed with the urge.

But just before he broke his concentration, he noticed something else hidden in the shadows.

A faint, pink glare between the trees.

His target.

Ero lunged toward it—and snapped their connection in the process.

"Aw, fuck!"

He fell from his place hovering in the air.

Instead of crashing to the ground, he soared.

"All right, let's go," he cheered.

A gentle night breeze lifted him back into the sky, and he flew with it over cities, forests, and rivers. He traced the mental map that had filled his mind before, trying to rediscover that soft pink spot in the dark.

The reason for his duty.

His purpose.

Ero found it.

He found *him*—deep in the forest mountains of Appalachia.

Just like the visions he'd had while meditating, thick iron rocks and layered cliffs started to surround him. The rusted aesthetic of the mountains spread out as far as the horizon. A sea of trees blanketed everything that Ero could see, oaks, maples, hemlocks, pines, and poplars, alongside sassafras, sourwoods, redbuds, and juniper. Here, outside a remote town nestled deep in the tall trees and mist-shrouded mountains, his senses sharpened, and he descended gracefully into it, landing on the multihued moss-covered forest floor.

Among the ancient trees, one of them with a blackened, hollowed-out hole in its side, he caught his first glimpse of the soft pink shadows from his vision.

Yes—everything was suddenly powder baby pink, like an aura over the entire mountainside. Anything else faded away.

Ero let out a quiet gasp with a strange sense of relief and familiarity.

He'd found the effigy.

The devil he was made for.

"Finally," he whispered.

He studied the devil cautiously as he rounded the hollow tree, eyes and mind searching for signs of the emptiness that had plagued his days.

None rose. Only the pastel haze of pink.

His thoughts were preoccupied, anyway. He was busy thinking of devils: the ones he knew of, the oldest and strongest of them all, the original Fallen Angels who led the demonic Corps. Ancient beings, both beautiful and grotesque, they were twisted in every sense of the word.

The devil in the tree couldn't be further from that image. He had a lithe, sculpted form, with bluish black curls that melted into the shadows, eyes somewhere between grey and brown, and a fixed, saturnine face. The only real thing that marked him as a ghost was the pair of those huge, dark wings towering behind him. They struggled against a series of thick, tarnished chains, a storm of defiance and desperation in every twitch. It was all just survival, raw and unrelenting, nothing done for show, only to live.

"Found you," Ero said.

"Fuck off," the devil snarled.

Ero didn't flinch. He was too focused on the dire fangs that glinted between the devil's full lips, twice as many and twice as long as Ero's own angelic fangs.

"Sir?" he said cautiously. "Do you know who I am?"

The pink shadow aura around the devil started to drain away. In its place, a hollow materialized where his usual aura should've been. Like a pale shadow. Empty.

"No," the devil sneered. "Don't care, neither. Leave me the fuck alone."

Ero couldn't stop himself from grinning, just a fraction. "Sure, that makes sense for me to do. I leave you the fuck alone, you leave me the fuck alone, and we both go on our merry way, never to speak of this fateful encounter ever again. Because I didn't come all this way just to find you or anything."

"I said, fuck off!"

A few things happened at the same time.

The devil's wings ripped powerfully free of their chains. They flared up and splintered the hollowed tree trunk, shadows swallowing moonlight. Bark scattered in all directions. His eyes locked with Ero's.

Ero summoned his weapon, the axe-headed halberd, almost automatically. Still, it wasn't fast enough. Before he could even use it, the devil bit viciously into him. Everything went black as the deep ocean after that.

He stayed under... then came to in long, slow swells.

By the time he could think straight, his body was still too heavy to move. The sound of fluttering wings from crows watching nearby beat against his eardrums, drowning out everything. There were so many wings, but not a single quell. Then, all at once, he snapped into focus.

The devil was pinning him down, fangs at his throat, draining every ounce of blood in his body.

Ero's head whirled with a dense fog. He tried to shove back a bit, but the devil casually shrugged him off, biting deeper. Nothing worked. His thoughts ran rampant without direction, and the devil kept taking more and more and still somehow even more...

This time, he couldn't resurface. Ero had to let himself drown.

When he next woke up, it was in a dark room. He lay on an old, nonexistent bed, and his neck, chest, and shoulder were covered in deep purple bruises. The pain lulled him. Ero'd never felt anything like it, even while training. He sat up carefully to keep the weight off his wounds.

A presence simmered at the door, limned in backlight, but he couldn't discern its mark very well. It was as if the faintest, liquid smoke stood in place of its aura.

Of course.

It was the effigy of evil—the devil whose despair echoed into Ero and brought them together at last.

The devil stepped slowly into the room. He stood tall in a pair of black boots, a wrinkled white shirt, and an old navy blazer. His disheveled blue-black curls, gathered loosely behind him, escaped to frame parts of his face. Now that Ero saw his features more clearly, they were striking. Warm brown skin, cutting eyes, long, thin eyebrows, and full lips that concealed his characteristic canines, slightly larger than angels' fangs. It bizarrely made him seem gentle despite it all. Even his dark wings appeared totally clean, with no evidence of his earlier violence. He was staring at Ero's face, searching and watching closely as he approached the bedside.

"What are you?" he asked in a voice close to steel. It was hard, but light, drawn out with a classic cowboy drawl. Not at all like the mountain accent out here, but smooth, sugary, and soft-edged. *What're ya?*

Ero didn't answer at first. His halberd had gone home, his neck and shoulder deeply stung from the attack—why hadn't he healed yet?—and the devil's voice was all he could think about.

"What?"

The devil pulled lightly at Ero's collar to expose the wounds. "You heal well."

"What do you mean, well?"

Ero lost his train of thought to a sharp pain. He touched the side of his neck and found the threads of his body were healing up, as the devil said—just extraordinarily slowly. He couldn't believe how slowly.

"You tried to kill me," he blurted.

"Usually do. But you heal well." The devil spoke so simply, as if everything he said made perfect sense.

It didn't. Nothing about this situation made sense.

So many reasons flew through Ero's head. He couldn't keep up with half of them. Hadn't the devil taken his blood? If so, why wasn't it working? Why could he still not detect any mark or mastery that wasn't his own? And, fuck, why did the devil's bite *hurt* so much? He didn't know what to do with all this pain and confusion.

"L-let me start again. I think we might've skipped a couple steps. I've been searching for you. You can call me Ero. What do I call you, sir?"

The devil narrowed his eyes in another frown. "Sir?"

"What else can I call you? You won't give up your name. You keep it pretty viciously hidden."

Ero's senses stretched once again, searching beyond himself for purchase where something—a mark, an aura, *anything*—should be. Nothing responded except for the quiet where the devil stood in front of him, not even the pink haze from earlier.

It just wasn't right. Something should've been there. An impression that signified the devil was more than human but a ghost from hell with a demonic design. Without these subtle shifts and underlying currents in emotion and energy that usually surrounded him, over half the information Ero was used to working with simply wasn't there. He was adrift.

He suddenly remembered Lios, remembered what it meant to feel another's extrasensory presence, to acknowledge their feelings and intentions without a word passing between them. Her warm, sparkling aura.

This moment, with the devil right next to him and still barely perceptible, was a sharp contrast.

"And no matter how hard I try, I can't seem to find it..."

"No name to give. Never had one. If you're Ero, who's Cerviel?"

Ero froze. He never mentioned Cerviel.

He finally feinted out of the devil's reach, called on his wings, and summoned his halberd again to press between them. The tip of the intricate, beaded axe blade pointed at Sir's solar plexus.

"Sangromancer."

"Oh?" Sir said, standing straight and still.

"Yes, fucking sangromancer. You saw into my blood. I know what you can do."

Sangromancers were blood manipulators. Sir had taken more than just blood from Ero—he'd accessed memories, feelings, gained insights. For someone without a mark, he must've found his own way to wield his powers. Ero couldn't have known the devil's abilities without being able to get a read on his mastery, but he wouldn't be caught off guard next time.

Sir's wings stirred in agitation. "Don't know what the hell you're talkin' 'bout, but you better get that fuckin' weapon out my face."

"I'll put down my weapon when you stop playing these cute little games with me, attacking me on sight and draining me half to death. I'm just defending myself at this point. Now tell me who you are, *Sir*—and why I can't sense your mark, while you're at it." Ero licked his lips. "My service doesn't mean a thing if—"

"Oh?" Sir said again and grinned enough to show his fangs. "Your service?"

Ero swallowed, but he wasn't about to wilt when he finally had Sir's full attention. "Don't tell me that's news to you after the meal you just made of me. I'd think you would know my whole life story after all that. Yes, my service; I was created in service of you. It'd be nice if we could serve each other. I'm simple to please. Just don't prey on me or lie to me. Those are my only standards. Tell me yours."

Sir's expression flattened out. His wings went eerily still, too. "You lookin' for standards, sugar, keep it steppin'. Now move this thing, or I will."

He glanced at Ero's glimmering halberd and guided his finger up to the sharp tip in defiance.

Ero held still for half a second.

"Guh!" Sir recoiled.

A great light instantly exploded into the humid room, sending a shockwave into Sir that smacked him against the far wall.

"My bad," Ero said. His grip was iron, though.

He'd trained for this. Despite his doubts, a ghost weapon like his halberd would never harm a human.

So, it was clear. Sir really was the effigy of evil that Ero had been created to find and save. There was just something about him that made his mastery, his mark, and his aura impossible to detect beyond a passing breeze.

"You...!" Sir muttered.

His wings were as swift as they were powerful. He used them to tackle Ero back across the room. They both grappled against the rotting wall until Ero kicked free, using his halberd to wedge space between them. The long shaft shoved Sir back.

"Hey, chill out! We can still talk!"

"You attacked me."

"I didn't attack you. My weapon is divine. Of course it would repel you on its own accord if you touch it!"

"Bullshit."

Sir was back on Ero in a second. He fought with raw strength and speed, like a kickboxer or martial artist, meeting blow for blow and targeting Ero's defenses. The power of his strikes was actually staggering.

How—seriously, how? Ero didn't expect to have to fight on more than one front with an opponent whose aura he couldn't even fully sense. Although, fighting close quarters like this, hand to hand, he probably wouldn't last much longer if he didn't use his mastery, too. It was an easy defense to reinforce his attacks with holographic shimmers of spiritual energy. All he had to do was re-engage the eclipse matrix in his mind that had scaled off his power.

"No bullshit. Trust me, you *will* know when I attack you."

Light bloomed, then vanished, like fireworks, as he force sealed Sir's eyesight.

"Argh!" Sir crashed onto the dusty wooden floor, scratching at his eyes, but immediately got back to his feet with his wings. He glared straight at Ero even through his supernatural blindness. The veins around his eyes were dark against his brown skin. "The fuck'd you do to me...?"

"Force seal," Ero said, keeping watch.

He followed Sir's eyes as his breaths evened out. Sir's fangs disappeared behind his defined lips, and the cloudy, muted grey of his eyes steadily reemerged. In no time at all, Sir had lifted off the floor—his wings didn't even twitch, this time—and closed a hand around Ero's arm.

"Force what?" he repeated, somewhat calmer. He still couldn't see anything, but the cold focus of his gaze on Ero's face said otherwise.

"Watch your grip there, lover boy. I'm glad to see you're so comfortable doing what you want with me already, but like I said, it was just a force seal. You know, like handcuffs. Can you fucking see me already?"

"Yes. Blurry, but... yeah. The hell is that sealin' shit? Almost attacked you again. Thought I was permanently blinded." Slowly, Sir tilted forward and sagged a bit against Ero before pushing away, like the entire ordeal exhausted him. "You got a shake or two. Talk."

Ero didn't know where to start for a moment. They both stood quietly in the dark, sagging room. Sir's questions started to confuse him less and less as they went on, though. Any ghost should've been able to recognize the use of mastery, especially a force seal. Mastery was just a part of life for ghosts. It was energy. If Sir had no idea what a force seal was, their problems had just multiplied. They would have to start from scratch.

"I'm sorry, Sir, but I think we're gonna need a lot longer than a couple of shakes. Let's hope you're a fast learner—for both our sakes."

Chapter 7

SIR—FORMERLY A

Oh. He liked the way Ero kept callin' him Sir. Not Alex, or Alexander, or "Hey, you piece-a-fuckin'-shit."

Sir.

Somethin' 'bout that name said by Ero made him wanna make it his own. Even if he burnt off and never saw Ero again, he wanted to keep this new name with him.

The name given to him by an angel.

For the first time, he could be somethin' other than someone else's nightmare or distorted reflection. He could be his own.

He swallowed the name down, took a beat to center himself, and planted his eyes back on the enigmatic Ero.

Sir told himself he waitin' for his eyesight to fully return. But he could see just fine now.

He just couldn't look away.

Ero looked so much like the sun. Gold wings, red eyes, and a single pair of short fangs. He rubbed his neck wound absently, too. Back and forth, firm pressure, like a lil massage. Sir'd be hard pressed to believe that wound even hurt Ero anymore with the way he was touchin' all on it. Did anything hurt him? Did he feel anything? Sir'd filled himself to burstin' with his expansive blood, and Ero'd just passed out for a while before poppin' right back up. Bruised, but otherwise right as rain. Clearly somethin' more than human. Maybe, another monster—like Sir.

He'd bristled when he first met Ero, his instincts warnin' him to attack this maybe monster. Now that he'd tried, and Ero hadn't gone nowhere, all Sir could do was find himself trapped in Ero's eyes.

Strange eyes, too. Brilliant red-gold—ruby surrounded by a thin gold ring. Wide, round, and all-seein'. Eyes like an owl. Right from the start, they'd fixed on Sir with such soft intensity. It was unlike anything else. The eyes of a hunter, rather than prey.

Sir had no clue what the fuck to make of these sun-colored wings, intricate eyes, and eager smiles on Ero. There was somethin' indescribable 'bout it all that made him stop, think, and shiver; somethin' he couldn't help but wanna sink his teeth into, too.

His head started to pound as he studied Ero's face. Those crystal eyes slowly warped and morphed into a hazy red cloud that fell over his vision. He closed his eyes and turned away, tryin' to fight the bizarre sensation.

"Sir?" Ero said, lazily, almost sleepy.

Sir snapped to.

That right there. That's why Sir took this name.

His eyes met Ero's again, hesitantly at first, testin' to see if that red haze'd return.

There wasn't none. Just Ero. Wide eyes clear and focused.

Sir tensed, feelin' foolish for expectin' anything else. "Fine, you got long as you need if that'll get you on out my hair. What d'you want with me?"

"Get me out your hair?" Ero repeated lightly. He started tuggin' at the ends of his own coils, stretchin' them far, lettin' them spring back. "Why would you want to do that? We just met."

Sir expelled a dry cough. He'd meant to laugh, but couldn't. This guy was unbelievable. "Adorable," he said, instead.

Ero popped his tongue. "Thanks, actually, I'm glad you noticed. Do you want to take a tour?"

"Answer me."

"I will. Later. If you answer me first." Ero did a slow, sinuous spin on his heels. It really was adorable, for as much of a show as it was.

Takin' a second look, Sir ran his eyes over Ero's frame again. If he had an ideal, Ero might've been it. Tall as hell in a black turtleneck, gleamin' white lab coat, and fitted jeans. His brown skin was dark against the long rose gold curls that faded to silver at the fringes. Fit and competent. Casually warm. A small smile exposed his short gold fangs again.

Sir did not smile back. It was a dangerous gesture that dug at him. Burrowed deep. "Angel. Quit searchin'. I see how beautiful you are. Move on."

Ero paused, for the first time, barely more than a second. "Well, thank you! I just needed to hear you say it. Since I can't sense your aura or anything, I wanted to be sure that you like me. I'm yours, after all." His wings and shoulders squared out as he went to attention. All he lacked now was a salute. "Sir, I know you to be called 'the effigy of Lesser Earth's last evil.' That is, you're a vestige from a time that doesn't exist anymore. An anachronism. I've been looking for you so that I can make this right."

"Better." Sir's lips twitched at the corners. He couldn't tell if he was irritated or entertained anymore. No wonder Ero was so pearly and shiny—pure facade. "Ya here to kill me."

Ero waved both hands in front of his face. "No, not at all, not at all! Sir, did you hear anything I said? I'm yours. I'm not here to kill you, love. I'm here to marry you."

The fuck?

Sir had no clue what he was hearin'.

"Marry?" he said, with zero inflection.

Why would he *ever* get married?

He'd seen what marriages could do to people, and at no point did it look like an improvement on his current circumstances. Alexander and his tumult'd boiled over onto Sir for years, burnin' him right on up. And for the past week or so, he'd been cooped up in this lil goddamned shack in the mountains tryin' to figure out how to get control of his wings. "Unpredictable" was 'bout far as he'd gotten since he'd killed Alexander with them. If he added a random marriage to the mix, he would probably never gain control of anything again.

Oh, yeah, and he'd be fuckin' married.

"Yes," Ero said, whippin' out an unbothered lil smile. Suns and moons could rise and fall, and that smile probably wouldn't even dim a shade. "You can marry into the Right Hand of Protection if you accept it. That way, we'll have every guarantee we need that you can't endanger this world anymore—because you won't be a devil of the Left Hand of Destruction after you Rise."

Oh, that made even less sense.

For real, though—the fuck?

Sir was a devil of the what? And he was supposed to fuckin' marry this random who?

Angel? Left? Right? Hands?

Rise?

So he'd basically stumbled across a giant missin' facet of his identity, but in the same breath, was bein' told to abandon it. Change it, change himself, for this angel he'd just met who told Sir that everything 'bout him was wrong. That everything Sir worked so hard to understand 'bout himself meant nothin' now.

He'd killed his only friend for this information. Abandoned his humanity and finally understood himself for a change.

Get the hell out of town.

"Angel."

It was all he could think to say. What else could he do? Bolt?

He'd never met someone, or somethin', that he couldn't reflexively conquer. His senses were strong, sharp, and deadly accurate. His need had left a trail of bodies behind him and every one of them had molded, festered, and disappeared right in front of him—just like Alexander, Sgt. Esmeralda, and even the fallen star, eventually.

Only Ero was different.

Ero held his own against Sir, and Ero'd healed from Sir's bite already.

Ero was a goddamned angel.

"Yep, that's me. The Last Angel. Nice to meet you again, Sir." He grinned and extended a hand—unbothered.

Sir didn't take it. His eyes followed, though. Pinned there.

Sir was... a devil. He just knew if he moved even a single muscle that he'd get another "unpredictable" reaction from his wings and dig himself in deeper with all this angel business. He really just wanted out of everything, at this point.

Nah, that wasn't even true. He wanted out, but still needed answers. He still existed. Alexander'd told him what he wasn't, but never what he *was*—or why. Not human, just other; a monster from nowhere.

Then there was Ero: another other, yet full of legacy. Another natural enemy of humanity—in the form of an angel.

Ero's big eyes flickered down to his own unshaken hand before he stepped up to just take Sir's hand for himself. "I said, it's so nice to meet you, Sir. I guess I'll keep calling you that. For now."

Sir went cold everywhere, still frozen solid as Ero gripped his hand.

At least his wings didn't snap. Progress.

But he only barely kept himself from dartin' away. Ero squeezed his hand tighter 'round Sir's, leanin' in closer with that dauntless smile.

"Can I call you Sir?" he asked in his cute, coy way.

Sir stared into his eyes. There wasn't no red haze at all this time. In fact, this close, Sir could only notice that he was shorter than Ero by nearly half a head.

"S'fine. Don't got no other name, anyway."

"You keep saying that, but once I find your mark, I'll know the truth. You can't keep it hidden from me for too long. I'm The Last Angel, after all. I'm made for you," Ero said with a wink.

Sir 'bout rolled his eyes. "And you keep sayin' that, but I got a real hard time believin' all the heavens'd sacrifice their last and only angel to me."

"Oh. Is that what my marriage to you would be, a sacrifice?"

"Quit flirtin', and fuckin' answer me." Sir's lips parted, revealin' his long fangs.

Ero just smiled again, close-lipped, honey, and composure. "Good to know you're paying attention, at least. You're not all wrong. The Last Angel is my title—because I am the only angel in my order—but higher powers than me still exist. They're angels, too. Just like you're not the only devil, as much as you probably think you are, skulking around here on your own. Leagues of devils exist. There's always someone bigger, someone quieter, watching from above or below. That's why, no, I'm not a sacrifice. I'm more like a gift, from my superiors to you. Get into it."

"A gift." Sir couldn't help but echo all the nonsense.

'Cause slowly, deeply, he realized Ero was right. At least, right *enough*. It wasn't new information—just unfamiliar. Every word Ero spoke 'bout these ghosts and these worlds unfolded like a pearl from a grain of sand. Somehow, Sir did have some idea of the reality Ero painted even though he ain't have a single memory to support it. Somethin' 'bout it all just made sense in a way that didn't make sense. And yet, he had no hope of fightin' its logic with his own.

Ero, the last angel of his order, was a gift.

For him.

Sir was a punk. A predator. *Devil*. His past was an illusion that didn't exist before Alexander came into his life: a void he filled with blood, meat, and bones whenever it most convenienced him. The blood was never enough. He always needed more.

"What, you don't believe what I'm telling you or something?" Ero blinked his golden-red eyes innocently. "I'm just a gift to you, Sir. It can't be that hard to accept that we're showing you mercy, can it? All you've ever really known is apathy, emptiness, fear, and hate—all these emotions I know now because of *you*. Now, if you choose me, you can know peace. We're spiritual beings, ghosts. All we are is energy: the energies of destruction and protection, war and peace."

"Hate and love," Sir said. He didn't feel like the spiritual embodiment of hate, or destruction, or nothin' else, though. Just a constant, vicious hunger.

"Exactly. All I'm here to do is help you. You'll see it yourself as soon as you give me the chance. A marriage is just a contract. We both have to enter it on our own free will. I can't force you to do anything you don't want to do. It wouldn't work, even if I tried. That's not how mastery of the Right Hand works. All you have to do is reveal your mark to me, and I can help you to Rise right now. You don't have to live like this ever again. Hunted by humans, killing just to live, doing more harm than good. All alone..."

Ero glanced 'round the dim spartan room, his usual grin saggin' for just a moment. The last word echoed off the walls.

Sir'd squatted in this lil beat up shack only a few nights. The first night, really. The rest were spent chained to the biggest, strongest poplars 'round, and durin' the day, he'd roam the roads, forests, and lakes of lil Appalachian towns. Most times, that was safest. He didn't wanna risk tippin' off Georgia State Patrol now that he'd skipped Texas. They'd link up and descend on him in a second if he gave them the smallest chance.

But he wasn't none too eager to go easily wherever Ero told him to go. Even Alexander never had a hope of controllin' him. Alone was best.

Alone was safest.

"'Don't have to,' or 'can't'?" Sir finally asked. "Make it sound like a choice when it don't seem like much of one to me."

With a shrug, Ero said, "It is a choice—for you, just not for me. I already told you I was ordered to do this, so I'ma do it regardless. You're just gonna have to meet me halfway, and trust me. We have to trust each other."

Sir'd been burned by words like these before.

"Trust, huh," he mumbled to himself.

Last time he'd trusted somethin', it was that doggone urge to devour the fallen star. And in turn, it'd tried to devour him instead. The bite force of the fallen star'd blistered. The pain'd been broken only by a bright red flash of light.

Suddenly, Sir couldn't shake the feelin' of familiarity. Like vertigo, unease and confusion swirled 'round inside him.

The fallen star and that red light...

That was another part of what bothered Sir 'bout Ero. While he'd been trapped by the fallen star, a red-tinged ring of light'd shone—like gold drippin' in blood—and Ero's eyes were a perfect match of it.

Ruby red, surrounded by a thin golden ring.

Sir felt like fallin' and drownin' in those ultra-red eyes. Sometimes like crystal, sometimes like blood. They were so big, owl eyes, temptin' him down into forgotten and unknown visions. Another red haze.

"Sir?"

His head started to hurt, like before, the red haze fallin'. He blinked and came back to himself—back to Ero—before it got any worse.

What the hell were these headaches and visions he kept seein' in Ero's eyes? Every time that red haze crashed down, he disappeared in the fog of it.

"Fuck," he muttered. "You want me to trust you... Can't even get a straight answer out you. Your eyes're the most honest thing you got goin' for you, and I can't look into them without gettin' a migraine. At this point, me trustin' you'd be like you trustin' me. Now don't that make a fucked up picture? I ain't goin' anywhere. Not with you, boyfriend. Time's up."

His head was still poundin'. He didn't know what he'd been 'bout to say before he said it. Now that he had, he realized how close he was to Ero, and backed up to strengthen his stance.

Right. He ain't want no part of it, 'specially if he only got new questions and no answers from the whole thing.

Ero was frozen, unblinkin' and wide-eyed. "What do you mean time's up?"

Sir looked 'round without seein' much of anything. He just needed to split. Right now. He needed out of this cramped fuckin' room and away from this mysterious fuckin' angel with his insane fuckin' demands before he went crazy.

"I mean, don't follow me," he said, and stepped.

Thankfully, Ero didn't budge.

Sir couldn't fly all that well. Still couldn't control his wings enough yet. So he ran instead: faster than flight.

He zipped through the forests and rivers of the mountainside, makin' his silhouette sleek and slender as he slipped between them. His breaths were as even as always, but his chest felt tight from porin' over the visions in his mind.

The images changed again and again, broken by lightnin'.

Ero's crystal-red eyes surrounded by a ring of golden brown. *Flash.*

The red light of a small, cold sun. *Flash.*

A gold ring glossy with fresh blood. *Flash!*

Midstride, Sir sank into murky sand. He'd run clear out of Georgia and all the way to the Atlantic coast.

To the overgrown shore of Bulls Bay.

South Carolina, sweet and golden, sprawled all 'round him. He clearly recalled passin' through dense, mist-shrouded forests and rivers like threads of silver. Somewhere 'round the flatter foothills, he'd blanked. Now he tried to picture the patchwork of the Piedmont fields spread out quilt-like, interspersed with thin, windin' roads. He'd never seen them before, but the images pressed into his mind in real time when he concentrated on them: miles of Lowcountry, pine and marsh and tidal creeks, 'til the old salt marshes stretched into the ocean, where he stopped cold.

Salty water splashed his ankles and mingled with the earthy scent of the forest behind him. They came right up to each other;

a thick canopy overlooked the secluded clearin' by the water's edge where Sir stood. His reflection shimmered on top of the silver ripples, full of warmth, color, and vitality.

Damn but he looked good.

Felt good, too.

Felt fan-fuckin'-tastic, actually.

He'd never run so fast in his life.

As if drawn by his bein' there, a small mob of deer come up from the nearby shadows, their dewy eyes meetin' his own dead-on. An unsaid understandin' passed between them pretty quickly. He was hungry enough to eat, probably, but he didn't have any taste for them. He'd been spoiled rotten by Ero's luscious blood.

Blood of another predator, like him.

Sir shifted his gaze back to the shore, flanked by a row of colossal uprooted magnolias, like primeval sentinels. The shoreline was scattered with bleached white skeletons—whales, dolphins, crabs. The giant trees'd been their guardians for centuries. Now the exposed roots, thick and twisted as lichen-covered snakes, sprawled across the dirt and bones in tangled patterns.

Relics of a forgotten time. Anachronisms.

The first light of mornin' slowly started to break up the dark.

By now, Sir already figured he couldn't outrun Ero. It was no surprise to hear the angel approach. Even between the wind in the trees, he could clearly pick out Ero's silent footfalls.

"Sir..." He sounded tentative, for the first time. It didn't suit him too well, 'specially as he kept strollin' on up. He shined too bright. "You didn't go very far."

"Not gettin' rid of you anytime soon. Am I, Angel?"

Ero sighed calmly. "Not really, no. Do you want to accuse me of lying some more, or are you ready to listen to what I actually have to say? I think I figured out where I lost you before, if you'll just let me explain. You really stand to gain a lot by accepting my offer, you know."

"Like what? Your hand in marriage for the rest of my miserable life?"

"Among other things. Why, you've never not gotten your way before? What else do you want?" Ero swept the silver tips of his curls over his shoulder as he leaned closer to Sir. His wings glimmered a bit under the washed-out moonlight, not yet true mornin'. "Do you want our marriage to be blissful and loving, instead? I can give it to you. Just ask."

Sir's eyebrows twitched as their eyes met.

In an instant, a stillness swallowed everything 'round them.

Red red red.

It was the same as those times before, which gave him those headaches: Ero's eyes found Sir's, and the red haze came fallin'.

This time, for the first time, he concentrated on it, instead of fightin' it off.

Just ask, huh?

Ero's golden-red eyes morphed into a dark ocean. Memories for waves. The whole world paused and reddened. The tide quieted, and the wind held still. Only the fadin' moon remained unfazed, a stoic onlooker while Sir waded through the red currents of Ero's unguarded gaze.

Could he trust this angel's mercy?

No, initially. On the surface. Glint, like a reflex.

But if he waded just a lil deeper...

"Haa," Sir finally sighed.

The red haze dissolved. Ero hadn't moved, a statue while Sir searched his gaze, but after a second, he half-smiled.

"You're staring so hard. Are you thinking of what you want out of me?"

"Yeah," Sir said.

Ero's smile cracked a bit.

It was true, though. As much as Ero downright bewildered him, Sir had to admit his intrigue with the angel. More than he felt comfortable admittin' to himself. And his gut pulled him in separate directions. Trust the angel, and love him. Don't trust the angel, and hate him.

Could Sir trust the angel and still hate him?

...Did he have to?

He'd always wanted answers to all the questions that Alexander wouldn't—or couldn't—give him. And here, suddenly, in a manner too good to be true, an all-knowin' bein' just landed in his lap.

With a ball and chain...

"Why marry me?" he asked.

"Oh"—Ero recomposed himself—"I told you. To save you. To make you an angel of the Right. If you choose me—if you choose love and reject the Left, you'll free yourself of the evil influences rooted in the Left Hand of Destruction. You won't have to kill to live anymore. You won't have to wander alone. You won't have to wonder who or what you are, or where you're supposed to be. You won't need to live like a devil rejected from your own world." He paused to top up on his smile. "Marriage is also the least violent way for you to Rise. I mean, they were gonna drive a giant metaphysical sword through your heart, or even just drag you home to the Empyrean Spheres and have the evil divested from you by force, but..."

"What the fuck," Sir said, unimpressed.

"You're an evil ghost," Ero replied mildly as he shifted onto his side. His shoulder and wing brushed against Sir's. Feather touch. "I guess it's not too strange I have to explain that to you. You've been stuck in this world a good long time. Do you remember, I said I know you as 'the effigy of Lesser Earth's last evil'? Let me tell you a little something about this world you're calling home right now. Lesser Earth is small, and more than that, it's young—freshly revived from ashes of the last world that was destroyed however many eons ago. This is how reality persists here, in the material realm, where creation and destruction, birth and death, coincide everyday. Greater Earth already died. Now the Lesser needs time to live. It needs time to build for the first time again. You're not really accounted for in that larger picture. It can't grow when you're causing all this chaos you're not supposed to. These people—this reality—it deserves a fair chance. This is their place, not yours. You don't belong here, not really. You never have, and no matter what you do, you never will."

"Anachronism. Roger." Sir moved to split again—he ain't know what else to do anymore—but Ero caught him 'round the wrist to stop him. He almost bared his fangs. "Let go of me, Angel."

"If I do, I'll just find you again. You can't run away from me now that I got you. I'll look for you, and look for you, and keep on looking for you, until I find you again—the way that I'm meant to always find you. Don't make me beg, Sir. Just fucking come with me." Ero tightened his grip, reaffirmin' it, then paused. "Why is your wrist broken?"

Sir went offline for a second.

Many of his injuries, some earned over his week on the lam, never had a chance to heal properly. The others were from his life before the fallen star, or even before Alexander. How'd the angel always notice the smallest, oldest shit that Sir'd usually push aside like water?

"What?" he said, comin' back online.

Ero stood in the sand. "See, you can't afford to brush me aside. Your wrist, your shoulder—" His eyes indicated each injury as he pointed them out. "You're suffering these injuries because you think you're human. You've been taking care of yourself like a human. You run on instincts and lack finesse, spreading yourself too thin to properly recover. Recovery is the only way to grow. Lesser Earth needs it, and you need it, too. All this running around that you do to try and find yourself, I can help with it. I have the answers to your questions. You know I do. You just have to come with me. Start by letting me heal your wounds. Please—as part of my gift to you."

Sir wanted to laugh. Ha-ha-ha. When was the last time he'd even felt a glimmer of pain from these old wounds? Next to the fire that fueled his need, physical pain didn't exist. But he couldn't deny Ero's accusations. Even up 'til a few short weeks ago, he'd mistaken himself for human.

Alexander'd been the first to accuse Sir of havin' no such humanity.

He was trapped, all over again.

"Do what you want. You will, either way, right?"

"Yeah~!" Ero clapped. "Thanks!"

He dropped down, pinned Sir to the sand by the shoulders, and sat on his stomach with a maniacal grin etched on his face. His wings silhouetted him like a giant shadowy halo.

"Holy shit, I've been itching to do this to you since you attacked me earlier."

"Comin' for the kill," Sir groaned, almost wishin' for it. He'd felt this way once before—in the arms of the fallen star. Trapped, but at peace. He gritted his teeth.

Ero put on a deep gasp. "Kill?! No, not that. Maybe kiss, if you let me, but not kill. You're sturdier than you look." Another wink. "I can't wait to get a hold of your mark so you can stop hiding your true colors from me. You know, I didn't see it at first, because your freaking aura is completely hidden, but I think you actually are pretty well-suited to handle me, Sir. Probably more than you think. Definitely more than I thought when I first met you."

"Still got no idea what you're talkin' 'bout," Sir muttered, caught between irate and dismayed while he stewed.

If he had anything to gain from havin' this angel drag him along for a while, at least he could use that time to figure out how to put an end to this senseless arrangement.

He wouldn't stay trapped too long. His jaw relaxed.

"That's all right, you don't have to know yet. You don't have to do anything. Just hold still for me..." Ero trailed off and carefully lifted his hands from Sir's shoulders. Paused to wait.

Sir considered boltin' one last time. Surprised himself when he didn't.

"Good boy," Ero whispered, then said, "Try and relax. I know with mastery of the Left, you can do whatever you want to anyone without their knowledge or consent, but that's not how the Right works. You have to let me in. The more you allow me, the less resistance you'll feel. I meant it when I said we had to trust each other."

For once, the gravity of Ero's words settled into Sir. His eyebrows drew down as Ero's weight pressed on him. Lighter than expected—but still remarkably heavy. Strong and sure.

"Come on, let me in," Ero said again.

Sir balled his fists. "Just go."

Ero nodded. They were leanin' towards each other, close enough that Sir could surge forward the slightest bit and knock foreheads.

He forced himself to relax, instead.

He really did have so many old and poorly healed fractures, sprains, and bruises, with bones set wrong in some places. Over time, he'd adapted well. Changed the way he moved. Compensated. It became even easier after he'd devoured the fallen star. Nearly negligible.

"I wonder why you don't heal like you're supposed to," Ero mused as he massaged Sir's solar plexus—the center of his chest. Damn angel'd aimed at that same place with his weapon just a bit ago. "Devils can self-regenerate as well as any angel. You're just shadows of the Empyrean, after all. The dark side of the same moon. I wonder a lot of things about you. Don't forget to breathe, too. You're still kinda tense."

Sir breathed in and out, in and out, drawin' enough air to drown a whale.

Ero shifted his hands down to Sir's stomach. "From here. You need to breathe from here."

Sir damn near jumped out his skin. "The hell you always touchin' me like that for?"

With an innocent pout, Ero said, "Like what?" and pushed in with the heels of his palms.

Sir breathed out again, directed by the press of Ero's hands on his stomach.

"You were breathing like an animal, you know. Your heart naturally doesn't beat. You don't need to breathe so shallowly like that. You instead should breathe from here, Sir—that's right, open up. See how that's better? You may not be human, but your body responds well. I wonder if I can do..."

A small stream of tepid energy suddenly passed between them, smoothin' out bones, mendin' blood vessels, and re-structurin' muscles in just a few moments. Sir felt it all at once.

"This," Ero finished.

"Ah...!"

"You're okay. It's just me. Breathe, baby."

Ero's energy against Sir's skin melted into him like strong sunlight, so sharp and hot that it stung, with a lingerin' warmth left behind. A bright, clear burn. Soft incisions.

"There you go," Ero whispered again. "Almost done..."

Some of the bones had to shatter apart before they re-formed. The pain came quiet, muted. Ero's energy stretched Sir's muscles 'til they fit in better patterns, untyin' knots and knittin' up tears. Tendons, cartilage, fat, and fresh skin eventually buried all his old scars. All exceptin' the oldest—a thin, faint line that arced from Sir's collarbone over his shoulder.

He felt like he was bein' healed on several levels—inside, on the surface, and outside, all at once—by the fire-poker of Ero's energy. Like spiritual surgery. A transcendental tattoo.

"Fuck, s'weird," Sir groaned.

Ero chuckled, but the sound came out flatter than usual. "It's funny you should say that, 'cause you're the one I think is weird." He sat back on his haunches, heavy on Sir's hips, and took his time lookin' Sir up and down. Tryin' to figure somethin' out. "It's not just the tension in your body that's blocking your mark from me. You really... Tch. I've heard of ghosts who couldn't properly wield their mastery before, but I don't think I've ever heard of one who had no clue at all about mastery. That's why you don't know your name, you can't heal properly, and you can't control your wings. That's why I can't sense your mark or your aura, either. It's all because you don't have any memory of nonhuman life. You don't even remember how to call on your mastery, do you?"

Sir took in a last deep breath, propped himself to sittin', and tried not to look Ero in the eye when he didn't budge even a bit.

"I ain't call nothin', and I know myself well enough without all that shit," Sir said. "You done fixin' me up or nah? S'hot as hell."

"Sorry, yeah, I'm done healing your old wounds, but, Sir... I can do so much more now that I know what the real problem is. I can show you who you really are, if you let me." Ero was always on a hundred, but the new revelation made him seem almost feverish. His excitement sparkled.

Sir bucked his hips. "Get off me."

"Say less." Ero finally rolled off and shot up to his feet. "The sun is almost done rising. Stretch out, see if you feel well enough to head back. I have a lot to teach you when we do."

"What? 'Bout mastery?"

"Naturally. But I really mean, about yourself, Sir."

Chapter 8

ERO

"T HIS IS A GLAIVE." Ero grasped the holographic shaft of the weapon in his non-dominant hand, extending it to Sir in the large, overgrown yard beside the shack house. He wanted to keep this as brief and painless as possible. They had already wasted enough time backtracking the landscape from Bulls Bay to the Georgia mountains. Bits of dawning sunlight shone against the dew at the tops of the tall grass around them as he said, "I'd like to see you in action again one last time to get a really good feel for what would be best for you, but this is as good a place to start as any. It'll help you call and control your mastery if nothing else. Here, take it. Swing it around some. See how it fits in your hand and how it'll complement the way you fight."

The curve of the glaive's heavy blade would make for some powerful cutting and slashing strikes, similar to the blows from Sir's fists. Sir sliced through the air with it a few times, catching the light and throwing it around, but it didn't take long for Ero to figure out it was off-balanced.

"Tell me what you think," he said.

Sir shrugged as he weighed the glaive. "S'a weapon."

"Ghosts usually have one, or two, or three, yeah. They're indispensable in a fight—and an achievable manifestation of anyone's mastery. Like your wings." Ero glanced at them briefly, always taken with their dark veins and subtle lines. "Choose any weapon, a rifle, a shield, a whip, whatever, then mark it and call it. That's all you have to do."

"I have weapons." Sir flashed his fangs in an uninspired smile.

"You sure do. So think of this as a backup. You already called your wings, but you can't send them home, right? After you call your weapon, you should be able to retract them both. Like this." Ero seamlessly sent his own wings and the glaive away, dissolving into particles of light, and then summoned his wings again. "No more having to sleep in chains."

Sir tried to hide his startle—he had a bad habit of playing all of his reactions close to the chest—but Ero saw straight through it. Most of the time.

"I'm not blind. It's not lost on me why you were sleeping with your wings chained up—you have no control over them. Like an errant limb, or a pair of breathing lungs, our wings function subconsciously. They probably got you into trouble, huh? Did you hurt someone you loved—or maybe yourself? I told you you stand to gain a lot. This doesn't have to be a sacrifice for either one of us," Ero said, then summoned a prismatic punch dagger, and pressed it into Sir's hand. "This isn't just a weapon. What I'm really giving you is control, Sir. Please, take it."

Sir shuffled away from Ero even as his eyes fixed on the punch dagger. The T-shaped handle of the dagger protruded between his fingers when he gripped it. The plain silver blade was short and stout, a perfect complement to the way he liked to hook, cross, and uppercut.

"It's yours now. Go on," Ero said.

Slowly, Sir flexed his hand around the punch dagger. It shone silver-grey then vanished as if in crumbles. Before Ero could say anything else, Sir reformed the dagger out of a hazy, flickering smoke into a blue-black blade with a titanium tip.

"Sick," Sir said.

"Very," Ero said. "That was... fast."

"I can fight with this."

"Yeah, you can. Your natural style is a bit, ah, athletic, so this should mesh well with those jabs you like to dish out. Just aim for the parts of the body that you already do—they're the same energy centers that will do the most damage with your dagger here. The kidneys, the clavicle, the nose, and the sweet spots between the ribs." Ero lifted his finger to the last area on himself, pausing to consider. "Soon you'll see you're already smarter and stronger than you ever were before."

Sir raised his eyebrow. "Before what? I had you?"

"Yeah! Great, I'm glad you pick things up so quickly, because now you're gonna have to do something about your wings." Ero pressed ahead without a care, his smile wide. Without meaning to, he was getting comfortable here—familiar in a way that seemed to come too easily.

"What d'you mean?" Sir suddenly snapped. "My wings don't do nothin'. They can't. Just got them one day." He rubbed at his shoulders, rolling them as if that would disguise the dark wings looming behind him. Nothing could hide those weapons.

"You can control them, you will control them, and I'm gonna show you how. It's easy. See?" Ero hummed, and his white-gold wings vanished once more. He could still feel their weight, but they had gone home, safe from plain sight, until the next time he called them back. "You just have to will it. Trust me, remember?"

Sir scoffed. "Right. Trust ya."

"I already said it once—I'll give you anything you want. Just keep up with me for now. It's important." Ero grinned more mischievously now, exposing his short gold fangs to the sunlight. "You have to retract your wings, Sir. Show me that you can."

"Back up," Sir said, and raised the punch dagger to eye level.

He thought so loudly and focused so hard that Ero could almost hear his ire: *Let's see if there's any truth to this bullshit.*

"Retract."

The dagger disappeared like ashes in the wind. Sir's wings slowly warped behind him as they shivered then vanished in the same way. The whole time, he kept his face flat, but the relief melted into his shoulders the instant he noticed his wings were gone.

And all he'd had to do was trust.

"Excellent," Ero cheered. "Didn't I tell you you had a lot to gain? Ghosts are limitless beings. I can teach you to control anything you want."

"And you can't do your job if I don't." Sir smiled mirthlessly.

Ero paused, but he still returned the hollow smile with his usual warmth. This was familiar, for sure. "Right again. I wouldn't be able to do my job if you didn't know how to master. But I can now that you're getting control. How do you feel? Still want out?"

Ero bit his lip. He shouldn't have asked. It wasn't an option, just a tease. He took a note from Sir's playbook and tempered his expectations somewhat. If Sir rejected him, again, after all this…

He watched carefully as Sir held out his palm. The punch dagger and his wings reappeared as if they'd never gone; like reflex, muscle memory, and second nature all combined. They disappeared again just as quickly. He was practicing.

"Say I'm in. What then?"

"Pledge your undying love for me, of course, husband."

Sir waited.

He did that a lot, rather than respond. Ero adjusted without even blinking. After a lifetime of dealing with Tsais, Sir's stoicism set him at ease, reminding him of simpler times. He almost couldn't help it.

"Okay, fine. Take what you want. You don't have to wait anymore. I can tell you're getting restless."

That was clearly what Sir wanted to hear. His fangs peeked from under his lip in an immediate, hungry scowl.

The fangs of devils were so much more menacing than the short, decorative pair that angels had. Silver, instead of gold, with bewitchingly long, sharp tips. Sir ran his tongue across them.

Ero's heart broke into a sprint. "Come on. I can take you."

Sir walked up, pressed Ero back into the tall grasses until they were swallowed whole, and brought their faces close enough to feel his breath. He stopped just shy, though, tightening his grip as Ero's chest brushed his arm on each inhale.

Ero expected this. He'd trained for this. He wanted it all along.

"You don't have to stop," he whispered.

"I won't."

Sir began to lift his hand and lower his head. His heavy gaze wandered down to Ero's neck.

"Yeah, I won't stop," he said again.

His nose grazed Ero's warm, trembling throat as Ero bravely tilted his chin up to make more room. Sir dragged his fangs from root to tip along the same spot he had bitten into before. It had completely faded already, but he still sank slowly back into the old wound, leaving his mark yet again.

Ero clutched onto Sir without saying a word. What could he say, while he was being drained beyond the point of death? What nice or pretty things would lighten the burden? All he could really do was sigh, try to breathe through the pain, and occasionally shake.

As promised, Sir didn't stop until Ero had no resistance left.

This time, he came back much more quickly than the first time. Probably only a few seconds had passed. Ero didn't even think Sir had noticed—he was too busy rubbing his lips and tongue against the closing wound. He healed the punctures he left behind.

That was a good sign. Devils weren't generally capable of healing others. Sir's mastery was already heading in the right direction.

At least.

"Sir?"

"Angel," said Sir with blood on his breath.

"What are you doing, healing me?" Ero tried to laugh, even though it was the last thing he felt like doing. "I can do that on my own. I'm fine. Just let me up."

He pushed at Sir's shoulder, and Sir released him. Ero stumbled a bit when he did, sending him into a mild coughing fit. Droplets of blood and small, ripped chunks of red muscle splattered against his lips as they came up. His black pants, the grass all around them, and even a bit of Sir's face were dotted red. Sir licked his lips.

Ero wiped his mouth with a sleeve. "There, do you feel better? You always take so much."

"S'always so much to take," Sir said, a lilt to his drawl.

"I'll take that as a yes. Good." Ero coughed one last time, then straightened himself up, presenting as regally as he could muster. He even surprised himself with how well he could pull together. "Now try to attack me."

Sir barked a single, incredulous laugh at that. "Ha! Right. After I just drained you like that. You can't hardly stand."

"I'm standing! I told you, I'm fine. I heal on my own. You haven't killed me yet, have you? So call your wings and your weapon, and attack me. I want to show you something. Trust me, remember," Ero added, gently.

The less he telegraphed how deep the pain of Sir's bite went, the less Sir could question it. He just had to put up with whatever it took to raise Sir. It would only be a moment in the grand scheme.

His pain meant nothing and everything at the same time.

Sir had gone quiet, unanswering. Again.

Ero huffed. "One thing's for sure, you may not look like a ghost, but you damn well act like one with the way you love taking your sweet time. Come on, already. Attack me."

Sir's face remained unchanged as he scanned the surrounding tall grasses, the distant mountains. He seemed to evaluate the request for another long while.

"Fine. Your wings," he said at last.

"What?"

"I'll attack you. But call your wings first."

"Oh, no, I don't need to. You'll see. Just come on," Ero repeated.

Sir shook his head, a clear *Here, damn*, and with a sudden burst of movement, he lunged forward. His fist was aimed for Ero's jaw.

Ero sidestepped, his movements fluid and well-trained. He countered with a swift kick to Sir's side, but Sir deflected it back.

Sir's attacks had been wild and powerful before, underscored by his natural need for self-defense, but Ero got an entirely different sense for them now. He struck like a focused force of nature, each blow more calculated than the last and sometimes accented with the punch dagger.

"So far, so good!" Ero called, pulse racing. He had never taught anyone to fight before, and watching Sir's refined strength unfold delighted him way more than he expected.

It looked like Sir was taking to his eclipse matrix perfectly well.

Between the bloodletting and exchanges of energy, Ero had found the perfect opportunity to attach an eclipse matrix to Sir's dormant mastery. The eclipse matrix was an ancient wartime technology that had rarely been used since. Cerviel had built Ero one of his own, as a way to tolerate his life's mission, and he had, in a way, done the same for Sir when he healed Sir's old unhealed wounds. He had used the only opportunity that Sir had given him to touch him, and the rest was history, so far. The installation was painless and invisible. Ero made sure of it.

It was Sir's own eclipse matrix that had wrenched his bones and stitched his skin until nothing remained but health and life in him. There was no way he and Ero were at the level of trust where Ero could do that on his own. Sir just underestimated his own nature since he was so ignorant to it.

Ero aimed to changed all of that. He finally called his wings to break free; they shimmered around him in an instant. "See if you can keep up with me."

Sir stumbled a bit, landing square on his feet as he glared at Ero from the ground. "Let's see," he said, calmly, and then jumped.

Ero summoned his halberd and attacked at the same time, but Sir spun out of the way. He evaded well. His grey-black wings unfurled in the same fluid motion, keeping him airborne.

"Good! Keep going!" Ero said. Dropping altitude, he attacked again.

Sir was faster than before. He dodged aside. "I won't stop."

"You don't have to, remember?"

His attacks went on, more precise, more controlled, aimed at finding Ero's weaknesses.

Ero narrowed his eyes as he fended off the intensity of Sir's assault. It was both impressive and increasing. As the fight wore on, he had to focus harder. He pushed himself to keep up with Sir's relentless barrage.

"All right, now—ahh—!"

The titanium tip of Sir's dagger sliced across Ero's temple. That was all it took for his own eclipse matrix to suddenly engage.

"No, wait!"

He couldn't stop it.

Sir disappeared.

One second, Ero was reaching for him, scrambling not to defend himself, and the next, Sir was on the ground, buried in the tall grass.

"Shit! Sir!" Ero dashed down beside him, wings stowed.

What had he done?

Sir was passed out, his skin split and torn open, with new wounds layered on top of the ones that had just been healed.

Ero struggled to think back on his feelings and intentions during the fight. He had been sure to keep from going all out. Honestly, all of his focus had been on countering Sir's blows. Was that enough to trigger his unconscious self-defenses—that negligible strike next to his eye?

Sir probably wouldn't come to for a while, if so.

"Oh, Sir..."

Ero had stunned him, likely with an automatic but undirected force seal. Force seals were meant to bind ghosts convicted of a crime, divesting them of the powers responsible for such betrayals, in preparation for their final judgment. Sir had triggered his own arrest.

"I'm sorry," Ero said, leaning in toward Sir as if he could hear. "I'll be right here when you wake up. Try to rest while you can. We got a long way to go."

He reached for Sir's hand. Before he could do anything else, Sir's eclipse matrix kick-started the healing process, like other devils. His wings gently retracted. All Ero had to do was watch as the fresh blood of his wounds slowly faded, too.

Finally. Sir was behaving more like a ghost in the ways that mattered.

Eventually, all his injuries disappeared—everything except the long, but shallow, thin scar at Sir's shoulder.

Ero ran his fingers over it. "Why won't this one heal, I wonder?"

The same one he couldn't heal before, neither could Sir's own mastery. He glanced up to Sir's face and studied it as if to find the answer there.

It didn't take but a moment for him to lose track of time, memorizing Sir's face. The simple lines and inviting shapes that composed Sir's features were precise and fine, almost androgynous. Fox-like eyes, full lips, and these long, thin eyebrows had emerged from underneath all the blood and balefulness. Without his hair and bruise-colored wings in the way, he didn't look like any kind of devil at all. He didn't look like an angel, either. He almost looked... human.

A drop of bright red blood fell on Sir's face. Ero flinched and touched the cut on his temple, still slowly healing. "Damn it."

Sir's eyes flashed open, and Ero was caught staring.

He didn't have the decency to avert his gaze.

"That was quick. Are you awake? Usually it takes a lot longer to rise from that kind of hit."

For a while, Sir didn't reply. He just looked back at Ero, quietly.

Angrily.

Ero adjusted his grip on Sir's shoulder and gave a gentle squeeze. Clear head. He wasn't afraid. If anything, Sir's ability to strike him in a fight was encouraging—they were well on their way to Rising together, if he could already do something like that.

Sir's eyes slid shut again, and for a moment, Ero thought he'd actually drifted back into a coma.

But then, with a low, dragging groan, he said, "Fuck you."

Ero almost laughed. "Sure. Fuck me. You don't even have to ask."

Sir's jaw flexed as he licked his lips and ignored Ero, pulling away to sit up on his own. His endless curls draped over his back and shoulders like a black shield, in place of his wings. "The fuck was so important to show me about that, hm? Damn well been knew I can't finish you off yet. Trust me, I been thinkin' on it."

This time, Ero did laugh. It startled him, but he couldn't help it. "'Thinkin' on it,' he says, like it's not pretty much a matter of time. I don't think you realize what just happened—I subconsciously force sealed you after only one of your attacks drew blood. Sorry again, by the way, now that you're awake. That was on reflex."

"Force sealin' again. S'why I passed out?"

"More or less. You fight hard, Sir, like I said, but not hard enough—no, not informed enough. Not against me. You need to fully master the energy inside and around you before you have the hope of actually overpowering me. Because I understand force seals—I understand mastery—and you don't. Yet. That's what I wanted to show you."

"I thought..." Sir grabbed his punch dagger as it resolved out of thin air, like, *See?*

"Yes, you have 'control' now, but you don't just need 'control' of energy to master it. You also need to 'understand' it. Put this away." Ero fit his hand gently over Sir's around the punch dagger. It dispersed, leaving only skin on skin. "This is nothing compared to what else you can do with your mind once you 'understand.' Here, listen with me. Don't speak. You don't have to think, either. Close your eyes, and just be still for a moment. You're good at that, anyway."

He demonstrated, taking the world into his lungs with a single, sacred inhalation. The stretch of his mind was nearly religious. Keeping his latent talents boxed away while he'd been in the company of humans had been so stifling, now that he had full range again.

He shook out his shoulders and then squared them.

"It's in your blood, Sir—the need for your spirit to not only control, but also to connect to all the energies of the world. You can do it easily. Here. I am right in front of you. Would you still sense my presence if I wasn't holding your hands like this and you weren't holding mine? What if I stopped speaking and breathing? And further, even beyond me, the wind rushes through the trees—they all have separate vibrations of their own. Would you still know they were here with us if you couldn't see the vines sway and feel the air against your face?

"You already know the answers to all of these questions. I'm just asking them to speak to their presence in your mind. All you need to do to access the truth is concentrate on it. It always comes—the truth of reality."

The monologue fell like a memory from his lips, saccharine, nearly second-nature. They were the same words that Cerviel used to train him, the same words that pushed him to understand *every-thing*—to manipulate and harmonize with the world.

To create reality. To be god.

The most foundational plight of the angels.

"Start small. Focus on me. It'll come naturally sooner than you realize. You can sense everything you'll ever need to know about me in my aura—even how I feel in this exact moment. The same goes for you. The same goes for everyone and everything. Just concentrate. Look for me. I'll find you."

Finally.

Another awareness flickered at the edges of Ero's own, ushering in Sir's spiritual presence.

The elusive mark of the devil.

Here it was after all of Ero's searching. From the Bridges of Chaos, to Galveston Island, and even when they met in the misty Georgia mountains, Ero had searched for Sir's mark all over the realm of Lesser Earth. He'd found strangers, nightmares, fears he never knew he had, but not a single sign of his devil's mark.

Until now.

Insignificant, unassuming, the mark of Sir's mastery started to take shape. It gave his aura an indistinct and enigmatic edge, with a dim, muted glow, like a vanishing shadow.

Most auras were as discretely individual as whoever they belonged to. Like Lios' had been, her lush, pastel purple hues, and Tsais' deep, even green.

Sir's was empty.

Void-of-course.

Ero let out a steadying breath and clenched his fingers around Sir's. He inched forward. "Uh... There you go. See, you already have full control. You just have to understand what you're feeling. This is how you're supposed to perceive the worlds around you."

"Shut up." Sir took a deep breath before a growl abruptly grew in his chest.

Ero went still as Sir leaned in, leonine and predacious, slowly pinning Ero in place with his body. A line of irritation cut across Ero's senses, as faint as Sir's low, hard voice.

"So heavy..."

"I know. We're built for it, though. And you have me. I'm right here, Sir."

A silver shadow, like grey candlelight, started to fill Sir's aura. It was nothing like the electricity and warmth Ero sensed from others. It was vacuous, instead; incomplete; a mirror of his mark.

"Sir, please say something."

Sir shifted forward more, bringing them about chest to chest with each other. "Angel..."

Ero's eyes almost rolled back. Sir was a solid weight on top of him; he'd cemented their hands to the ground on either side of them, too, so the press tightened any time Ero tried to move. He screwed his eyes shut to keep his heart from drilling through his ribs.

He wasn't afraid of Sir. He wasn't afraid. Clear head, clear heart.

"Hey, Sir... Remember to be still if you feel overwhelmed. You can direct your thoughts wherever you want them to go. Everything doesn't have to be such a struggle."

Ero swallowed. The trees around them flailed as if a storm was tearing through. He focused on Sir's smoke trails of a mark.

"Calm down. Take it easy on yourself. Everything's okay."

Sir didn't calm down at all. He squeezed, pulling more insistently, until everything in Ero lit up in his silver shadows.

There it was.

Sir's total, aura-filled mark.

His aura glimmered with the same silverish hue as before, but it flickered like a distant flame in darkness. He'd done it. This was the mark of Sir's mastery, without a doubt. It emanated with his power and energy—but also with malevolence, hopelessness, and a devastation that broke Ero's heart.

"Why are you so different," he murmured.

The tendons of his fingers began to cry out for reprieve, calling his attention.

"Shit! Sir? Sir, can you hear me?"

The thin shadows from Sir's newly manifested mark soaked into everything around them, a grey-black radiance that gradually pooled into the grass. A jolt of something like those old nightmares Ero used to have flickered up around them, catching an electric charge in the air. Like his worst dreams had come to life.

Sir was no Nightmare. Ero didn't recognize any name, rank, or class on Sir's mark, so whatever he was, it couldn't be a damned Nightmare.

Ero wasn't afraid, but his heart hammered as if he were. Sacrifice was nothing new. No matter what, he had to press ahead.

"Sir, listen to me—"

A colony of cicadas suddenly burst out of the ground like hungry, milling ants. They came to a rolling boil, black bubbles that broke open into insects. Thousands of dark shells transformed the ground into an oil-shine tar pit. As the cicadas trilled, a symphony from hell, static electricity burst over Ero's hands and forearms, crackling as it sent small pulses of pain under his skin.

Oh... He wasn't afraid. He wasn't afraid. He wasn't losing control. He was made for this.

He tried to yank away, but it was as if he'd been anchored in place. Sir was as unresponsive as a mountain on top of him. Currents of pain kept stabbing at Ero's forearms, shoulders—spreading to his chest, neck. Cicadas crawled under his clothes, fleeting, ticklish bristles against his skin. Vibrations echoed through his muscles. He choked on the damp, woody musk. They were everywhere.

He grit his teeth against the urge to gasp and turned his face in towards the back of Sir's head. The thick, dark curls shielded his mouth from the buzzing legs and wings.

"Sir," he tried. "Can you hear me? You have to answer me. You have to wake up. *Now*. Before you fall."

The screaming cicadas drowned out his voice. Nearby crows joined in the fray as they passed. He had to clear his head. He couldn't lose Sir to the underworld.

"Mhh..." Sir started to answer, but it stretched into a heavy growl as he gnashed his teeth against Ero's shoulders.

His busy fangs ripped open tears as fine as paper cuts across Ero's skin. They burned as much as if Sir had fully pierced him. Cicadas crawled all over his wounds.

Dazed, he tried to breathe through the worst of the pain, like before. His eyes closed as it began to overtake him. He was good at acting like it didn't hurt. His body could react all it wanted—his heart could pound, the cicadas could cover him—but he'd never budge, or flinch, or recoil. He could be the same stone that Sir had turned into. He could tolerate anything, even dying.

Sacrifice.

It was all about sacrifice.

Sir had taunted him with it, and Ero had denied it, but he probably shouldn't have. He really was a willing sacrifice. He was designed to shed blood and to dive into hell should he need to.

And he would.

But the drone of cicadas started to ebb. A small bundle of sparks flared at the boundaries of Sir's expanded aura. They cracked, screamed, and popped. Sweet rot dangled in the air, and then fire.

At first, only a few blooms caught flame—the Spanish moss and beard moss that hung gracefully from the branches. Then more and more lit up until the dangling mosses roasted in the air and spread from vine to vine. Dark, flickering shadows raced toward the canopy above. More cicadas flew into the flames, singeing sap.

"Sir?! Snap the hell out of it! You're lighting the forest on fire, and it's catching! Come on! Wake up!"

Black fire rained from the sky. Ero yanked at Sir's grip, but it was like pulling against a machine. Sir didn't budge. Flames licked at the trees, spreading fast, and Ero scrambled to shield the forest from the chaos. He didn't know what else to do. He could force seal Sir again, but Sir already wasn't responsive, and without following through with the final—fatal—seal, it wouldn't make much of a difference.

Maybe Ero shouldn't have installed an eclipse matrix in Sir, or even taught him mastery in the first place, if this is what he was capable of doing when left to his own devices.

He had had to—it was his job—but empowering Sir like this gave Sir access to as much capacity for benevolence as malevolence. It did the same for Ero. Between them, the eclipse matrix allowed a devil to use Right Hand mastery without Rising and an angel to use Left Hand mastery without Falling. Although, Ero hadn't been created in the seat of perdition and sent to plague the human world. He didn't dabble in much mastery from the Left Hand, either. Maybe under circumstances like those, the mark of his mastery would emanate chaos and destruction, the way Sir's did. Maybe he would shut down when he was confronted with the energy of the universe all at once, too. The angels wouldn't care about finer details like that. They only cared about getting the job done.

Suddenly, the cicadas disappeared—all at once, they retreated from under his clothes and scattered into the mountains. For a second, there was only the rapid buzz of wings, bitter, burnt sap, and the crackle of charred swinging vines.

Then a teeny tiny flickering aura approached the widening edge of Sir's mark, along with a small, scratchy "Rowr...!"

Ero shook his head. He almost hadn't noticed the interruption. "Hey, hold on! Don't come any closer," he called.

Somehow, a little black jaguar had gotten caught in the crossfire of Sir's unrestrained mastery.

"You'll get hurt! Please, run away. Run far!"

The cub didn't listen. She blinked giant, smoke-fogged eyes at them, and stumbled even closer.

Again, Ero yanked, and pulled, and tried to blast Sir away from him, but all he could do in the end was shield the cub from the catching flames as they continued to burn.

"Sir. Wake up. Come on, husband. I'm not gonna lose you here. *Wake up!*"

Chapter 9

ERO

S TILL, THERE WAS NO answer.

The little black cub that wandered its way into Sir's mark staggered along under Ero's protective bubble until it squeezed its chunky little body between them and cuddled up to Sir. Ero was speechless for a minute—bewildered. Who the hell was this little cub? If not for her aura—the same clean, clear aura that most animals had—and the fact that she kept warmly cuddling up to Sir, Ero would've guessed it was someone he knew. Tsais, maybe. They had the same green flashing eyes.

"Y-you—" Sir stammered.

"Ahh!" Ero looked up to find Sir staring straight at him.

He hadn't even noticed the little bit of space that had opened between them. The cub curled up and made itself a little throne there.

"You scared me! Sir? Can you hear me? Are you there? Cut it out already—you're burning everything alive around us."

Even before Ero finished, Sir's flames started receding. All
the flickering silver-black shadows steadily dissipated until only
the static electric currents between their bodies remained. He
wasn't totally free yet, but Ero still let loose a sigh in relief.

Sir frowned and spat out a mouthful of dark, purplish
blood. Ero shifted to try and shield the cub from spatter, but
he was still trapped.

"You... talk... so fuckin' much," Sir finished saying.

Ero didn't even care if that was supposed to be a neg. "True!
It's a good thing, too, or else we'd have even more destruction
to answer for. You heard my voice, in the end. I'm still not
entirely sure why I lost you."

He glanced up at the bleak, crooked branches that creaked
overhead. A rainfall of debris gently showered him, and ashes
drenched the mountainside around them. The acrid stench of
burnt wood, grass, and chitin hung in the air, stinging his eyes.
Even knowing Sir couldn't be a true Nightmare didn't make
the situation seem any less nightmarish.

"Do you know what happened?" he asked.

"No... Sorry..." Sir mumbled. "Never do. Wish I did."

Ero's heart cracked for a second. Sir looked so tired, his
hair limp as it veiled his face, and all his reactions were slow,
his responses even more spaced out than usual. Ero couldn't
imagine living life as a slave to his instincts, with no higher
knowledge to guide him. No wonder Sir clung so hard to his
roots—they were all he had. They were all that made sense to
him. Anything else may as well be a deep, dark cavern.

"Sir, are you with me?"

The words left Ero without him meaning to let them go. Once gone, he tried to swallow them back down, but his throat was too dry. More worry came up.

"Do you need anything?" he added hoarsely. "Do you need more of my blood?"

Sir tilted his head somewhat, as if considering the question, but didn't get a chance to respond.

The still mountain air was shattered by a commanding voice. It echoed through the scorched trees.

"Hold it right there! We got y'all surrounded!"

Sir suddenly retracted the last static electric mark of his mastery. "Texas authorities," he said, lips pressed.

Ero's eyes widened as he turned to see the clearing around them fill with the ominous presence of Texas State Troopers emerging from the haggard shadows. Their weapons were drawn and pointed right at Sir, forming a wide circle around him, Ero, and the unsuspecting cub. Ero was unused to registering humans as threats, so he had ignored any notions of them to contain the spread of Sir's destruction instead. He hardly registered them at all. Lios had spoiled him.

A surge of panic bubbled up in his blood.

Still recovering from the aftermath of his awakening, Sir struggled to hold himself upright, and he'd gone silent again. His eyes, once glazed over, narrowed to calculating squints. Ero would have to fend these humans off for Sir, somehow. He knew exactly why they were here—for the same reason as he was, more or less. Sir was a killer that needed to be dealt with.

"Put your hands on your head, and surrender!" another State Trooper commanded, voice amplified through a megaphone in their helmet. "We been trackin' you too long to let you go, so you may as well give it up now, boss!"

Eerie, how similar their goals were to Ero's, really.

Sir's lips curved into an absent, unseeing grin. The air around him seemed to crackle with intense pressure.

"Sir, hey, Sir, listen to me," Ero said. "I'll take care of them for you. Do you hear me? I will handle them. Just let me go, and you don't have to do a thing. Please... please, don't do anything."

A thick mountain accent cut through next. "Son, you're speaking with Lt. Ogbere. I'm here on behalf of the Georgia State Highway Patrol. My friends from Texas behind me here are the task force that's been dispatched to find you, John Doe AKA 'the Ghost Killer.' I'm giving them a hand. See, the state of Texas has been in pursuit of the Ghost Killer for the full week of March 28, wanted for the disappearance of one Dr. Alexander White Esmeralda and one Sgt. Jackson Esmeralda of the Texas Rangers, as well as several state police teams between Houston and Helen. Please comply with the call for your arrest, so we can all go home to our families, thank ya very much."

Cops.

Why, oh, why did they give Sir a damn nickname? They were so excited for the rare chance to pursue a violent criminal that they didn't realize they were pursuing the wrong one. Ero couldn't take his focus from Sir if he wanted even a chance in hell at keeping them alive.

"You should get out of here," he told them. It was as if he was nailed to the forest floor under Sir's weight.

"Lemme see those hands, fellas!"

The crunch of boots on scorched earth filled the air, a grim cadence that grew louder with every step the Troopers took. Each sound hammered against Ero's chest, driving dread deeper into his veins.

Sir canted his head back, languidly, but with an odd pause. His hair slowly fell back from his shoulders as he turned toward them.

"Please, run," Ero whispered, tears burning in his eyes.

Lt. Ogbere and the contingent of Texas State Troopers behind him hesitated, unsure of how to proceed now that they were face-to-face with Sir. "Just do as we say, all right? We'll get to the bottom of this together. Later," he added, pointedly.

"Oh, fuck it." Ero concentrated on his devil. "Listen, okay. You don't have to fight them if you're too weak, Sir. You never have to kill again, remember? There's another way out of this. You've never had me before, but you do now. I'm here now. Let me help. Drink my blood."

It didn't appear Sir heard a damn word.

With a sudden burst of speed, he lunged at Lt. Ogbere, moving faster than anyone could follow—even Ero.

The air resonated with a vicious *sssshhhg*, and Ero barely registered what happened before he saw Sir standing over Lt. Ogbere's decapitated body, his light eyes glinting like an animal's.

"Heard you, Angel," Sir said, his voice thick with fresh, dripping blood.

The Texas contingent collapsed into a clamor.

"Lieutenant! No!"

"Contact, contact!"

"Bellamy, get Georgia on comms! Engage ahead!"

The Troopers swiftly and resolutely opened fire. Bullets beamed through the air, but Sir maneuvered between them effortfully, dodging some and barely blinking at the impact of any others. He darted forward, drew blood from the Troopers, changed targets, rinsed, and repeated.

In the most sick, macabre way, Ero watched with awe as Sir unleashed a devastating display of his barely contained power. There was no hesitation, no remorse—just raw, unrelenting devastation that left no room for mercy. The little jaguar, sensing the danger, cowered beside Ero, even as she kept her eyes glued on Sir, too. It was horrifically magnificent.

In a matter of moments, Sir had reduced the State Troopers to one. He cornered the survivor against the burnt husk of a tree, her back pressed tight against the bark as she fumbled for her comms.

She bellowed, "Thomas! Commander! Anybody?! Comms check? Comms! Please, somebody come the fuck in!"

"Y'all should've never left Texas," Sir said, his voice low and cutting, a blade sharper than the air between them.

Ero rushed straight ahead before he knew what he was doing. He was just thinking about saving the only State Trooper left alive. Her name was Officer Niv Blake. Her birthday had just passed. Ero had to stop Sir from killing her, too, the only way he could think of—he used himself as a shield.

Sir's hand snagged tight around Ero's throat, instead of the State Trooper.

Ero gritted his teeth as blood sprang to the back of his tongue. Behind him, Officer Blake shouted into her mouthpiece, sending her yell through the distant mountains. He reached back with one hand to tap her, and urged, "Please, run, now."

Just like it had in Galveston with Lios, Ero's influence over-whelmed Officer Blake once he touched her. She stopped shouting at once, didn't even pause to glimpse his face, and sprinted off into the endless rolling mountains, clamoring until her final footfalls vanished into the quiet.

Alone, at last.

Ero put both his hands on Sir's, each breath a labor, tinged red.

"Are you gonna fucking let me go?" he croaked.

Sir said nothing. He just glared at Ero, his eyes the color of daytime clouds—too bright, too intense, to match the flat line of his frown. In fact, he looked almost like a statue, his eyes fixed on the way his own hand clamped around Ero's neck.

Ero couldn't even say it hurt. He didn't need to breathe. It wasn't as though he was choking to death or anything.

But still...

"You should... treat me better," he said.

Sir barely flinched. He still seemed distant, even though he could talk clearly now, and refused to look away from Ero's neck. Blood drenched his mouth and collarbones. It dripped in long, slow lines down his skin. "Angel," he said after some time.

"Angel... yes... I'm your Angel." Ero had never been more delighted to call himself that name. "Now let... me... go."

"...Sorry," Sir said, and released Ero.

He collapsed, clutching his throat as he coughed. The air crashed back into his system.

The little cub he'd left behind crept back up to his side, eyes complete circles as she bumped herself against him. He scratched lightly under her chin. Thank goodness for her, something to distract him from gasping. It was still unpleasant having to live through strangulation. As he tickled her, she started purring—loudly—like an old car engine, and it lulled him into a contemplative pause between relief and unease.

Well, if Ero hadn't fucked up.

Sure, he managed to keep Sir from killing Officer Blake, but the rest of the small Texas task force lay torn apart, their bodies quickly crumbling in the burned-out clearing around him. Even without the flamelike shadows of Sir's mastery, a dark, eerie glow lingered over the field like scars through the ash.

"Sir? Can you still hear me?" Ero asked, heart pounding. "Is 'sorry' really all you have to say?"

In the least surprising move yet, Sir didn't reply. The cub flippantly broke away from Ero to go to Sir. Ero almost stopped her, but by the time he had reached out to grab her, Sir's hand blocked the way.

Sir had kneeled down to pet her. He mimicked the earlier way that Ero had pet the cub's chin to help ground himself. Never in a million years would Ero have guessed that Sir had such a soft spot for animals. He sagged.

"Honestly," he sighed, "I don't even know what to expect with you anymore, Sir."

The closer Sir came to Rising, as he adapted to integrating his implicit powers, the less preoccupied he became with ditching Ero. That should've been more than good enough. And yet, here they were, in a blackened graveyard.

Ero had to do better than this. He had to be better than this.

He took a deep breath.

"Well, thank you," he said in such a small voice that it could've been a prayer.

Sir kept petting the cub. It didn't seem so absent anymore, more focused. Ero pressed on regardless, his voice a bit louder. He couldn't hesitate now. It had already cost too much.

"I'll take the apology. In return, I want to thank you for what you did earlier. For letting Officer Blake go and for listening to me even if you didn't want to. I appreciate that you did that. I was afraid, for a while there, that you had changed your mind about trusting me."

Then he called on his wings and halberd in the same easy breath.

The cub looked up and growled at him.

Slowly, Sir glanced up, too. He even opened his mouth, as if he had something to say.

Ero smiled.

"Let's talk later," he said, took aim, and hit Sir with a force seal.

Sir landed on his back without even a sound. The cub jumped a foot in the air, hissing her surprise. She ran over and yanked at Ero's pant leg.

"It's all right, he's all right," he assured her as he scooped her up. "There really is something about him, huh, princess?"

He had to stop himself from immediately going to check on Sir. He didn't have long. Sir had already proven that he could rise from a secondary force seal in just a few minutes. With the help of Ero's blood falling on his face, too, of course. Ero couldn't really guess how long it would be before Sir rose with no interference.

However long it was, it would have to be enough for Ero to get his shit together. He had to clear his fucking head.

As of right now, he'd done everything he could to ensure Sir was up to par for the Ascension ritual. Even if his mark never manifested as anything more than empty flickering shadows, it was still Sir's mark. If anything, its use against the State Troopers only confirmed that.

So.

Now they just had to get married and follow the path toward Sanctuary.

He'd have to work quickly if he had any chance of offsetting Sir's natural inclination for straight up malice. Especially if this was what Sir accomplished with his first stabs at mastery: another string of murders in a list of others.

He had to get Sir to want him.

He had to get Sir to marry him.

He still had to get Sir to Rise with him.

These were the last steps left. Three small, simple, inconsequential steps.

Ero bolstered himself. Reflexively, he checked his temple, but the small wound Sir had landed on him earlier was gone. Good. He still healed from Sir's attacks—no matter how slowly.

"Time to clean up this mess."

He put the cub to sleep and paused for only another second before rolling her gently onto Sir's chest. It seemed like the place she'd like to be most. With both hands free, he held his halberd crosswise. The decorated axe head almost tilted out of his grasp, but he held firm and rebalanced it. He focused on the breadth of the damage done by Sir's fangs and effervescent flames—the mark of his mastery was unmistakable across the landscape. He took a slow, deep breath and cut through the air in a swift horizontal swipe. An arc of light sliced into the grass, trees, and half-decayed bodies. Everything the light touched rapidly revived into the expansive exhibit of vibrance from before. The State Troopers vanished, and the forest glowed with resplendence in the aftermath.

He couldn't undo their deaths, but now that everything appeared sparkling green and gold again, he almost felt silly for being so fearful earlier. He had to remember: There was no damage Sir could cause that Ero couldn't handle. He had been made for it.

All these chaotic, negative emotions that funneled into him from Sir's direct influence must've started messing with Ero's internal wiring, if he seemed to forget that.

Or maybe it had just been the intimate combination of calling Sir's mark forward, the black flames that devoured everything, and being trapped underneath him that had made Ero's heart shudder.

It started pounding again as he stowed his halberd and approached Sir's side. His fingers twitched without it. He knelt carefully, hands hovering over Sir's sacrum, where Ero had hit him with the force seal. The sacrum controlled the overall flow of energy in the body. Ero wanted to ensure the blockade there would hold before he tried to disable Sir's eclipse matrix.

Because he had to... didn't he?

"Somehow," he murmured.

It was the only way forward if Sir kept straying so far away from the Right Hand. If nothing else, it was the *safest* way forward. Now that Sir could access his mastery autonomously, Ero could remove Sir's eclipse matrix without removing that autonomy, but also without giving him anymore access to unnecessary power.

A low groan pierced the silence. Sir's eyes started to roam behind his lids, and Ero's blood ran cold.

"Damn it...!"

Sir always woke up so goddamned quickly. How was it possible to be that strong?

Another spike of panic stabbed at Ero.

Was he the one who was too weak?

As Sir's eyelids fluttered, Ero bit into his bottom lip hard enough to draw blood. The metallic taste rapidly became a familiar flood in his mouth. Something about it comforted him.

His blood was probably the least violent way he had left to sway Sir. He'd use it until he fell apart if he had to—since it seemed he was supposed to do just that.

A thin stream of blood escaped the corner of Ero's lips and dripped onto Sir's.

"Nnn..." Sir moaned.

"Open up, lover. If you won't take it, I'll give it to you."

Slowly, Ero leaned in, pressing his mouth against Sir's in a warm, wet kiss. The wave of blood stretched between them, and for a split second, Sir stiffened in surprise. There was so much blood that it overflowed from the smallest spaces between their lips. Sir wasn't drinking.

"Come on...!"

Ero almost panicked, his heart throbbing as he pressed his blood against Sir's tongue with his own. The first touch shocked him, but he didn't stop. He couldn't shrink back. He had to surge forward. Come on. Clear head. Clear heart.

He licked into Sir's mouth again, sliding more blood across Sir's tongue. A strained moan hit his ears, as if from a distance at first—from the faraway mountains, like Officer Blake's screams.

It took another moment to realize, it was all Ero. He was the one moaning.

And Sir had both hands latched around his ribcage.

Sir was awake. He pulled Ero closer.

Ero stopped moaning and posted his arms to keep from falling flat on top of Sir. Finally, as Ero kissed more blood between Sir's lips, it started to disappear. Sir drank it all, with a shade of his trademark hunger, then he opened his mouth, and kissed Ero back.

It wasn't as though anything quite tangible had changed between one thing and the other. Nothing except for Sir leaning in to steal more of Ero's breath. With the blood gone, all that was left was the press of their lips and tongues, and the dark behind their eyelids.

Ero shivered as Sir squeezed his sides like he wanted to break them. His touch was rough, like a vice, and as he tilted his head, deepening the kiss further, his teeth grazed Ero's lower lip. The sensation sent another shiver down Ero's spine until he moaned again. The kiss went so deep, lined by blood, their mouths moving together in an agitated to-and-fro. He could feel Sir's heart thudding against his chest, deep as a bass drum, and trying hard to match the frantic pace of his own. The world around them disintegrated, leaving only the two of them, locked in the moment, trapped in each other.

Until Ero backed away, breathing heavily.

Sir's lips lingered against Ero's, and for a fleeting second, the heat of their shared blood wasn't the only thing connecting them. He pulled back, too, his gaze clouded with something unreadable, but his grip on Ero tightened.

He was still calm.

Despite his red, bruised lips, like the center of a storm, he held himself chillingly still, while just below the surface of his placid face, a hurricane raged.

Ero's heart ached all of a sudden. "Are you awake?" he asked breathlessly.

"Yes. I'm awake, Angel."

Sir said it in such a way that telegraphed his every expectation to set this conversation aside, but Ero wasn't about to let that happen now that he had Sir's attention.

He grabbed Sir by the collar. "Then answer me, damn you. Why do you keep killing State Troopers who come after you? I get why you felt like you had to in the past, maybe, but I told you you could depend on me now. I know you could hear me—you said you could. Why didn't you even try?"

"Doc was my friend," Sir said as a matter of fact. "Or my father, I dunno. Texas'll keep lookin' for me 'cause I killed him."

Ero grit his teeth through a smile. "I know that. I'm not saying any of that is your fault. I know what he put you through. I just want to know why you didn't listen to me when I told you not to act."

"S'hard to hide from them outside of stayin' off-grid. They're like flies. Can't ignore them, or else they'll just keep comin' back." Sir shrugged without moving his shoulders, then dragged his gaze down Ero's body—still straddling his lap. "Their tech's good. Local governments cooperate all the time. Think I killed ten or twenty Rangers across Louisiana, Mississippi, and—"

"Stop!"

Ero grabbed a handful of Sir's black hair and covered his mouth with the other hand.

"Just stop it, Sir. As long as they look for you, you'll just keep killing them? How can you say stuff like that so heartlessly? You're talking about people whose lives have ended like they're nothing. Do you even realize that your actions have consequences? You can't just say whatever the hell you please and do whatever the hell you want. Maybe you could before, when you were the only one responsible for your actions, but not now. Not anymore. I'm also responsible for you now. I have to answer for everything you do."

"What d'you mean," Sir asked through Ero's fingers.

"You know what I mean! You take the meaning straight from me every time you drink my blood! Angels don't needlessly kill humans like this, Sir," Ero said, panting. "If you want to have any hope of Rising, you can't kill anymore. I'm your ticket to ultimate mercy. You said you would take it. You said you'd *take me*."

Almost as if to mock him, Sir grabbed Ero around the waist, yanking him close again. That wasn't enough for Ero.

He balanced himself on top of Sir for a second time. "Marry me."

Sir barely moved his uncovered mouth. "Sure. Said I would."

"Right now. I mean, marry me right now." Ero mirrored Sir's blank look back at him. "Then we can Rise together. You don't have to love me. That was never a requirement. I wouldn't ask that of you on top of everything else. Just marry me."

He couldn't force Sir into marriage, but it couldn't hurt to insist. Tsais' warning flashed in the back of his mind: *We'll keep a close watch*. It'd already been a day and a half since he found Sir. They wouldn't have many more.

Ero hated keeping so still, waiting for Sir to answer him. In a way, they were holding onto each other and keeping one another held in place at the same time. Sir dug his thumbs into Ero's sides through the layers of his clothes, but Ero didn't budge. He kept his hands and knees firm on the ground on either side of Sir and let his hair cloud around them.

"What's even in it for you? Marryin' someone like me," Sir asked.

Ero let out a long breath. His blood settled, and he relaxed on top of Sir. Clear heart. "I already told you—it's my job."

"I mean, for real. Your job the only thing that matter to you?"

"No, not the 'only' thing. It's just that my feelings don't matter because they're not relevant. That doesn't mean *your* feelings don't matter, though." He shifted on top of Sir, and gently added, "How you feel about me very much matters to me."

The truth was, his feelings fucking smarted. Sir kept rejecting him, only accepting in the smallest ways, when he was supposed to be perfect for Sir. For all the value of feeding his blood to a sangromancer, Ero had taken the kiss with gratitude. He wasn't weak. He wasn't broken.

He *could* do what he was made to.

Sir's grip on his waist tightened again, eyes narrowing slightly as he held Ero in place. "If it matters so much, why you pushin' so hard?"

Ero's expression softened to a gentle plea. "Well... because I believe you don't have to change to be good, Sir. You weren't always a killer. You learned to live like this. You can learn another way. You're being given such a rare chance. It's a small ask not to kill, isn't it? The merciful have found that if you and I commit ourselves to marriage, you'll have both reason and the ability to seek redemption. To find a better purpose than killing."

"The merciful, huh? That what the angels think of themselves? Someone to show mercy to the merciless?"

"I— That's what we call ourselves, yes, but that's not what I call you. You are not merciless," Ero said firmly, his resolve stalwart. "You spared Officer Blake. You spared me. You even spared the little princess from the mountains, even if you don't want to believe it was you who did it. You're a devil, Sir, that part is true, but you are not merciless like devils are. You want to know what I really think? I think deep down, no matter who you think you are, you want everything I'm offering you. There's no way you'd keep me so close if you didn't see something you wanted for yourself. Maybe you don't trust it outright, but you know I'm telling the truth. You can see it clearly in me, in my blood. You just don't know how to reach for it yet. I've already shown you the way. Think of marriage as a business deal or a political arrangement all you want. Your heart doesn't have to be in it. You just have to say yes to it. It's an offer we would extend to more devils if we thought they would take it. Instead, they're too in love with the Fall to even want to save themselves."

As usual, Sir stayed quiet a while, his gaze distant. Ero could almost see the internal battle raging in him—the conflict between the evil origins that held him captive and the faint glimmer of hope that Ero kept extending to him.

Ero prayed he'd take it, once and for all. Everything hinged on it.

Finally, Sir's eyes refocused on Ero, a blend of determination and resignation mixed into the cloudy grey. "In Texas."

"...What?" Ero shook his head. "I mean... why Texas?"

"Miss Officer back there reminded me to clean up my mess back that way. Somethin' I wanna check on 'fore I go with ya. If you lemme head back to Texas, then I'll marry you all day long," Sir said, adding, with half a fanged smile, "Trust."

The terminal *T* vanished in his southern drawl. *Truss.*

Ero's first reaction was to reject it. His cells protested, recoiling from Sir as if on an instinctual level, and the only thing that kept him in place was Sir's hands cemented around his waist.

Ero had to sit and face Sir's willingness up close. It unsettled him.

"Trust," he repeated slowly, testing it.

Me trustin' you'd be like you trustin' me, Sir had said at Bulls Bay. Ero didn't think anything of it at the time, brushed it off. He could give up any part of himself at the drop of a hat if need be.

His mission had been a lot clearer back then.

"Fine," he said after a long while of staring back. "We can go to Texas. We can go wherever you want, Sir. I'll follow you anywhere. But if you cross any police who are still pursuing you, you cannot kill them. I don't care if you're hungry, or agitated, or overwhelmed, or if you think they fucking deserve it. Every life you take makes our path forward that much harder—the path you *agreed* to. Let's avoid any more bloodshed while we still can. Just use me. Leave all the rest to me. And goddamn, but when we get to Texas, or wherever you decide you want to go, finally, please, marry me."

As Ero's words trailed off, Sir's faint smile disappeared, replaced by his usual guarded expression.

"Don't you know my warrant's still out? They'll come," he said. "Ready for that?"

Ero licked his lips, tasting the smeared blood that stained Sir the same red color. "Yes. Are you ready? If you treated me the way you should, you would know exactly what I can do for you, and how, by now. Say you will. Say you'll marry me after we leave here."

"I said, I'll do it." For the first time, Sir wrenched his gaze away from Ero to glance around the lush mountainside. His eyes were back on Ero in an instant. "All the damage's gone. Do that while I was out?" he asked. That eerie, eye-of-the-storm calm resurfaced across his face.

Ero smiled wide despite himself. He didn't want to bring any attention to that death scene. "Of course."

In the back of his mind, talking with Sir had taken his thoughts off the madness of his earlier panic. Now that he'd been reminded of it, he realized he hadn't been able to do anything about Sir's eclipse matrix. Nothing at all. He had been able to revive the surroundings, but Sir had started healing—breaking the barrier of Ero's force seal—before Ero could even attempt his sabotage. Now, he truly only had Sir's word to rely on if they hoped to accomplish the mission.

"You're not upset because I force sealed you again, are you? Or because I kissed you while you were sleeping?" he pressed innocently.

He had to make Sir want it.

Sir looked unamused, which probably meant he was having a blast, because the way he glued his hands to Ero's waist never changed. "If I was?"

"Hmm. Not possible. You're too enamored." Ero cocked his head as he leaned in without even a hint of shame. As long as he kept Sir's mood up, he could get away with as much as he needed to. He could even have some fun. "You can kiss me now that you're awake, if you want," he added.

He swallowed, thinking back to his failed attempt to sabotage Sir's eclipse matrix and the kiss that followed. After drinking Ero's blood, Sir had come alive. He had held Ero tight. He had kissed back. Could Ero even handle the full force of Sir's attention if he had it?

He wanted to know.

"Nah," Sir said slowly, "I'm good."

A quick exhale escaped Ero, sharp and incredulous. "No, you won't kiss me?"

"Nah, I'm not angry. You said you'd do what you want. I'll kiss you when I want, too." Sir slipped his hands under Ero's shirt to hold him skin-on-skin; they sent chills through his body. "But you keep force sealin' me—blindin' me, knockin' me out, and shit, and I'm just s'posed to sit here and take it. Why I can't do any of that to you?"

Ero leaned away from the contact. "Easy. Only angels can force seal other ghosts. Devils don't have the authority. They exchanged it for raw, lawless power a long time ago. If you want to force seal me, love, you're gonna have to earn the authority to do it. Sorry."

"Ah. All roads lead back to the Rise."

"You may not want to hear it, but it's true." Ero moved one of his hands to cover Sir's heart through his stained shirt. There was a long, slow *ba-bump*... or two... the drawn-out sound of Ero's blood moving through Sir's veins.

Strange, even for a devil. That was Sir to a T.

"Every ghost has a chance to Rise, some just refuse to. We believe you're worth convincing. We believe it so much that I was made for you." Ero smiled around the old refrain.

They fell into a quick silence again, Sir with his focus trained on Ero's face. He seemed to be looking beyond Ero, or into Ero, without seeing what was in front of him. He did it in moments sometimes, and in minutes other times, but he took so many opportunities to stare like this that Ero couldn't help but notice.

"What do you see when you look at me like that?"

"They gave you to a devil to marry. I could've devoured you," Sir said, as if it didn't make sense to him.

"But you didn't. You spared me. Tell me what you see when you look at me like that."

"You were pissin' me off."

"You still could've tried harder to kill me. And yet I lived so that I could usher you into your power. Funny how that worked out. What do you see, Sir?" Ero pushed his fingers into Sir's chest, insistent.

Sir glared as he snapped to attention. "You should get up off me. Can't give you what you want."

This time, it was Ero who held Sir in place, refusing to shift from his position. "What do I want? Is that what you saw? Are you reading my mind or something?"

Sir sighed, but softly, long-winded. "Inez."

Ero hesitated.

Who was Inez?

Unimpressed with his confusion, Sir pried himself from underneath Ero and marched over to scoop up the little princess. Ero regarded her from the grass—he'd forgotten about her for a while. Poor thing was still limp from exhaustion in Sir's hands.

With a *whoosh*, his wings appeared and wrapped gingerly around her as she rested in his arms. "Inez," he said, facing Ero. "Name of your princess. She's comin' to Texas with us. Reckon she'll keep you company."

His gaze lingered on Ero, expression unreadable. For a moment, it seemed like he might say something more, but as usual, he simply turned away, his wings folding protectively around the cub.

Chapter 10

SIR

IN THE HEART OF Texas, hills, woods, prairies, and rivers thrived with the same unrestrained abandon as always. Everything became a blur in the air. Sir'd only been gone a short while, but it may as well've been a lifetime. Honkin', interconnected cities dotted the plains he flew over. Dim solar lights glimmered in the distance right 'longside towers of reflective skyscrapers and vertical gardens. The highways snaked 'round with sleek, self-drivin' cars glidin' effortlessly across the state. Ancient oak trees lined the long, windin' roads, and hundreds of wildflowers painted the meadows in the margins thousands of colors. In the dark, fireflies, nighthawks, and moths found the light. Nearby creeks and bayous reflected the stars in the night sky.

Home, sweet home. H-Town. The scent of wild tarragon and creek water reached his nose, mixed with the faint hum of solar lights below. It was all too familiar, yet as novel as the first day he'd left Alexander's house.

Closer that Sir sped toward the city, the more he understood 'bout its scenery zippin' past him than ever. He'd never seen this place from above before. He didn't have control of his wings back when he fled. It made everything he'd experienced here seem... small.

Everything exceptin' the single, phantom heartbeat that'd changed his life forever.

The heartbeat that'd belonged to the corpse he christened a fallen star, for the way it glowed even in its death.

The heartbeat that'd called for him to *eat it*.

Ero's insistin' that a marriage could redeem Sir from somethin' like that seemed so ridiculous at first.

Now that Sir'd fed on Ero enough to chew on the floods of ancient info brought with his blood, nothin' seemed ridiculous anymore. His life as he knew it really was over—the life that made some sorta sense. Shit, that life was over before it even started. He'd been born to some kinda evil world that lorded over the human world. The place he used to know only as "home." This place.

So much of him still remained here: the deranged, molested son and the ignorant, apathetic monster. His lonely life built with bricks of abuse, blood, and violence. It'd been all he knew his whole life. But he couldn't deny—the root of his ceaseless curiosity'd always been linked to his search for his true nature. His memories, his origins. Anything that explained *him*. Every time he took blood from Ero, Sir inched a lil bit closer to those answers. He felt it like his own risin' pulse.

If only that was all that Ero was offerin'. Instead, the angel came with all kinda clauses. *Fall in love, trust your natural enemy, betray everything you are because we say so.* Far as Sir understood things, it was pretty classically angel-like of Ero to hear this command, and just say, *Yes*.

Above everything else, angels obeyed.

Devils rebelled.

That was the distinction between the divine and its shadow. Every time Ero spoke about marriage, Sir's instincts screamed to rebel.

A future sewn together with love, trust, angelhood? With these other angels—Ero's so-called family? Even without meetin' any of them, Sir already couldn't stand a one. Ero'd grown on him, or been forced to, anyway, but nothin' he'd learned from Ero suggested the other angels would be so welcomin'.

They had no reason to be. Only Ero did. Right, his job.

What other option'd Sir have, though? Submit himself to divine punishment? He could take the flimsy forces of Texas State Troopers all day. An army of angels like Ero, though...

So then marry.

Forsake himself, shed his godless instincts, and waltz over to the Right Hand. Marry into it.

When Alexander first found him, Sir ain't resist. Before Alexander ever hurt Sir, he'd been a half-decent person. A half-decent guardian, or mentor, or friend. Enough to keep Sir in Houston, in that house, even when Alexander left him there.

For some reason, with Ero, who swore never to leave, Sir couldn't help resistin'. Reflexively, like a hair trigger, he tested the cage that closed 'round him. But the cage—if Ero's arms could be called a cage—only softened, over and over, givin' Sir everything and anything, just as promised. Givin' him answers, a new purpose, and all sorts between.

Ero was so smart. So strong. More than anything else, Sir took a shine to that quite a bit. Ero understood the world.

Well, that, and the fact that he was told to marry a devil, and he set right out to do it. He even shared his strength and other sacred gifts to do so. Freely. Smilin' all the while.

What if he was right? What if Sir could just trust him? The more the learned, the more he wanted to.

"Slow down, Sir... I still have Inez," Ero said, voice cuttin' through the rush of wind.

Sir retracted his wings a bit and turned to face Ero as he glided on his back. Flyin' was like sprintin' underwater, but glidin' was easier. Glidin' was closer to runnin', and Sir was a runner. He'd run this route when he first fled Texas—he knew the way. The Alexander house wouldn't be too far now. He kept his eyes on Ero.

The angel held Inez carefully in his arms while he caught up. "What's the rush?" he asked when he did. Measured, his gaze distant.

Sir felt like sneerin'.

He really should treat Ero better. Try a lil harder. If they were fixin' to unite themselves for all time, or what have you, the least Sir could do was fake an attempt. Usually, when Ero posed them cute lil questions, he could find the answers to them easy enough. Right there, smack dab in Ero's sharp, red eyes, clear as day. He used to get those migraines from it, a scarlet brain fog—but he'd blocked the answer out or just let it overwhelm him. Now, he saw the visions unfold for him, like a subconscious film playin' in his head. A gift Sir got from the Left, no doubt. Ero couldn't've known too much 'bout it, seein' as Sir still ain't know too much, neither.

"Inez'll wake soon," he answered.

He was already exhausted, and Ero'd win any fights he started, anyway.

Ero sucked his teeth, even as he smiled back. The same, dauntless smile, emergin' victorious. Came in different degrees, but always sayin' the same thing: Ero wasn't scared. Ero wasn't bothered. Ero wasn't fixin' to be run off by Sir's piss poor attitude or otherwise.

"You know, I wanted to tell you, I think it was sweet you named the baby Inez. Pure and innocent—is that how you see her? I didn't know you had enough of a heart to feel that way about something without preying on it."

"Better'n lettin' you call er Ma'am," Sir said.

"Ha! He's sassy!" Ero laughed. The sound bounced off clouds, effervescent, but he cut himself off abruptly. "About that, Sir. I'm sorry I couldn't find your real name. I swore I could, but... Honestly, your mark should've revealed a little more about you than it does. As is, it barely reveals your aura, much less your rank, class, or name."

Sir never cared about names or classes in the first place. Clearly it mattered to someone somewhere, but here, in this life, it'd never meant a thing. And he had a perfectly fine name now.

"All good, Angel."

A crow descended to fly beside him.

Ero paused before grinnin' again, that damn, short-fanged grin. He glanced at the crow over Sir's shoulder, and it darted off, like it'd been caught causin' mischief. A dragonfly followed suit. Ero looked away again.

"I think you really are different, Sir. You're cooler, gentler, than you think. I mean, this world seems to love you so much. Most devils only give a damn about the things they can use to carry out their whims, and so they're usually rejected by those things. Forests die, people scare, oceans dry, and animals flee around devils. But it's the opposite with you. You even adopted Inez after you protected her from *your own* mastery. I see all the time why you were chosen to Rise."

"Only once we get married, though. Not good enough 'til we get married," Sir said.

The dreaded inevitability.

Ero sighed. "It's just a contract. A promise that you'll fulfill your chosen role. Try not to think about it in terms of worth. I already told you I'm here because you're worthy. But we still need some way to hold you to your word, that's all."

Sir twisted onto his front again, puttin' some space between him and Ero. As if it could distance him from the weight on his shoulders, too. Every second at Ero's side was another second wasted findin' his way out this mess. Worse still, it was another second Sir minded less and less.

Somethin' 'bout Ero made even the most absurd possibilities seem desirable. Sir found himself searchin' for his guidin' voice, all the time, without even knowin' it. When Ero'd called for him, he'd listened. It'd brought him back to himself. Every time.

Could he be Ero's husband? Stand on divine ground with him as an angel? Could he live like that?

He spent so much goddamned time porin' over these kinda questions. Ero'd hounded him 25/8 for barely a day or two, but it'd worked. Sir thought 'bout Ero so much that visions of white-gold wings filled his wakin' hours. If Ero was the only angel in the world, then Sir'd've probably jumped at the chance to marry Ero at least twice over by now...

But there was always a vague, nebulous presence loomin' beyond them: the unspoken army of angels.

Ero tried not to talk or think too much 'bout them, but Sir felt them there, more and more, their eventuality, worsenin' the precarious balance between his past and his uncertain future.

"Sir." Ero latched a hand around Sir's wrist and kept him from driftin' too far away, like the crow earlier'd done. Their eyes finally met. "Interrogate more into what you know now with the information from my blood. That's what sangromancers like you do—they divine the truth from blood. If you look, you'll be able to see for yourself. I mean it when I say I won't let anything hurt you. And once we're married, like I said when we first met, you won't be a threat we have to mitigate anymore. We're almost there. It won't be long now."

Sir's senses spiked. Had he better intentions, he'd've listened to Ero and sorted through the fountains of knowledge he'd gained from all the bloodlettin'. Could probably spend his whole life porin' over that stuff and still not get to the bottom of it all.

Instead, with a sudden surge of restlessness, he veered outta Ero's grasp.

"True. Not long at all," he said, and burned off.

Toward the Alexander house sittin' just on the other side of the horizon. 'Cause as they came closer, he realized, *there was someone inside.*

"Sir! Hold up!" Ero shouted.

Sir ain't pay him no mind. The familiar old circular driveway came into view as if magnetized to him. A small white Toyota parked exactly where Alexander's F-150 used to sit. He picked up more speed and took a nosedive towards the ground when he hit the bald cypress trees over the roof, bustin' his ass on the way down. Guess he couldn't really expect the exhaustion to stay away too long, no matter how powerful he was now. Waterlogged leaves and outreachin' branches tangled up in his clothes, limbs, and hair, and the ground shuddered when he hit.

He'd landed outside the window of the room he used to share with Alexander. Inside, it was empty. Dark, quiet, and viscerally gutted.

But just a bit farther...

He had to steady himself against the windowpane first. The trees were swayin' 'round him. A fire opened in the pit of his gut that he hadn't felt in what could've been millennia. Somethin' so explosive that it brought him to his knees and corrupted him from the inside out. His old friend: the need that slumbered inside him. He'd burned through Ero's blood or encountered somethin' similar.

His wings ached so damn bad when he retracted them that his muscles trembled. After, gaspin', he focused on gettin' himself centered.

Grounded.

Here.

He'd thought of this place soon as he saw the impenetrable look in Ero's eyes, sayin', *Marry me*, and *You are not merciless*. All the death and destruction he could inflict now, thanks to Ero, it'd started here: His home with Alexander just outside Houston, before he'd found the fallen star.

Sir's heart thudded in his chest. As he slid his hands across the familiar sidin' of the ranch-style house, his need intensified, and his vision blurred with a dull red haze.

Someone was definitely inside.

He walked right through the frosted front door, like Alexander'd be the one waitin' for him on the other side.

Ding. Welcome, guest.

Ha. Law already wiped the home network and everything. Last time he'd been here—only a few days or weeks ago, right?—Alexander'd been a pile of red bones and meat on the livin' room floor, with Sgt. Esmeralda smeared across the wall. The room since then'd turned into a haunt. The once cozy, cluttered library, filled with them old medical and legal books, had been stripped to its bare bones. The elegant shelves were empty, the lush, lonely furniture gone, and the billowy white curtains now hung lifelessly, castin' a ghostly glow on the polished cement floor. Only a few forlorn items remained: an ornate formal dinin' chair and a mirrored radio connected to an extension cord that snaked into the kitchen. The transformation was stark, unsettlin', a shadow of its former self, leavin' an overwhelmin' air of abandonment here.

None of that had Sir's focus. He'd never felt less attached to this place. His heart still stuttered, though, and his fangs ached in anticipation.

In the center of the livin' room, a goth Black lady was sleepin'.

She lay tucked away in a lil pallet between long, wiltin' vines, moody makeup still baked on her face. A short, unwrapped soft-pack of smoke sat clutched in her tattooed fingers. Lacy chains, silver piercings, and black cotton covered her body. Her aura was a calm blue; blue like the sky, shaded by the same stormy clouds of deep exhaustion. Her name... was...

"Vincent," Sir whispered.

Vincent Bell. 29. Favorite color orange, sometimes green, like the Mexican flame vines she horded 'round her. Thin, flaggin' blooms, faded starbursts. The sight of her calm, stormy-blue aura pulled at somethin' deep inside Sir. He didn't know if it was hunger or somethin' else, but it terrified him all the same. He'd felt this way before—lured to devour somethin' otherworldly.

But he'd promised to control himself. He thought long and hard 'bout breathin', and centerin', and waitin' for Ero to make it here.

His body moved before his head could catch up.

Before he realized it, he was on top of Vincent. Every step closer to her was a step closer to himself—and away from Ero. Ero's words echoed in his mind, but they couldn't drown out the instincts that roared louder with each passin' second. His fangs brushed against her bare neck.

She didn't stir right away. Her skin did flush warm, though, as she recognized the press of Sir's mouth on her. "Kieran? S'you...?" she mumbled.

Sir backed up a pace, snappin' his teeth together.

Vincent's aura kept calm. She thought he was someone else.

Again, Ero's goddamned voice needled at the back of his brain: *Every life you take makes our path forward harder. The path you* agreed *to.*

Sir'd promised to behave.

So why then did he struggle so much with just fuckin' doin' it?

Vincent's eyes cleared. Her breath got rabbit-quick, and her heart slammed blood through her body. "Y-you..."

Spit gathered in Sir's mouth. He was hungry. "Don't shout."

Ero's voice was still there. *Just use me. Just use me.*

For some reason, Vincent didn't bolt away once she realized Sir wasn't who she'd thought. "It's... you...?" she whispered.

What?

Was she still confused? Did she recognize him?

How would that even be possible?

"Who're you? Why're you here?"

Vincent's voice was thin, faint like her aura, as he crushed her close again to keep her from fadin' away. She barely even gasped. "It's... you..."

He had to get into her head. He barely even had to acknowledge his new abilities now. He just had to do it, and it happened. His brain worked so much faster than he could consciously keep up with now that it was up to par with that of other ghosts. If he tuned in and followed Ero's words, lettin' his subconsciousness do most of the hard work, ideas snapped into reality as if out of a vision. Sometimes, he was amazed with what he could accomplish based only on his own knowledge and the instruction Ero'd given him. He didn't feel or look any different, but somehow Ero'd woken up this power in him that he hadn't even known he'd had.

The power to see the truth in others' eyes.

"Look at me," he said.

Vincent was already under his spell before he cast it. "It's... you..." she kept whisperin'.

"Tell me. How d'you know me?"

As she gazed up at him, Sir's senses washed away in her memories. The precious fragments of her life showered down over him. He stretched his mind and found hers in the rainfall, followin' it all the way to her heart.

He sunk in an instant.

Chapter 11

Vincent Bell

H ER NAME USED TO be Vasariah. The name she had in the First World, when she had a family and lived underground. Far underground, far enough to brush the underside of the crust, she lived surrounded by the pressure and glow from molten magma mountains.

She lived there because she was an Angel.

She and her siblings made up the central command of the Angels, but they lived in isolation from their soldiers under the surface of the Earth.

They only saw the sky when they trained. Aboveground, surrounded by plush, dark nighttime clouds, Vasariah loved to train. She grabbed her usual partner, Malikim, and they would spend their endless days with their huge, gleaming swords crossed in clash after clash. She enjoyed it so much, not only because it was her specialty, but also because, one day, this world—her home—would burn in the flames from their armies, and she'd get to be the one to do it. The armies they hadn't met yet would fill them with all the power they needed to be gods and alter reality.

Until then, Vasariah just had to train. And so she trained damn hard.

Her swords, like Malikim's, were made of Empyrean Damascus designed to last all of eternity without breaking—more than could be said of Vasariah. At the end of each training day, she and Malikim retreated underground to assess their most stubborn wounds. They were Angels, the same rank and order as their unseen armies, but as the commanders of those legions, they held a higher station. Sometimes, they could beat each other out by leaving a scar that wouldn't heal. Still, as many scars as they had, it was rare to end in anything but a draw between angels of all the same rank, order, and class.

Vasariah gritted her teeth. Today would end in another stalemate, like all the rest, if she didn't do something. She had already lost her first weapon.

Malikim stood across from her, a tower of dewy bronze skin while his eyes of the same color locked in on her. In the split-second where she lost focus, Malikim teleported right past her defenses.

"Wake up, Vasariah!" he shouted. His voice resounded in her ears, and Vasariah's grip tightened on her sword. She hated his lofty tone—it wasn't mocking her; he was right. He sheathed one of his swords, beat his powerful bronze wings, and tackled her to the ground with his second sword raised to strike.

She was too late to do anything except lift her own weapon in defense. She deflected with the last of her strength, hard enough to knock both of their swords from their hands. Malikim calmly re-drew his first one.

"Enough. Move again," he said.

Vasariah hesitated, thinking of going after the sword in Malikim's hand, but he clocked it and nested the business end against her throat.

"Dare you," he added.

"Or else what?" Vasariah spat.

"Move again, and find out."

"Oh, fuck all the way off, Malikim. Get that thing away my neck, or soon, you'll be the one finding out."

"Sure, I'll back down," Malikim said with a wide grin. "Just give up first. Admit that I got the better of you fair and square—twice, already. While you're at it, try thinking less of prolonging the fight just for the sake of it, too. You might've actually gotten somewhere today if not for that shit habit of yours. Instead, you lost, and now you got my steel on your throat."

"Sorry," Vasariah said through the blood in her teeth, "I just don't know how to give up. You know that."

"Oh, I know. I know it better than anybody. That's why..."

All at once, Malikim flexed, and Vasariah barely saved her head from Malikim's sword before she lifted them both off the ground. Together, they plunged into the depths of the nearby river without a hope of floating.

The weight of the agitated Euphrates dragged them down. At the bottom of the river, Malikim pinned Vasariah with a hand locked around her throat, and the razor edge of his wings stabbed through her own underwings.

"Argh!" Vasariah roared. Dark reddish bubbles billowed out of her mouth. "Malikim, you bastard! Are you trying to damn me? Get off my fucking wings!"

"Give. Up. Vasariah," Malikim said, rock steady. He wouldn't give her an inch, even with her solid, pearly wings struggling to tear free from his.

Vasariah's wounds spouted cloudy puffs of blood into the water, turning her sight dark and milky. Malikim's face disappeared behind the trails as her struggle ripped up her wings more and more. Exhausted, she tried to reach out with her mastery under his restriction, but they could only coerce admissions of defeat out of each other, as they were.

And all the blood in the water made it clear Vasariah had been defeated.

Her mouth finally relaxed into an effortful grin. "Goodness, Malikim. I didn't know you were such a show-off. Did I push you into that much of a corner?"

"Who's in a corner? And I'm not showing off. I'm restraining you the only way that you'll listen—by your grace. You're the one who said it: I know better than anyone that you act like giving up is impossible to do. So I thought I'd give you a real reason to give up." Malikim didn't smile back.

"By shredding my wings and threatening to curse me to damnation? What the hell? Enough, already. You won, you won. Malikim, get off me. It fucking hurts!"

"Maybe after I teach you some patience, huh?" Malikim said easily. His wings stabbed further into Vasariah's, pinning her even more firmly to the riverbed. He finally started to smile back.

A sudden tidal wave dislodged them both from each other, and Vasariah went flying downriver in a tumble of dark, ruddy water and tattered wings. She choked on the air that struggled into her lungs until a force lifted her, coughing, from the depths.

She landed on the bank nearby, covered in wet soil and dense grass. "Malikim—!"

"No. It's Andras. Here," said youngest Andras, his distinctively bright black eyes shaded by worried eyebrows. He pressed some of his energy into Vasariah so that she could heal up faster, gain her bearings. There was a strange urgency to his movements. "Salem is taking care of Malikim. She's the one who freed you with the tide. She probably overdid it a bit. Sorry."

"Ya think? Why the haste? Malikim and I were doing fine."

Technically, they had been doing fine, anyway.

Toward the end... Vasariah's vision had clouded over. She didn't know what to make of Malikim's "lesson." Her pearly underwings still ached, despite her own self-regeneration and Andras even helping her. The wounds eventually closed up, but they left long, thick scars near her wingtips. New tallies. She traced the jagged edges with trembling fingers; every lesson she'd yet to learn.

"It's Salem," Andras said as he wrapped up. "She keeps hearing chatter from higher-up, even though the Sixth Angel still hasn't reached out to her directly yet."

Salem—their leader, the oldest—was the only one allowed any contact with other angels. Vasariah nodded.

"So she thinks The End is near."

"She knows The End is near. It's just a matter of time until we're called on," Andras said. "After that..."

Neither one of them had ever said it aloud. When The End came, the Sixth Angel at the Trumpet would blow on their horn and summon Vasariah, her siblings, and their legions. They'd be called to task for the destruction they spent their lives training for. After that...

"What's gonna happen to us?" Andras asked softly. "Are we gonna die without a purpose? We're so isolated. We don't even know the forces we'll be commanding out there."

Vasariah flinched, as if struck by the words. She didn't have an answer. This minefield of thoughts had always seemed too impossible to consider, too unimportant and distant to matter more than their role in the Sixth Angel's mission. Their ultimate mission. That was the only moment that had ever mattered to her.

Before she could think of what to say, a tornado wind swirled down over them. Andras took cover behind Vasariah until the wind gusts dissipated, revealing their leader, Salem. Her presence was commanding and enigmatic. Tall and feminine, with the same long, black silver-streaked hair as Andras, she moved with an uncontested strength. Her deep violet eyes cut through the dark night, betraying none of the ancient secrets she shared with the Sixth Angel. Her loose, formless clothes marked her as a mystery in the shadows, and her aura buzzed with energy as she gripped Malikim's arm like a misbehaving toddler.

"Vasariah," she said, stern and strong. "I'm glad you're looking better. This one has his own lesson to learn, still—don't you, Malikim?" Salem tugged on his arm. "But I can see his heart was in the right place trying to teach you the same damn lesson as always. Get it through your thick skull already. We don't have time for this. You're a commander. Have some awareness when you fight, don't just scrap tooth and nail, trying to strong-arm your way to the end."

Malikim said, "I told you, true power comes from control and refinement. Not raw strength, brute. You should get a handle on that before The End comes and really can't control yourself. It'll be too late then."

"Enough of that." Salem pushed Malikim over toward Vasariah and Andras. "This right here is why we have each other. It's why we exist together. Now make up already so we can head back. We've all made enough of a mess for today, and I know every one of you feels that The End is already here. Don't you?"

Here.

The End is already *here.*

Vasariah helped Andras to his feet, but he wouldn't meet her eyes. It was rare to talk about The End so much, so openly. Maybe that was testament to how close it had come—right under their noses.

It was a concept Vasariah had trained for her whole life, yet hearing it spoken aloud made her chest tighten. She almost hoped for it, now that it had finally come, regardless of what it meant for the First World or the next.

"Right. Vasariah, you're okay to return underground?" Salem asked.

Vasariah cast a last glance at the sky, slowly turning blue. "Yeah, I'm fine. Let's hurry home."

In the small hours, feeling The End creep up as if it was inside her, Vasariah stroked her scarred wings, and said, "I love you."

No one answered, at first.

Then Andras whispered back, "I love you."

Malikim and Salem quietly followed, one after the other, "I love you."

It was the first time any of them had ever said the words aloud. Vasariah prayed it wouldn't be the last.

As usual, no one responded to her prayers.

——————————— —— ———————————

Vasariah was probably the last to know. She'd been inspecting her scars from the fight earlier, safe at home in the warmth of the magma flow, when all of a sudden, she was forced to breach the Euphrates River into a land of bloodshed.

The fallout from the previous five Trumpets had already laid waste to thousands of grand, thriving cities when she rose. The Fifth Trumpet had brought a star falling from the sky. It left a crater—the Bottomless Pit, the home of locusts and bats that plagued the winds—and sent plumes of ominous smoke into the air. The atmosphere was heavy with the stench of decay and death, as ominous, flickering shadows engulfed the world. The ground beneath her where she'd risen from the Euphrates split open, revealing deep chasms that seemed to reach all the way home. Massive waves rose and crashed on land, bitter, poisoned, and reeking of rotting corpses. The remaining waters roiled with fury, a lot like the tide that Salem had created to free Vasariah just the other day. With the sound of the Sixth Trumpet, she was part of a new set of cataclysms to befall the broken world.

Salem's voice suddenly rang out, her tone clear and steady. "Vasariah, there you are! I've been looking all over for you! Have you seen Andras—?"

"Andras is gone," Malikim gasped, appearing beside them. "I can't find him at all. We've already been summoned. What should we do?"

"I can't sense him, either," Vasariah said. "Salem? It's your call."

Naturally, both Vasariah and Malikim turned to Salem. She had always led them, ever since the very beginning, when their bodies were first made in the waters of the Euphrates that had taken over the land.

Salem was silent for a moment. "Let's trust him. Let's trust ourselves, and the faith we have in each other. Nothing else has ever mattered before. Besides, if he's really missing, it's probably better that he won't be involved in the battle, anyway—our youngest, always worried about The End. Right? After we've done our job, after we've completed our duty, we'll come back for him wherever he is. There will be an after. We'd know if he was really gone. We would know. Do you hear me? It's too late to question shit like this. Now, it's time to focus. Get your weapons! The Sixth Trumpet already sounded!"

Salem had just drawn her sword when, with a presence as commanding as the cosmos, Andras and the entire legion of Angels arose from the far reaches of the ruined Euphrates River.

"Andras! We thought you were safe somewhere! What the fuck?" Vasariah barked.

"Here!" Andras shouted back.

He held out bridles that resembled long, shimmering comet tails adorned with microscopic stars. The horses they led had coats as black as the void between galaxies, with heads reminiscent of lions and eyes that gleamed like the fire of exploding stars.

Salem, closest to him, grasped the bridle reins with a question in her gaze. A fourth of the legion of Angels that had followed Andras fell in line behind her as she did, a single body of hundreds of soldiers.

"Our armies," she said.

"Yeah! I was summoned away to prepare them. And these," Andras explained as he took horses to Malikim and Vasariah. The legions divvied themselves up accordingly. "Together, we fully become emissaries of fate for The End. They're ours to command as the Four Apocalyptic Angels of the Euphrates."

"Say less, little brother!" Malikim mounted his majestic horse with equal parts reverence and excitement. "The Four Apocalyptic Angels of the Euphrates...! Let's go! Lock in!"

His legionnaires cheered behind him, as if attuned to his emotions, reflecting them back at him. He gazed at them in wonder for a moment.

Aside from Salem's secluded briefs with the Sixth Angel, none of the other commanders had ever so much as spoken to another ghost, and here they were, celebrating the birth of a new Earth together with support from the entire order of Angels.

In awe herself, Vasariah first reached out and brushed a hand over the flank of her horse before she mounted. Her spirit merged with the horse, as if expanding her self to include it, fused in energy and purpose. Through her mount, she absorbed the power from the legion pledged to her. She searched their eyes, but none answered with anything outside of loyalty and determination.

"Wow," she sighed.

"Let's get it!" Heartened, Salem took charge once again.

The horses' manes rippled like auroras as Vasariah and the others tore off after Salem. She raised her swordhand, just like before, and everyone followed her lead. Their legions wiped out entire populations of humans near and far while the waters of the Euphrates surged again with deep, arcane resonance. It was as easy, quick, and simple as that.

Malikim spread his wings wide across the horizon, forming an incandescent trail that ignited the impenetrable plumes emanating from the Bottomless Pit. Vasariah fixed on it.

Endless nightmares, torments, fears, and other monsters poured from its endless depths. The fallen star who had created it had vanished, swallowed by the smoke and sorrow. Their destruction was just another chord in the symphony of cosmic forces unfurling all around Vasariah. The very fabric of reality had started to waver, and with each beat of her wings, she traversed the boundaries between chaos and control.

"Vaz? Your judgment?" Andras steered in close to her on his mount, concern in his glittering black eyes. "I'm ready on your cue. Are you good?"

Vasariah replied with a vicious grin. "Thanks, baby brother. I'm absolutely good. I'm better than good. I'm divine! Come on, friends!" she called, and set off. Under her focused gaze, earthquakes tore across the mucky, muddy earth that shifted mountain ranges and split far-off oceans. Hundreds of valleys yawned open to reveal the hidden veins of the world beneath, like dozens upon dozens of little Bottomless Pits.

It all seemed so well guided. Perfectly predestined.

The End of the First World.

It was then, enthralled by the vision of the world—the Universe—gone cold and dead, that something happened to Vasariah.

As her legionnaires slaughtered every third human under her command, an unknown force gripped her, and she suddenly felt a sharp sting from inside. Like the stab of a needle, it pierced through her.

Bloodlust.

There was glory in this. Indulgence, power, and glory.

She'd waited her whole life for this hour, and here it finally was, the moment she was born.

She was made for this.

"Vasariah!" called a distant relative.

She couldn't tell who. Just a face and an aura that blinded her when she turned toward it.

"Vasariah!"

"Vaz!"

Vasariah struck with her sword, but her horse pulled her away before the blade connected. The trails of starlight it left behind blinded her even more. She rose up and kicked off the seat. Her horse cascaded into the depths of the churning corpses floating in the riotous rivers below. Steam from its mouth lifted to the water's surface, then went out.

"Vasariah!!!"

"Vasariah!?"

More shouts of her name. Her name... Was it her name...?

Warm blood nearby. Vasariah sniffed it out and snatched it out of the air. She had one of Andras' legionnaires by the throat. They clawed at her arms, straining.

"Vaz, stop! What are you doing?" Andras choked. "If you kill that soldier, you'll Fall! Do you understand? You'll Fall and never, ever return. Don't tell me everything we went through was for nothing. What got into you?"

Poor, sweet Andras. Still worried about Vasariah when one of his legionnaires was caught in her grip.

She was stronger and faster than ever, primed for her life purpose, and running on empty. Her fangs ached as they grew, sharpened, and in the next second, she sank them deep into the Angel in her hands. They let out a painful cry. Vasariah pressed in deeper, drinking down all the blood that flowed freely from her bite wound, unable to break away. She kept consuming the Angel's essence with no end in sight to the urgent void inside her. She was another Bottomless Pit, the fallen Wormwood, a crater that unleashed hell onto the world.

Just as she'd been designed to do.

"Quit it, Vaz!"

Suddenly, she was torn away, and she turned the force of her bite on Andras, too.

Somehow, realizing it was Andras she had captured didn't change her hunger or curb her need to drain him. She just kept on drinking, and draining, and devouring.

Another, greater force wrenched her off of him, as if blasted apart. Vasariah landed against the brick wall of Malikim, her back to his chest and his hands clamped around her arms.

"Let me go! Let me fucking go!" she cried.

Malikim kept her restrained while Salem investigated what remained of Andras and his soldier. When they'd been forced apart, Vasariah had ripped open so much of Andras' shoulder that the arm nearly separated from his chest. Salem bowed over him, but only his body was left. As if torn pieces of paper, the other Angels under Andras' command also withered without his leadership.

"What did you go and do, Vasariah?" Malikim fought to keep her under control, but spoke calmly. Coldly.

Salem laid a kiss on Andras' fading forehead. Andras had always been the favorite. The most cherished and spoiled rotten. Even now, despite being the one who had killed him, Vasariah missed his pensive black eyes looking to her.

"You goddamned devil," Salem said.

Malikim tensed. "Salem, no—!"

Unlistening, Salem charged.

Malikim just barely managed to spin in time to take Salem's blade instead of Vasariah. The shock of the impact broke Malikim's hold on Vasariah, and she finally tore away as Salem dropped her sword as if it burned.

Vasariah didn't get far. A dozen Angels from Malikim's and Salem's legions blocked her path, brandishing all kinds of weapons.

"You won't get any further."

"You've done enough harm."

"Look at what you did to your family."

"No one will ever forgive you for this."

Vasariah glanced back at Malikim and Salem behind her. Malikim was hunched over, clutching the sword that speared him through the back, while Salem attempted to patch him up.

"Why'd you do that, Malikim? Why would you ever do that?" she whispered.

Malikim tried to laugh, but coughed up blood instead. "So you... won't Fall... too..."

"Shh, quit talking! I'm healing you, damnit. Concentrate!"

Salem mumbled prayers into his hair, pressing energy into him feverishly, but his wings steadily drooped into the blood collecting around their legs. Malikim was dying.

The legionnaire Angels attacked while Vasariah was distracted. It took her a while to get out from under their combined assaults. She couldn't even double back to monitor the situation with Malikim and Salem. As soon as she tried, an Angel blocked her, cursed her out, and tossed her like a ragdoll to the next.

A fire blast finally interrupted, coming between Vasariah and the Angel that she grappled with. She glanced around and found it had come from Malikim's horse before crumbling, as Andras' had, into the abyss below.

Salem let out a grievous, "No!"

But Malikim was already dead, his legion was dismantling before their eyes, and Vasariah the opening she needed.

She dove headfirst into the water covering the earth, near the edge of the Bottomless Pit. She loved being close to it, fueling up on its power and devastation. A blaze of fire followed her beneath the surface, then a second, third, and fourth, so she dove further down, where the pressure increased around her.

The attacks had to have come from Salem's horse and legionnaires, the remaining defenders of Vasariah's family.

Fine. So be it.

Holding her position below the dark, riotous waters, Vasariah summoned a precision rifle. Salem's horse was circling overhead, poised to counter as soon as Vasariah revealed herself.

She took aim and fired. The horse recoiled when hit.

Salem appeared at its side, too late, and a rain of poisoned, flaming arrows sliced into the water after Vasariah. She dodged the majority of blows from the barrage, but she couldn't dodge Salem, who followed, clamped a hand around Vasariah's throat, and dragged her from underwater.

Together, they crested through the brackish ocean back into the sky. A handful of Salem's legionnaires descended as soon as they did.

At once, Vasariah understood that only a handful of angels were restraining her because the rest of Salem's legion that survived had started clashing with Vasariah's own legion. They'd been busy executing their mission on her behalf, pumping her with more existential power, and Salem had put an end to the stream of energy constantly inflating her strength.

"Clever lady," Vasariah said with a snarl. It seemed odd to antagonize her oldest sister, her leader, the head of her family, whom she'd always respected so much, but the entire experience had divorced Vasariah from her sense of self a long time ago.

Nothing made sense anymore.

"Quit, already," Salem said. Exhausted, and angry, but never losing the last of her hope. Her trust. "You've fallen, baby sister.

I don't love you any less. But you need to quit. You've killed too many. You fell too far. Please, let go. Just Fall."

"Only if I can take you with me." Vasariah flashed her long fangs and pierced Salem's neck.

Salem didn't scream. Her hold around Vasariah tightened, and the Angels at Vasariah's back grabbed hold of her wing joints.

Vasariah went cold, pulling away as much as she could. "Salem, hey, what are you—"

"Just getting started, really. Now!" Salem commanded.

Vasariah struggled and squirmed, but with half her overinflated strength diminished, Salem was more of an even match for her. She blacked out while trapped between Salem and her legionnaires, fearing she'd be divested of her wings, and so, stripped of her very nature.

She only came to once she descended to solid ground from the sky for the first time since the Sixth Trumpet had sounded.

Vasariah landed in a pool of blood that dribbled from the toes of her bare feet and, with a shake, retracted her powerful wings.

The carnage that surrounded her was a stranger, at first. Confusing, in a way. She didn't remember anything that happened after Salem drew her sword. She'd seen this same scene before that, and it had been just as devastated as it looked now—tainted skies, evil waters, mountains turned to volcanoes.

But now something was missing. Inside of her. No. She was fuller than she'd ever been before. Full of...

Something was wrong…

Where were her siblings?

Reflexively, she stabbed her sword into the pool of blood beneath her and half-collapsed to her knees.

Something was wrong! Was she dying? She wasn't in any pain—in fact, she felt incredible, stronger than she'd ever been—but couldn't support herself anymore. Like her mind lost control over her limbs.

Slowly, she lost her grip on her sword and planted both hands on the ground, splattering sticky red-black blood everywhere.

There, in the thick layers of blood that soaked the murky dirt and ashes under her, a reflection peeked out as if from the other side—Andras' big, bright black eyes.

Wide open. Glazed over. Lifeless.

"Aughh!"

Her wings suddenly reappeared, summoned as if by someone else's will, flickering in and out of flex as she gnashed her teeth and gripped the blade of her sword with her free hand to stay upright. Now she felt pain—like a spike driven through her spine and skull, this pain cemented her to the bloody ground. Overpowered, she toppled to the side.

Andras' dead eyes stared back at her in the dull bloody reflection.

"What happened?" she bawled furiously. "Where is my family? Why am I alive? Who did this? Tell me!"

"See for yourself, Angel," a voice called out—a gold light that filled her senses, carrying the mark of the Sixth Angel at the Trumpet, a fearsome figure with a fiery aura. "We'll wait for you."

In the light that enveloped Vasariah, an oppressive prism of awful, wonderful colors restored the events that she couldn't remember despite standing there in the aftermath of it all.

She saw herself burning, killing, betraying.

Losing everything.

Falling from grace.

Her gaze shifted to the Bottomless Pit, the yawning miasma that both birthed evil and contained it. The legions she and her family had commanded, once luminous beacons of hope, had followed every one of their commanders into its depths in pieces.

"What did I do...?" Vasariah whispered.

A terrible crescendo answered her—the Seventh Trumpet with a grand chorus of divine voices saying, "*The kingdom of the World is now gone.*"

Alone, the Seventh Angel at the Trumpet descended, and looked Vasariah in the eye. They were a radiant angel, with divine dark skin that glowed as if under iridescent lights. Their vast wings refracted brilliant rainbows, and their blank eyes held pools of infinite wisdom and power. This strange angel, wrapped in tight black leather and armor, marked the dawn of a new era—the ruin of the earth.

And the ruin of Vasariah.

"Your services aren't required anymore," the Seventh Angel said. "Go to your eternal resting place quietly. Now."

Vasariah recoiled.

"Wait!"

The Seventh Angel paused, and Vasariah glanced over as the Sixth Angel made herself known.

Vasariah's commander.

She had never met, seen, or heard from the Sixth Angel before. Only Salem, as the leader, had been allowed, despite all four of them being under the Sixth Angel's direct command. Salem had had the utmost respect for all Seven Angels at the Trumpet, and so naturally Vasariah did, too. She couldn't help but feel enormous awe at the feet of the very entity who was probably winding up to kill her.

"Thank you for waiting, Trumpet Seven. I know we're on a tight enough schedule as it is. I just want to meet my subordinate face to face for once. It won't take too long." The Sixth Angel stood as tall as her counterpart, her skin a deep, metallic bronze, and her huge wings crafted from sharp, polished steel. Being close to her made Vasariah tremble slightly from a dizzying mix of reverence and terror. Like the Seventh Angel, the Sixth Angel was strapped with pristine weapons, clad in dark armor, and carried her trumpet on her hip. Hers was dark iron. It made the sound that had woken Vasariah up.

The Sixth Angel looked down at her without changing her static expression. "You call yourself Vasariah Prat of the Euphrates, right?"

"The one and only, at your service," Vasariah said, half-dazed.

The Sixth Angel reached out to help her onto her feet. "And you've been busy, too, I see. Here, up you go, sugar. Are you in any pain?"

Vasariah didn't know what to say. She flexed the wing joint that Salem's legionnaires had almost torn off, but no, she wasn't in any pain. None at all. She didn't feel anything, in fact—not pain, not grief, not malice; just nothing.

Slowly, she shook her head. "No..."

The Sixth Angel nodded. "Good. Good. You fought hard. It's okay. It's not your fault. If anything, I'm glad this happened sooner rather than later. You were created like this, after all. I had always hoped that by keeping y'all in isolation, we could limit the world's influence on you, but I guess there wasn't any getting around it, in the end. You're Angels. We should've probably seen something like this coming from the start. I'm so sorry. We'll take care of the rest. Come here. It's okay," she repeated, warm but detached. With an empty smile to match.

That's when Vasariah figured it all out.

Angels of upper ranks and orders were missing the emotional link that gave so much humanity to Vasariah and her small family. Probably, too much humanity. She felt it subtly, but persistently—that as strong as she was, compared to the soldiers beneath her, Vasariah's strength paled against the angels above her. And the more powerful angels didn't seem to give a damn about anything.

She was about to die for doing what came naturally to her. No one cared about saving her—or her family. She had hijacked the first apocalypse, wiped out all the angels below her, and the angels above her barely even blinked.

Andras' voice echoed in her head: *What's gonna happen to us? Are we gonna die without a purpose?*

It was funny how she could've felt so invincible such a short time ago. Now, she felt no more divine than a human, an animal, or a speck of earthen dirt.

The Sixth Angel stroked Vasariah's face, her golden eyes unchanging. Slowly, she wrapped her hands around Vasariah's back, her grip firm and final. Vasariah barely had time to register it before her wings dissolved. She wanted to drop to her knees but couldn't because of the Sixth Angel's steel embrace.

"I seal your forces of destruction," the Sixth Angel said evenly, while Vasariah screamed in silence.

She couldn't make a single sound. Her mouth and throat slammed shut. It was a wonder that she could still hear or see anything.

"Now, rest," the Seventh Angel said. Hard, like a command.

The Sixth Angel stepped back, releasing Vasariah.

As soon as she did, Vasariah Fell.

She didn't feel fear or pain—just an overwhelming emptiness. The bright fire that had always driven her flickered and floated away, like her wings. Together, they were left hollow and aimless.

The ground flipped over so that she plummeted through the sky in an explosion of prismatic sparks and flares. Wind burst against her face and body. She fell, fell, fell, from high in the air to waters below, then disappeared into a crater of her own.

The Fall incinerated everything around her. A tidal wave exploded in her wake, adding more destruction to the chaos. Monsters, rats, and snakes howled in the distance. Vasariah's body twitched violently in her grave, one time, then never again. Blood pulsed through her veins as slowly as gravity drew a bird's feather to the bottom of the ocean floor.

There, in her final resting place.

After the End of the First World, where devils and danger had reigned, the Empyrean orders of angels moved on without the low-class legionnaires that had succumbed to evil. They mercilessly took control of the Universe and the newer, lesser worlds born out of the ashes of destruction. Inevitably, evil, enmity, and the Infernal orders of devils seeped back in, and the balance of power shifted again. But without the Apocalyptic Angels of the Euphrates, the Universe went on expanding and contracting in an Endless Cycle while Vasariah slept.

Until the day a child was born with fragmented memories of her Fall. A child named Vincent Bell.

Chapter 12

SIR

S IR DRANK LIKE A fiend. Almost automatically. Vincent's thin blood fueled his senses and briefly eased the ache in his veins as a short history of her life settled into his memory. Not just this life, either, but her past life, too—as Vasariah. Everything swirled together, switched back and forth, drawin' Sir further down into the insanity of the angels.

Vincent hadn't known of her first life. Just got tortured by it. A lightnin' rod for trauma who no one cared 'bout, no one protected, and no one believed. In the end, just another neglected, rotted wound of a person: that was Vincent Bell.

And she'd satisfied Sir's hunger, but it felt different from usual. No, actually, not that different.

More similar than different...

Similar to when he drank Ero's blood. Angel's blood.

More images and memories rapidly flooded his mind—the evolution of the First World, the War and the Separation of Ghosts, the Fall of Humanity, and finally, the destruction caused by an angel named Vasariah at the End of the World. All watershed moments Ero never experienced. But Sir had. Through *her*.

Well, shit, how could he not've seen it before?

Vasariah was his fallen star.

The hellscape that Sir'd seen while devourin' her had been one of her last memories, as an Apocalyptic Angel at the End of the World.

This grey, vague history of the Empyrean Angels settled in his consciousness through Vasariah. A missin' piece of the puzzle—includin' the foundations of Ero's grand little mission. It wasn't just 'bout savin' Sir, the way Ero always framed it. It was just as much 'bout Ero as it was 'bout Sir. Maybe even more so—Ero was The Last Angel, after all, not him.

Sir didn't harbor this naggin' sense of responsibility for Ero's fate on his own, but 'cause of Vasariah.

An angel possessed by bloodlust who corrupted her entire order.

He suddenly saw somethin' strange, a vision of himself through the Fallen Angel Vasariah's perfectly clear senses, despite everything 'round them soakin' in darkness.

He was lured straight to her restin' place.

Called to consume her.

Covered in her meat and plasma.

Trapped in her arms.

And suddenly freed by a gentle, distant voice...

Sir'd always known the fallen star was more than human, 'cause it'd helped him to see he was more than human, too. And wouldn't you know it, he'd turn right 'round and meet an angel with eyes the same blood-red as the light that flashed in his mind when he devoured that fallen star. Disappointin' he hadn't seen it sooner.

All of it.

The Angels of the Right Hand'd suffered a loss they'd never recovered from when Vasariah, one of their most gifted, trusted, high-rankin' angels, Fell. Half the class'd been wiped out while the remainin' few rose to higher stations, leavin' no Angels in her wake. If Ero was The Last Angel, and Vasariah of the Euphrates'd been the last before that, what'd that end up makin' Sir? Some kinda fucked up guinea pig?

What was the real reason he had to get roped into this Empyrean mess? His lil human world couldn't matter *that* much to all these so-called infinite beings.

Ero'd said it a million times—he'd been commanded to marry Sir. Who were those commanders? And what'd they want from Sir? From Ero?

Ah, Ero.

...Did he know these answers? Did he even wonder 'bout them? Or did he just smile and say, "Yes" no matter what?

As if summoned like a storm, Ero barged in on a gust of warm, humid air that stirred the spare furniture. Sir caught the reflections of faint gold light on the walls before Ero ripped him away from Vincent's body.

Ding. Welcome, guest.

"Sir...?! What the fuck?"

Ero immediately went to check on Vincent. Naturally, it was way too late for her. A thick black crack stretched out from the edge of the bite wound on her neck.

The room was silent except for Inez's snores.

Sir coughed. He'd landed against a nearby wall, crackin' it when his wings'd rapidly extended to cushion the impact. Thanks to the blood, he'd recovered from his earlier exhaustion, and he stared straight into Ero's ruby eyes. They didn't overwhelm him anymore or make him see waves of red. No, he saw them for what they really were now—Ero's shield.

Ero kept everything hidden away behind his eyes, only lettin' through what Sir wanted or needed to see. Must've thought he was real slick.

"Welcome home," Sir mumbled, spittin' out his own blood.

Ero took a minute to find his words. His aura never changed—he had tight control of his wilder emotions—but his face went blank while he searched. "What the fuck?" he said again.

Sir laughed; a dry, bitter hack.

"Don't you dare laugh right now, Sir. I'm serious. What the fuck?" Ero shot straight to his feet, stabbin' a knife-hand at Vincent's limp body as his voice cracked. "Because this looks like a fresh fucking corpse, and I could've sworn we just talked about not killing anyone else. What exactly is your fucking problem? I'm trying to help you! Don't you get that? Why do you keep doing this? All you have to do is tell me what you need, and I'll give it to you. Anything. I'll give you anything. Just stop the fucking killing! Stop it! Use me. Eat me. *Kill me.*"

Those last words stabbed Sir in the gut. He held his breath as they tore into him. Dared him to deny their weight.

Then, he got on his feet, too, plaster crumblin' behind him.

"Kill you?" he repeated.

Ero's eyes flashed. Those dangerous owl eyes. They always made Sir feel so guilty for just existin'. Like he was moments away from doomin' the whole world at all times, unless Ero kept him in check.

"Would that I could," Sir said, and paced forward, into pools of dryin' blood. "I tried, remember? Ate you right up. And yet, here you are. Day after day. What, you want me to try again right now? I can."

Ero flinched. "No, I just—I wish I could have gotten to you sooner. Days sooner. Years."

Sir paused.

"I wish I didn't have to save you at all. I wish I knew you from the very beginning. I wish I grew up with you, and trained with you, and loved you all your life, so that you would never have to live like this in the first place. Because otherwise... now..."

Always with the fuckin' evasion.

"Now what?" Sir pressed.

Ero sighed hard. "You're a sangromancer—you already know everything!"

"Not everything."

Sir stepped up again, and when they were close enough to touch, he wrapped his fingers 'round Ero's bicep. His grip knocked Inez from Ero's arms, but Sir caught her with his free hand, tossin' her safely aside.

When Ero reached for her, Sir yanked him back.

"Just say it, Angel. Quit hidin'. I been honest. Now's your shot."

Ero glared at Sir. The silver ombre of his curls fell across his face, closin' over his eyes even as his lips stretched into that god-damned grin of his. "Why do you need me to parrot things back to you so much when you already know them? I'll have to arrest you, Sir. It's that simple."

Lightnin' traveled up and down Sir's body. "Simple."

"Of course, it's simple," Ero said. "Unless you plan on fighting me to the death just because you're stubborn."

Sir licked his lips. *To the death...?*

Finally.

"And you'd do it," he said.

"Yes. I would fight you. No, not to the death. I keep telling you, I'm perfect for you. I mean it. I can protect you, and I can defend myself from you. I'm not scared of you." Ero tilted his chin up and looked down at Sir with glitter in his eyes. His careful, heartless eyes. "You know, no one else is allowed to touch me like this, and yet you just—throw me into the wall. Imagine that. If only I had known the best way to get you to pay attention to me is by pissing you off."

"You are fucked up," Sir said. "Y'all fuckin' trapped me from the start."

Smirkin', Ero went on, "Of course we did. You don't have a name."

"Fuck's that gotta do with anything? Besides, you named me. Sir."

That goddamned lil name meant so much to Sir. Three letters and a plain ol' word. If he couldn't escape the comin' days, it'd probably be the only thing he took with him from this world into the next. He said it firmly.

And this time, Ero was the one to hesitate. His smile shrank.

"That's sweet, Sir, but... that's it? Just 'Sir'? I called you that because I didn't have anything else to call you. You don't care where you're really from or where you really belong? We do."

"Sir... Alexander," Sir added.

That was how it went, right? Take the name of the family you have. It was better than Esmeralda, Alexander's chosen last name. Better than Monster and Bastard. Maybe he should've said Houston, or Texas, or Southern Magnolia, instead.

But he shored up his nerve and said it again.

"Sir Alexander."

Ero's smile returned, always tolerant, even as his anger stormed behind it. "Names, we can decide for ourselves all we want. Ero Hartsend is my chosen name, too."

Sir scanned Ero's frame again. Even now, he saw all the details in Ero's golden aura that Ero kept sayin' Sir was missin'. A name. A rank. A class. He couldn't understand most of it, but he still saw it plain as day. Like holographs in an ancient, nonexistent language.

"Cerviel. Your name's Cerviel. The Last Angel of the Sanctuary."

"Yes. I call myself Ero Hartsend, the way you call yourself Sir Alexander—but you can see it as clearly as you can see my face that Cerviel is my true name. You saw it when we met. I know you did because no one calls me that. That name belongs to someone way more important than me. That's the thing, though. The way you are, even now after I've called your mark forward, I still can't see the same thing in you that you saw in me before you even knew it. It's like you're missing something vital that all ghosts inherently have and can't create yourself, something that informs your rank, your class, anything. I can't seem to get further than your mark..."

Sir slowly rolled his shoulders in irritation. "And? What's any of that shit gotta do with marryin' me like we're political fuckin' pawns?"

"Is that all that you're getting out of this discussion, *love*? It's just nature: Angels of the Right protect. Devils of the Left destroy. Regents mark their subordinates in a contract of service. Spouses mark their partners in a contract of trust." Ero's voice dropped on the last word. "Auras carry those marks. And I spent hours dragging your aura out of you—when it should've already been there, by the way—only for it to say none of that. Nothing except that you eat angels. So of course if we discover a devil eating angels, and we're afforded the chance to approach him with caution, we're going to act like angels and approach with the utmost caution. The only significant politics are between you and me after that."

Sir waited a beat, breathin' real, real slow.

Absolute bullshit, but it all just sounded so gilded and solid in Ero's warm voice.

"They should've just sent you to kill me. Fuck off with all these head games. Maybe you can't sort me out because I really ain't a devil, then. Maybe I'm somethin' else. Not human, not ghost. Nothin' to do with you at all."

"That's a cute idea. Well, even if that was the case before—which it wasn't, full stop—that's not the case now. The only thing that's true right now is either you Rise with me, or I arrest you. And I don't want to arrest you, so I'm going to have you drink my blood, and I'm going to marry you, then I'm going to make sure you Rise. Period."

Sir didn't follow up. He studied Ero's face, and clutched his arm like a vice, but he didn't follow up. If he did, he'd probably snap.

"Come here, Sir," Ero said coolly.

Sir took a look at himself and raised his eyebrow. He was sticky and dirty, and his skin and clothes were tacky with dryin' blood. Everything from his sleeves to his mouth had meat and blood soaked all in it. "Come here?" he repeated.

Ero cleared his throat. "Well, I would love it if I could court you at my leisure, but we're kinda out of time. We've been out of time. It's fine, I can still make you work for it later if you want. What can I say? I really like you. I don't want you to die."

Die.

Death, again...

Only time Sir'd ever come close to death was when he'd been trapped by the fallen star. He remembered the burnin' light, hotter than the sun, wrappin' 'round him, pullin' him down like he was nothin'. The pain was so intense that he thought it'd never end, that it'd consume him whole, that he'd be extinguished—a casualty in a war between angels he hadn't even known 'bout yet.

But somehow, he'd broken free from the fallen star's grave embrace. That faint, red light made sure of it.

Sir found himself grinnin' back a bit. The insanity of angels must really be catchin'. He felt like he was inchin' further away from reality by the minute.

"Really like you, too, Angel," he said.

"Ha. Don't sound so enthusiastic. I might get the wrong idea and think you actually mean it," Ero said. The twisted smiles on both their faces faded.

Sir did mean it, though. He liked Ero so damned much. Way more than he had any business likin' someone who was fixin' to ruin—maybe even take—his life. 'Cause he damn sure wasn't fixin' to wind up in prison. Ero just did somethin' for him, though. He hated to admit that a buncha strange angels in an invisible world could just conjure up the "perfect partner" to pacify him like a toy to an infant, but fuck if Ero ain't take him in stride so beautifully—even beg for more.

"I do," Sir said. "Like you more and more everyday. Ain't I s'posed to? Can't you tell?"

This time, Ero's eyes panned 'round the room. Sir followed them.

Vincent's body'd already turned to ashes. The leafy Mexican flame vines 'round her blanket pallet dropped under thick blood stains. Inez hadn't moved from the nearby corner where Sir'd deposited her earlier, still spelled to deep sleep. He envied her for a flash.

Ero shook his head and grabbed the roots of his hair. "This is my fault. I'm gonna fix it, though. I'ma fix it."

"Don't sound so enthusiastic," Sir echoed.

"Oh, I'm enthused," Ero said, anything but. "You still can't scare me away. I said come here, so please, Sir, come."

Sir gritted his teeth, stock still. Right. He really couldn't scare Ero off. Couldn't defeat him or reject him enough to stick. All Sir could do was accept the Rise. And that right there was why he'd never mistake it for love, what he felt for Ero. Everything Ero felt toward Sir just hinged on Sir doin' what he was s'posed to. If Sir refused to Rise again, Ero'd flip on a dime.

Ero wasn't "perfect"—he was spineless. What kinda creature fell in love on command? With a creature like Sir, no less?

Sir couldn't be loved.

There wasn't nothin' in him to love.

Suddenly, Ero folded his wings away and shrugged right out his lab coat. He tore the tall neck of his shirt to expose his shoulder. "Come here," he said again, this time grabbin' Sir by the lapel. Sir still hesitated, but Ero closed the space between them with purpose. His hand gripped the back of Sir's head, guidin' it to his throat without leavin' room to breathe. "Mark me. I'll mark you. We'll get this done."

"Enough already," Sir snapped, catchin' himself on the wall.

Wasn't no hidin' from it now that he'd come all the way here. Sooner or later, he'd have to quit runnin'. He had Ero. He had his mastery. He had Inez. He had all the answers he was probably gonna get here on Earth. And he still had no idea how to overpower Ero at the end of the day. Sir was trapped again, like he was in Vasariah's arms, waitin' for another voice to wrench him free.

He showed his teeth at the thought. "Enough," he said again. "You want it, take it."

"Yes. God, yes. I—"

Quick and sinuous, Ero sank right to the floor. His ruby eyes glittered with a vicious, hidden grin underneath—always obedient, but somehow defiant, too. Like he meant it when he said *god*.

Sir resisted his own small, dark smirk. Followed Ero down and rubbed his thumb over the angel's full mouth. "I will figure out how to hurt you. 'Til then, I'm yours, Angel."

"I'm okay with that." Ero licked his lips, catchin' the pad of Sir's thumb. A spark. "I don't know how many times I have to tell you you don't scare me, Sir. That's like saying you should be scared of me."

This time, Sir couldn't hide his smile. He moved his hand from Ero's lips down the long line of his neck, chest, and abs. Sir stopped there, strokin' Ero's flank as he stared down into his crystal eyes.

"I am scared of you," Sir said, and stabbed his nails straight through the skin. Up to the knuckles.

"Aghh!" Ero gasped, flinchin' a bit, his face goin' stale.

Sir dug in farther. "Sorry. Got bad blood in me."

"Yes, but—fuck!"

"Yes. Just yes. Hold still, Angel."

Ero was soft inside. Past tight skin and whipcords of muscle, the meat and organs underneath gave to the squeeze of Sir's fingers. Stronger than human, but not impenetrable. Hot blood pooled 'round his fist as it disappeared into Ero's side. The smell of it poured into the room like liquor on a lit flame, ignitin' Sir's senses. He couldn't ever seem to get enough when it came to this angel. He'd just gorged himself on a half-reincarnated ancient angel a bit ago—how could he have enough of an appetite to hurt Ero like this?

Like reflex.

He had to test the cage.

Sweat started to shine across Ero's forehead as he turned his face aside and rolled his eyes in pain. Blood and bits of red-colored fat dripped out from his wound. He really did scare Sir like this. Just his smile (his pushy, domineerin' smile) could chip away Sir's resolve and make him doubt his own strength. It wasn't just the power Ero held, either, but the way he wielded it, too, like it was a second skin, a part of him that could crush or caress with equal ease. Sir figured out he was playin' with fire from jump, and yet, he couldn't resist the pull. Even now, with blood slickin' his hands and the taste of iron thick in the air, he couldn't tell if he wanted to kill Ero or be killed by him.

"Angel, look at me."

Blinkin', Ero listened. His gaze drifted, as if his thoughts were slippin' away from him. "I always do," he sighed.

A spike of irritation ran over Sir's body. He'd have to try bein' nicer some other time. The way Ero softened up like that, it threw him off balance—right back into the deep end.

Sir snatched his hand back, spleen gripped tight, and drew his thumb over Ero's lips, like he did before, this time leavin' shiny trails of blood on Ero's brown skin. "It'll hurt, sugar," he said in a hard, even voice. "This's how I am. Full of pain. Nothin' worth givin'. Marryin' me will hurt, and it won't get easier."

Ero's breaths turned deeper as he collected himself. He swallowed hard and lifted his hand to hold against Sir's on his face. "Same here."

Sir let out a tense, short sigh, knocked Ero's hand out the way, and dipped down to press his lips to Ero's bloody cheek. It was so sticky red that Sir licked a path clean before sinkin' to kiss the skin again. "Doubt it. You're easy," he mumbled against Ero's cheek.

"Easy..." Ero said breathlessly. "Is that why you keep kissing me, even though you wanna kill me? You think I'm easy to love...?"

Their lips almost touched.

"You were made for me," Sir said after a grip. "Right? No matter how I try, that don't change. So quit talkin'. Fixin' to kiss you some more, Angel."

Ero swallowed his words again, tryin' to keep a brave face on despite the pain he was in. He was so good at hidin' everything, all the time, by reflex. S'why Sir always felt such a need to drag some semblance of the truth out the angel, careless or not. He sealed their mouths together like a viper. Ero moaned, and the smell of cloyin' blood flooded up over them, delightfully pourin' from his wound. Sir couldn't seem to calm down. If his heart could race, it'd be at a dead sprint right now. Instead, it pounded like thunder in his veins. Ero had to feel it, too.

"Come on, Sir," Ero said, and raised his leg to graze Sir's erection through their clothes. "Eat."

Sir shifted. He was rock hard and a touch lightheaded, too. *Eat.* He'd heard this command before, to eat. It'd guided his every move since he'd first heard it. The fallen star'd told it to him. Vasariah. *Eat.* A soft and sensual word, said by Ero instead.

Sir really ain't stand a chance. The minute he stopped runnin' from Ero, he gave himself over to a life that ended one way or another under the heel of the angels.

"No rush. Breathe deep, Angel."

Ero shuddered. "I'm breathing. I won't run away."

"You don't run," Sir said and shoved Ero to the floor. He followed as if they were tied together. "I run. Tried runnin' from you, but you chase. You try to hide—like you hide your face—but you always chase. You don't run."

Without hesitation, Sir brought Ero's spleen to his face. It was dark purplish-red, shimmerin' with plasma, its firm and fleshy texture iridescent in the shaded sunlight. He bit into it deeply, instantly reachin' the softer, blood-rich insides. A delicious squelch filled his mouth as even darker blood oozed out. With every bite, the sound of tearin' tissue and wet squishin' of blood intensified. Before he realized it, he was supercharged with angelic life after suckin', chewin', and swallowin' down Ero's precious organ.

Ero wanted Sir's body clear of influences other than angels, but Vincent hadn't been fully human, at least spiritually. Sir didn't need too much more from Ero than this.

Still, he ate it all just to make sure.

Blood dripped from his hand and face as he finished up. Ero met his eyes right away. Shudderin', dusty-rosy, Ero reached out for him, and Sir went. He brought their mired mouths back together in a silent crash.

Ero'd already committed to his role. Sir couldn't find a way outta his own. Now, he just had to admit defeat, with the angel's blood churnin' in his veins, and his future tied to the whim of the Sanctuary.

"Fuck," Sir said, his own breath a bit thin.

More than ever, it made sense why he always needed to give Ero such a hard time—maybe if he pushed hard enough, he'd get them both out this godforsaken contract—but no. Ero wouldn't fight to leave it. He'd only fight to stay in it. For some damn reason.

Sir found himself gnashin' his teeth as he drew Ero's arms over his shoulders. "How're we s'posed to do this shit? Recite a vow, say, 'I do'?"

"If you want. I do," Ero said. His legs slowly parted, bringin' him closer to Sir 'til the space between them vanished. He was hot to the touch and covered in blood as he rubbed against the stamp of Sir's cock in his jeans.

Sir pushed back, addin' friction to the heat. "Do that, and I'll get hungry again."

"Sir..."

Ero made fists in Sir's hair as a line of frustration bled through his voice. It sounded more strained than usual, and if Sir was thinkin' clearer, he would've noticed a waver in Ero's perfect aura sooner.

His head was too much of a mess to do anything exceptin' the first thing in front of him, then the next thing, and the next. And that thing was Ero.

Sir worked him out his clothes, layin' bare miles of deep brown skin marked with dark scar lines. Steel-strong, world-wise, but he still had a soft, chewy center. His angel.

"Watch yourself," Sir said.

Ero didn't say a word back. So rare to see him silenced. His face was flush, so brave, his hips archin' toward Sir in invitation.

Sir took it.

His fingers pressed deep between Ero's legs 'til they started to slip inside, slick and smooth. He hissed from the warmth of the squeeze. "Oh fuck."

"Hurry up... come on, hurry up," Ero said softly, shudderin'.

"Shut up," Sir hissed. He pressed another red, sticky kiss to Ero's damp face. He was remorseless as he started to press his fingers deeper into Ero's soft, damp core, then stroked in and out. "Just shut up for once."

Ero's earlier frustration fell flat, and his aura sparkled as Sir touched him, like a ripple effect. All the thoughts Sir had access to on his face went carefully offline. Only Ero could be laid bare like this and still find a way to hide his face.

"Then come," Ero said.

With a smirk, Sir licked his lips hungrily and lowered his mouth over Ero's hard cock, lookin' up as he did. The angel'd been beautiful from the start, the kind of beauty awarded by strength and competence, but he was 'specially pretty now with a harsh blush scattered over his cheekbones, darkenin' his damp, swollen lips, and spreadin' to his chest and shoulders.

Fallen star, Sir'd always called Vasariah, because she'd reminded him of a dyin' star that'd fallen to sleep with the Texas bluebonnets. This close, Ero had the same faint shimmer to his aura that made him golden. Just like another star. But bright, alive, and burnin', like the Sun: the closest star.

"Sir, come on..." Ero sighed again.

Every time he said *Come on* like that, Sir unraveled a lil bit more. Later, he'd make the angel pay for his impatience by takin' his sweet damn time. Later, he'd have the angel beg for mercy. But for now, Ero'd made a good point—they had time constraints and no time for drawn-out romance. They never had.

Sir's gaze was unwaverin', his attention entirely focused on Ero as he curled his fingers and swallowed 'round the weight in his mouth. Ero didn't say nothin' else for a while, just pressed up into Sir's touch 'til he couldn't take it anymore and started beatin' on Sir's shoulder, moanin' long and loud. His voice filled up the whole room. Sir couldn't hear nothin' else, not even the bass drum of his own heartbeat.

Just Ero. Always Ero. Surrenderin', in the only way Sir could get him to do it.

Finally, Sir pulled away. His lips were drenched. "Stay like that," he said, voice beat up and rough.

Ero nodded, his wide eyes clear, unmovin'. The hole in his abdomen'd already closed. Only the remains of bright, shinin' blood were left behind. Damn shame.

Sir climbed on top of Ero, took himself in hand, and rocked perfectly into Ero's body. He almost crashed out right on the spot. Ero shouted, the sound echoin' in the room and overpowerin' Sir's low groan. He pushed deeper inside, and even deeper, nonstop 'til Ero wound 'round him like a vine. They hugged each other for a long time once he was buried inside, their breath a clouded fog between them.

"I think..." Ero mumbled and sighed. "I'm gonna pass out."

"Hold tight. Don't let go, Angel," Sir said. He pulled back a bit and thrust in deep again. Ero was so hot and sweet inside—a concentrated mirror of the warmth and affection that used to make Sir pull back.

Now, it pulled him in, in, in, in.

The rhythm was ruthless. Ero's response lost out to a moan as Sir drove into him over and over. Sir's mouth covered Ero's again, their kiss a slip of blood-drenched tongues, and he only broke away to latch onto Ero's tender neck.

"No," Ero gasped.

Sir pierced skin. A fresh shade of blood rose to the surface. Ero's head canted back, and he shouted, but he ain't say too much else after that. Who knew it was possible to shut him up once and for all? Sir's other hand wrapped 'round Ero's hip, reelin' him in harder, faster, tryin' to invade him. Understand him. Tear him apart. Love him. Whatever happened now. Sir's body was more alive than it'd ever felt, every nerve endin' lit up with the intensity of his connection to his angel. He could feel Ero's power, through their blood, through their aura, everything wrappin' 'round him and drivin' him to stamp Ero's body with his own. He clutched Ero searingly close and chased his end inside the warmth. Too damn late to run now—yeah. It'd been too late to run since the day he stumbled across the fallen star and ate her. Maybe even before that.

"Please..." Ero whispered, his voice at a scarce decibel. "Hurry... Haa..."

Sir's laughter was as reckless and satisfied as it was brief. "Careful."

He worked his hips and rammed into Ero with renewed force. He couldn't hang on long. Each movement, each harsh caress, brought him closer to the edge. His mind was a fog of heat and turbulence. Always angels. Red eyes, thick blood, and drippin' skin. He released a rough groan and tipped over, spillin' himself into every inch of Ero's hard body before he finally pulled back.

For a short while, they lay together, their bodies slick with sweat, blood, and sticky pools of cum. It must've been less than a minute, but it felt so much longer that Sir laid there, starin' into Ero's eyes face and feelin' the same daze wander 'round inside himself.

"Angel..."

Ero's mouth was swollen, bruised from use, and still tinged bloody red, even though most of the wounds they'd made on each other'd already disappeared. "That was... I... don't know what to think..."

Even rarer than sex-induced silence. Sir pushed in closer to him 'til their noses bumped together.

"Still think you're perfect for me, Angel?"

He asked it without thinkin', like always, but he had no interest in the answer soon as he did. Was it really possible for someone—even an angel—to love a devil who loved like Sir?

Like Alexander?

It hit him all at once—Sir hadn't even got his clothes off all the way before tearin' into Ero like he did. It wasn't usually like that. He wasn't normally the needy one. And Ero was left quiet and bleedin', just like he'd been with Alexander. Alexander's shame lived in Sir just as much as the fallen star's. Somehow, he'd taken it all on.

"C'mere," he said abruptly. He traced another rough path of anticipation down over Ero's hip, under his shirt. "Push me back. You're stronger than me."

There we go. Alexander'd never let him win shit.

"Sir..." Ero's body responded instinctively, archin' and pressin' into Sir's touch with a mix of urgency and surrender as he grew hard again. Sir's hands were remorseless on him, strong and confident, drawin' Ero closer to the end with each deliberate stroke. Then he stopped. Ero blinked, his faint smirk falterin', replaced by somethin' more fragile.

There was somethin' raw 'bout a moment like this—the edge of his power balanced by the undercurrent of somethin' else.

His hands latched onto Sir's shoulders, nails in skin, while Sir held him firmly, groundin' him without givin' him room to escape. Not that Ero was runnin' nowhere anyway. He rocked Sir smoothly over onto his back.

"I don't want to overpower you," he said, and reached down to take Sir's cock in his hand, squeezin' hard. "I keep telling you, I'm not scared of you. I'm your husband. I can take it."

Sir pressed deep inside again, as if on command. He had no room to protest. Ero's voice, always so sharp with challenge, softened to a breathless plea, his body quick to seat Sir's.

In, in, in, in. Their bodies fit together like it was inevitable. Closer, closer.

Every short breath hit their skin, ragged and uneven, as the intensity built right back up again. Goddamn fuck. Sir was really here. He really promised to marry Ero. He *was* married. Married to an angel, and sworn to become one himself. Goddamn the whole thing.

His touch went harder, more insistent, Ero's wordless responses more desperate. They fucked like that for a good, long while, with shakin' hands and glazed-over gazes, Ero's fingers rakin' over Sir's chest and shoulders hard enough to bleed. His voice hitched on each jolt.

"I—think I—"

"Yeah, Angel. Let's go."

Ero's back flexed in a perfect arch, and Sir gripped him tight. Ero opened his mouth to shout, but Sir sealed it with his own to swallow up the sound. One fell, then the other, he couldn't tell who anymore. Mess splashed all over their bodies, combined with all the smeared blood. They crushed each other close enough to hurt, feelin' shudders and coarse gasps run through them. Ero stayed put for eons afterward, hair all in Sir's face. Sir twirled it slowly 'round his first finger.

He didn't feel any different from the first time—still vicious, still voracious, even though he had no right. Ero'd given him everything, and he could still do it all again in a heartbeat. *Always hungry.*

"Angel, you sure you wanna trust me?"

Ero hummed, his voice still raw despite being so quiet. "Well, you really didn't give me much reason to until now. I was afraid you wouldn't go through with marrying me, in the end. But you did, so I do. You can kick back, relax, and leave the rest of the hard work to me, as far as I'm concerned."

"S'more shit to *do*?"

"Just a bit. I have to draw up an incantation circle, and if we had more time, I would give us a cleanse first, too, but..."

No leisurely courtships right now.

Sir shook his head. "Still not sure I'm s'posed to be doin' this. Not sure it'll even work. Don't envy you one bit."

"Well, you are doing it, and it will work. I told you, I'll make sure it will. You trust me, don't you? You've trusted me so far. We're so close. Let me get dressed, and I'll draw up the circle now," Ero said, pullin' himself back together. It almost didn't make a difference with how much a mess they'd made of themselves. His skin was tinted peachy-red.

"What, no rings?" Sir asked flatly. He didn't wanna move. Didn't wanna leave the moment and confront the next.

Or the next.

If he could linger here—if this moment was all their marriage would be—he'd be so okay.

Ero shrugged as he inspected his lab coat for damage. "We can exchange rings if you want, but we're already married. You even have my mark."

That was true. Nothin' visible to the eye, but known to the mind, Ero'd marked Sir as his. Just like Sir'd marked Ero. Like bites: Consummation. Marks of marriage.

How was he s'posed to get his life back now?

Sir's face flattened out into an unimpressed stare as he watched Ero finish redressin'. "Say, Angel, this mission you're on. Always wondered 'why me?' but lately, I got to wonderin' 'why you?' You never think 'bout what we're really part of here?"

Ero did. Sir knew he did. Ero wouldn't be Ero if he didn't question it at some point. *The only significant politics are between you and me.*

Still, Ero turned his back to Sir as he shook out his coat, restorin' it to pristine condition before slidin' into it. "Yes. I thought about it every day while I was training under my command," he said without facin' Sir. "I thought about it every time I was ignored, or feared for no reason, or talked at like I'm no better than a monster. I thought, 'Why is everyone else perfect? Why am I the only one who's always alone? The only one who's been told to marry a devil or die trying?' I don't know. One day, I can't remember when, it just stopped bothering me. Like you said: No matter what I do or how I feel about something, it doesn't stop it from being true. So I'm sorry, but you could've been anyone, you could do anything to me, and I would still love you. Not because I have to, because I don't, just like you don't have to love me, but I think"—he smiled as he turned 'round—"I love you because I want to. Regardless of what anyone says now, I want to love you, so I will. You're mine."

Sir didn't need to check for the truth in Ero's eyes 'cause it was plain there on his face. False smile, real words.

Ero loved him.

Sir wished he could say the same.

When he tried to love Ero, all the distorted emotions he'd received from Vasariah—from her memories lingerin' in Vincent's blood—raced forward from the back of his mind. Emotions toward all angels of the Empyrean Sanctuary. Rage, betrayal, a bone-deep lust for their blood—

Ero ain't want Sir 'specially. He wanted to prove somethin' that had almost nothin' to do with Sir and everything to do with the goddamned angels. *You could've been anyone*, he'd said.

Sir stood and fixed himself up. "Look, Angel... maybe I wanna stay with you. Don't think I know what love is for sure, but when you ask me to do shit, you make me wanna do it for you. No one else makes me feel like that—but it's not *just* that. It was never just that. Sometimes, it feels like we ain't no better than a couple pieces on a board, in a game with rules we think we know but don't."

"What are you—?"

"Angel." His mind lingered on Vasariah's memories, her bloodlust rippin' up reality. Whatever answers she held, they didn't come any easier than they did with Ero. He had to hear the truth from the horse's mouth. "D'you know 'bout that woman I drained just before you pulled up? Vincent Bell? She was born with the memories of an angel named Vasariah, and I think she recognized me when she saw me."

Chapter 13

ERO

"OF COURSE I KNOW about Vasariah," Ero said. He hadn't said her name in so many years that it felt like rust as he pronounced it, cutting through years of silence. He hated the way it stung him, drawing memories he'd buried deep to the surface, where they could bleed anew. "How could I not know about her? She's infamous for ruining the First World's End. She's the reason I'm The Last Angel. What do you mean she recognized you, though?"

Sir rubbed his shoulder, as if he didn't know what to say to that. He had loosened up a bit, talking more freely, since ripping the spleen straight from Ero's side. Ero was even tempted to accuse him of an unusual eloquence. "It was Vincent who recognized me, but I saw Vasariah in her. Y'know, saw how she ended."

"Ended?" Ero said it slowly, surprised at that angle. "She broke her promise to fulfill her mission and, in doing so, caused the extinction of all angels across time—before me. She was ordered to massacre a fraction of the human population, not her entire family or the entire army of angels. Her powers were stripped away to prevent further chaos, and since her eternal rest, angels have been viewed as closer to humans than ghosts—vulnerable to the same corruption. She was beyond dangerous. She wasn't just 'ended.'"

Sir raised his eyebrows. "Sound like it to me."

"We actually don't have time for this," Ero snapped. "I didn't ask after Vincent Bell because I already knew who she was. Ghosts incarnate sometimes. It happens. But in her condition, she can't do any harm. You, on the other hand, in this life, everyday, continue to do just that. Come with me right now, Sir, or I swear..."

"Or you swear what? You finally get to make an angel out of me—whoop-de-doo. It's still just you and me, alone together, against everyone else, who've never fully trusted you, and who'll never trust me at all. Just said so yourself. You trust me enough for that? You trust your command enough for that?"

"What are you talking about, do I trust my command? Of course I do, every one of them." As the Last Angel, Ero's command could be said to be many. Either Cerviel, who had created and trained him; or Ireul, his guardian; or Gabriel, ruler of Angels, like Ero, if there were any others. The list went on.

And standing against all the names on that list to proudly defend Sir in the Sanctuary painted a pretty ludicrous image.

"Well, I don't trust them," Sir said, "and they're damn sure not fixin' to trust me. That's fact. Shit, Angel, they barely even trust you. I seen it all with Vasariah. You know they wait for you to fail. To Fall, just like her, right? You'll earn your place with the others by marryin' me just because they said it? I'd finally know where I belong if I let you Raise me? D'you even know where you belong?

You're the only angel in a whole host of motherfuckers who're scared of you and everything you stand for."

"I know already," Ero said quietly. "I know all of that. I still chose to accept my role."

"Huh? Chose? You didn't choose shit. I didn't, neither. We were told, and expected to execute without question. Thanks for everything you taught me, Angel, but I ain't signin' my life away to a bunch of puppet strings like that. Nothin' was wrong with the way I was livin' before you came 'long and said it was. And you said it was 'cause someone told you it was. I'll take my chances goin' back to what I know works for me rather than tangle with these angels who put down anything that's less than gold standard. You should, too."

Ero shot across the room to cover Sir's mouth, as if it would make a difference. "Stop saying that. Stop it right now. We're already here. We're already married, motherfucker. You just have to stay put for two seconds. Ignore Vincent Bell. Forget about Vasariah. Just keep your eyes on me. You don't have to trust all of the Spheres—I don't, either. No one does. But I trust enough to ask you to trust me. We both know our only alternative is arrest."

"Or death," Sir mumbled from between Ero's fingers.

Ero tried to find any measure of surprise in the answer, but Sir was right. He'd known from the beginning that Sir would fight mercilessly if ever placed under arrest. That was why he worked so hard these past few days to avoid it. He'd made the decision at the start to increase Sir's strength, to Raise him, instead of destroying Sir when it would've been the easiest.

But for a little while, when Ero first met Sir, there had been such a soft pink light around him. It had coated the whole mountainside. Ero was so hopeful.

"That's up to you."

Slowly, Sir nibbled at the tip of Ero's finger, brushing skin with his fangs. Ero had felt those fangs all over his body recently. He found himself stroking it all the way to the tip. Sir's eyes never left his face.

"Right. Choice," Sir said. "But then I heard your voice, before."

Ero pulled his hand away. "Before, when?"

"Before all this. When I ate Vasariah."

Somehow, it was still possible for Sir to surprise Ero with his dire appetite. Another vicious reminder of Sir's nails and teeth tearing into his skin washed over Ero. He shivered as he suppressed it.

"You... ate Vasariah?"

Sir nodded solemnly. "She was sleepin'. 'Round here somewhere, actually. I was weak back then. Lost. Findin' her seemed like findin' myself. Guess we were both sleep in a way. She woke up first. Thought I was dyin' before I heard your voice tellin' me to wake up, too. That's when."

Ero had no idea what to say. His search for Sir had taken longer than it should've—there was no way they had any contact with each other before he had found Sir.

Nevertheless, a knot tightened in his throat.

"Maybe... when I crossed the Bridges of Chaos... no." Ero shook his head. Sir hearing his voice wasn't the important part. It probably wasn't even true. "So you found the resting place of the angel Vasariah of the Euphrates, and you ate her?"

"You protect. I eat."

"Yes. It's nature..."

Nails. Teeth. Skin. Blood. Sir had devoured Vincent, the human incarnation, too. Why wouldn't he have devoured Vasariah first? It was what he did by default.

Instinctually.

Naturally.

Sir clamped his hands around Ero's waist. "Angel, after I ate her, everything made sense for the first time in my life. My heart started beatin'. My blood started movin'. I could string two thoughts together."

"Because you took parts of her and made it yours. That's what you do."

"Exactly. And you're like me, Angel—closer to the earth, closer to humans, than other ghosts. Maybe that's why I heard you." Sir's features almost softened as he frowned. "So why don't we just meet each other here in the middle? Instead of tryin' to return to the hell up in heaven."

Ero froze, his heart still. The last thing he wanted to hear was anything in opposition to Rising. His whole life depended on this.

"Huh?"

"We could stay right where we're at. Not here, not Houston, maybe we can go overseas 'til my warrant gets quashed, but it can be anywhere so long as it's *here*, huh? I don't Rise. You don't Fall. We just stay away from *everyone's* bullshit," Sir said.

Ero's mind flatlined. Was Sir proposing they... elope?

"What?" he whispered. He couldn't bring himself to say anything else.

Sir pressed his lips together, searchin' for a response, but then he went rigid and snapped into a defensive stance.

"What is it?" Ero asked again, now alarmed.

He sensed it all at once: a tidal wave of power headed straight toward them, right before it blasted through the metal frame of the front door.

Ding. Welcome, guests.

There were three.

Sir darted in front of Ero with both wings spread wide. Even without being able to see past them, Ero had already recognized the mark of the angels that appeared in the living room. There was so much power in the house that both Ero's and Sir's strength were eclipsed by the three who'd appeared.

"The fuck're you supposed to be?" Sir demanded, glaring at each of them.

Ero pushed his wing aside to view the angels' faces—Tariel, Angel of Summer, alongside her two subordinates, Gaviel and Gargatyl. As leader, Tariel stood tall in resplendent armor that shimmered like pure gold, and her eyes shone a dazzling shade of amber. Her molten gold curls flowed freely around her armor, decorated in intricate red designs that spanned her chest and shoulders—it was her rank, a Knight-of-Heaven.

"They're Archangels," Ero said gravely.

The room was so quiet, Inez's soft snores rolled into the silence. Ero's breath caught in his throat as he met Tariel's amber eyes, searching for any trace of mercy.

They had run out of time, just like he'd told Sir. He had no right to act so surprised. Secretly, he had been banking on the fact that no one, like Tsais, had come to yank Sir away and get the job done themselves. Ghosts visited the Universe all the time, and none of them had bothered with Ero and Sir yet. But now...

"Maybe you forgot, but we don't answer to devils, Ero," Tariel said.

Behind her, Gaviel and Gargatyl wore the same ranks beneath designs of flourishing vines across their armor. Deep green eyes and long, thin dreadlocks set Gargatyl apart from Gaviel's brown eyes and bald head. They both had their weapons clutched in hand, one a staff crowned with a brilliant crystal and the other a shimmering blade with a delicate circlet. Tariel's huge, razor sharp lance didn't make an appearance yet. She came closer and closer to looking like she would summon it as her wide eyes took in everything.

"I suggest one of y'all come up with a good explanation as to what the fuck is going on here before I put that devil under arrest."

"Arrest?" Ero elbowed his way around Sir to stand in front. "Who said anything about arrest? Were you ordered to do that?"

Tariel finally took her eyes off the savage scene to glance at Ero. He tried not to imagine what she was seeing, considering what she had interrupted. He'd just been doing his job.

"Well, no—" she started.

"See? So everything's on track. I was ordered to do what I'm doing, and I'm doing it just fine. I've got it all handled here." Ero glanced at Gaviel and Gargatyl behind her, neither of whom showed signs of budging or recalling their weapons. "Come on, Tariel. You know me. You know Cerviel. She would never let me have her name if I wasn't ready. Sir and I were just—"

Tariel scoffed. "Sir? That's his name?"

At his back, Sir bristled, but he didn't say anything. He was letting Ero do all of the talking for now, steer the situation clear if he could. In an odd way, Ero warmed up at the thought. He never would've guessed that Sir would allow him to take control of a situation he was unsure in. Ero couldn't betray that sense of trust. Once he lost jurisdiction of the mission, it'd be out of his hands. Then Sir would be, too. He wouldn't let Sir get arrested by anyone.

Gaviel and Gargatyl paced forward once, their movements swift and purposeful behind Tariel.

"You were 'just' what, Angel?" Gaviel tapped her fingers near the hilt of her pale sword and circlet. "What's the hold-up, exactly?"

"It's been almost three days. You were already warned once," Gargatyl added.

Tsais' words flashed back to Ero's mind, not for the first time. *Don't give anyone any reason not to trust you. We'll keep a close watch.* He hadn't exaggerated.

Tariel cleared her throat, commanding her subordinates to back up, then stepped closer to Ero herself.

Sir was perfectly still and quiet. He was observing, braced. Ero treasured it.

"Ero," said Tariel, her tone blunted, "you should tell us what the delay's been now. We need to make sure that everything's proceeding as planned if no one's going to make an arrest."

Ero's shoulders tensed as he sensed the weight of everyone's expectations on him. Sir, the Archangels, those above them—everything had seemed so manageable about an hour ago... or so.

He took a deep breath, attempting to compose himself.

"Everything's proceeding as planned. It absolutely is, it's just... complicated."

Before Tariel could respond, Sir's voice cut through the tension like a blade. "Not that complicated. Just figured out your angle's all."

Ero's frustration surged anew, his hand instinctively reaching out as if to stop Sir's words in their tracks again. "Sir, don't."

"Come off it. Y'all don't think nothin' of Ero, just because y'all are Archangels," Sir said. His eyes were focused directly on Tariel's face, probing deep into her psyche with his cutting stare. "Y'all think y'all're better, stronger, worth more, and deserve more. Y'all wanted me to kill him, or him to kill me, or the Fall to kill us both. Ain't that really it?"

Ero ignored it. Sir liked to gnaw on uncomfortable truths until they turned to ugly lies. Even if others in the Sanctuary might feel that way, Tariel wasn't one of them. At least, she wasn't anymore.

"Sir, enough."

"Devil," Tariel said evenly, tone tempered with more authority than before, "I thought you might be intelligent enough to keep your mouth shut, but it seems like you know a lot of words. Now you'll answer me. Your actions and intentions here are questionable, if not suspicious, despite being given more chances than most. Either comply, and Rise to grace now, or surrender."

Sir's lips curled into a smirk. "Yeah. Surrender."

Gaviel and Gargatyl's wings bristled, flaring wide in agitation as they prepared to strike. Ero had always known Tariel was hot-headed, but compared to these two, she looked like a cool, composed commander, perfectly poised in her position. And all three of them had cornered him, their eyes blazing with purpose.

Ero stepped forward. His heart raced as the air crackled from tension. "Sir, please," he said, his eyes locking with Tariel's. "Don't be fucking cute right now. If you say surrender—"

"It's too late for warnings now. We heard it loud and clear." Tariel's wings appeared with a graceful yet menacing energy. "Get out of the way, Angel."

Ero flinched.

Sir's words boomeranged back to him. *Y'all think y'all're better.*

Gargatyl took a step forward, brandishing his iridescent staff. "Seems pretty cut and dry to me," he said, and took aim.

Before he could fire, Sir lunged out from behind Ero to stop him. A cacophony of clashes and clangs filled the room as Gaviel dove to block Sir. Staff, sword, and daggers gleamed with ethereal light, each clash creating brilliant arcs that cut through the air.

Ero's heart pounded in his chest as he watched the battle take off. This was Sir—chaotic, relentless, and alive in a way no one else could be. His instincts urged him to step in, to join the fray and defend Sir from the Archangels, but he hesitated.

Tariel hadn't moved.

Instead she stood stock-still, glaring at Ero almost as if in challenge. She'd finally summoned her grand, glowing lance, too.

"What are you doing, Ero?" she asked. "Your mission has one goal: Save him, or destroy him. Either way, eliminate the threat. He's refused to be saved, and now he's attacking my crew, and you still haven't arrested or eliminated him. Why are you like this?"

Ero pressed his lips together. "Maybe it's because I'm an 'Angel.' Huh?"

Tariel flinched at the accusation, just as Ero had before. In a sign of respect and friendship, she'd previously pledged to only ever call him by name, since so few ever bothered. But just a bit ago, the word *Angel* had left her lips like a curse.

"I'm sorry about that. I didn't mean it maliciously or anything. That damned devil of yours... Don't you try to turn this around on me as if any of it's my fault. I'm just doing as I've been told, *the same way you should be doing as you were told*. So what is it? Are you going to keep defending your devil or arrest him, Ero?"

Ero gritted his teeth together. Why did it feel so wrong to just tell her yes?

He quickly gauged the temperature of the fight between Sir, Gaviel, and Gargatyl. The resonance of their weapons and the crackling of their mastery filled the Alexander house, creating a symphony of battle sparks against ceilings and walls. He could tell that Sir's strikes were swift, calculated, and powerful, his movements blending seamlessly with the two Archangels despite their differences in strength—but he couldn't tell how long Sir would last against them all alone.

"Make your choice carefully," Tariel said in admonition.

All things considered, Ero did exactly that.

"Sir, get out of here! Don't let them force seal you!"

In a burst of ethereal speed, Tariel pressed the edge of her lance against Ero's throat. His back smashed into a glass wall behind him. It cracked in half.

"You damned...!" Tariel growled.

Ero smiled as fresh blood bubbled out from the corners of his mouth.

Sir managed to break through the Archangels' defenses. With a single shout, he landed a kick that sent Gargatyl flying into Gaviel. Ero's heart leapt into a sprint as he watched from over Tariel's shoulder. Sir seized his opportunity and made a quick escape through a shattered window without even pausing to meet Ero's gaze.

"Get up, you two!" Tariel's amber eyes flashed with fury briefly as she focused her attention back to Ero. "And you. What the hell was that? You really choose to defend him? I'm going to put that devil's eyes out myself if he did anything to you to make you lose your graces!"

"Already on it." Gaviel helped Gargatyl to stand, exchanged some restorative energy with him, and took off to pursue Sir.

Gargatyl did the same, wordlessly.

"Good. See? This is what's best. Let Gaviel and Gargatyl handle the devil, then we can all go back home. Together," Tariel said.

A surge of urgency rose up inside of Ero. "I can't do that. I can't go home yet. Tariel, please, just listen. Sir hasn't done anything wrong to me at all. If anything, it's the other way around."

"What are you talking about?"

"I—I don't even know how to explain this, but when I first found him, he had no mastery. Just none."

Lost, Sir had said he was. *Found*, after devouring Vasariah of the Euphrates. And yet, when Ero had met him, Sir still had no name, no mark, and barely a wisp of aura. Vasariah's blood in his body must've been like dumping a handful of water into a volcano.

Tariel sneered. "What does that even mean? He had no mastery... of the Right Hand?"

"No. He had no idea that he even *could* master, at all. I almost didn't, either—at first. He'd been isolated pretty much his whole life, living like a recluse in this house in the woods with no idea he was even a ghost, much less a devil of the Left Hand. I had to call his mark forward and teach him to master it before I could even try to Raise him. I had to sneak him an eclipse matrix, like mine, just to get his mark to appear."

Tariel's gaze softened. Despite her position, she had always been more willing to listen than others, and she slowly recanted the death grip she had on him as she absorbed his words. "That's... new. I've never known of a ghost who had no idea he was a ghost."

"Okay? So you see what I'm working with here." Ero wiped the blood from his face, although it blended in with the rest of the gore and sex still smeared all over him. He shook and shimmered until he was clean again. He almost didn't care enough to bother anymore. If Tariel thought two ways about it, she could take it up with his creators. Right now, he just cared about making it back to Sir and keeping him safe.

"So what?" Tariel said, slowly folding her arms over her chest. "You're saying you spent all this time getting him up to speed for the Ascension, and now you want some more time to finish the job?"

Ero met her gaze with resolve, his words pure earnestness. "That's exactly what I'm saying. We're so close already. There's no way I can stop now."

"I can certainly see how close you are," Tariel said and paused. Her eyes trailed over Ero's newly presentable appearance. "How much time do you need? Doesn't his eclipse matrix work like yours? Shouldn't it, like, max out his mastery of the Right straight away?"

Ero swallowed his knee-jerk surprise. It wasn't as though he'd ever told Tariel any details about his eclipse matrix. He never told anyone. He just kept his head down and worked his ass off to master its use.

"The eclipse matrix isn't that rigid—or powerful. It doesn't max out anything. What it does is allow me to reach across the invisible barrier that separates us ghosts and use mastery of the Left, doubling my strength, stamina, and understanding of mastery as a whole. You already know the cost of that."

"The Fall," Tariel said, almost automatically. Every angel in the world knew of his inherent weakness.

"Right. I don't use it a lot because it's not natural to me, and I'm not going down that route. But since I had to teach Sir what mastery was from the ground up, I figured an eclipse matrix was the only way for him to adapt for the Ascension in time."

For a while, Tariel just nodded as she took a subtle step back. "You two sure will make a pair, won't you? The two youngest spirits in all of the Spheres primed with the oldest technology in the universe."

"Maybe. It doesn't seem so bad to finally have what everyone else has—someone like me, in a way. And it worked. You've seen it work." Ero let the weight of Sir's fight with Tariel's subordinates flood back into their minds. Sir had held his own well. It was more than enough proof his eclipse matrix was competent. "My eclipse matrix helped me get him this far. His eclipse matrix will get us the rest of the way there. We just have to try first. Please, give us the time to try."

Tariel's wings shifted as she considered his words, her amber eyes reflecting a hundred thoughts but revealing none. Sir would see right through them if he was here. "You've always excelled above the preconceptions that others might have had of you," she said with a sigh and a decisive air. "You've come a long way, and despite everything, you always represent yourself exceptionally well as an Angel. You represent Cerviel and the entire Third Sphere well. Ero, listen to me. You should be proud of yourself. I know you're more than capable of mopping up here soon. Just get it done, all right? I trust you. You have my permission to continue the mission. Gaviel and Gargatyl, though—"

"I understand. I'll deal with them on my own."

She lowered her eyebrows in reproach. "Return my angels home in one piece. And find a way to eliminate that devil of yours—immediately, Ero. We mean it. You're on thin ice."

"Yes, yes, I know, I know. Now let me go to him. Please."

As Tariel stepped aside, Ero's heart swelled with a mix of relief and determination. He really bought himself some more time.

But as soon as he summoned his wings, the world started to spin. A relentless whirlwind of vertigo swept over him. His surroundings blurred into a chaotic space of colors and shapes, narrowing into a dark, warped tunnel. The edges of his vision grew hazy, like a fading memory, until everything collapsed into a faraway prick. The last thing he remembered was Inez's dark talons clicking over to stand beside him. She had finally woken up, cranky and confused.

He tried to reach out for her—to comfort her—but he fell down a black hole before he could.

———————   ——   ———————

From between the rosy gold curls of his hair, Ero's eyes creaked open and roamed the room around him. All he could see was a glass wall—a large crack webbed across its surface from where Tariel had thrown him against it when he dared to defend Sir.

Shit—where was Tariel?

He sat up, but she pressed him back down to the floor.

"That devil you serve really put you through it," she said, steadily feeding him a stream of her decadent energy. As a rule, Archangels were stronger than Angels. Her strength was even clearer to him while she healed him. "You were barely on your feet. How exactly were you planning to go after him?"

"Shit," Ero said, aloud this time. "Sir's still out there. He's fighting your angels. I have to go help him—"

"And you will, once you're well enough. Just give me a second."

Obediently, Ero settled down and allowed himself to take in Tariel's restorative strength. He would need it in order to be any help to Sir, anyway, since she wasn't in the mood to stop her subordinates.

They fell into a bittersweet silence as Tariel worked.

"Inez?" Ero called out carefully. She had disappeared some-where. He couldn't even sense her aura anymore.

"Your jaguar friend took off a little while ago. She seemed intent on looking for your devil. Did he spell her, too, or something? She's fucking fiesty," Tariel said.

Ero suppressed a laugh, imagining how Inez could've possibly intimidated an Archangel. "Sir's not like that. I keep telling you, if anything, I'm the one forcing things."

"I highly doubt that. You're a dime, Angel. Anyone would be lucky to have you. Only he doesn't know it because he's blinded by his origins. It's just how devils are. They fuck and they feast. Damn animals." Tariel eyed him meaningfully, but Ero ignored the stab.

"It's true that he's a devil, but he's different somehow, too. Vampiric, or angelic, or maybe something more, maybe less, I don't know. I just know that he's embraced by Lesser Earth even though he preys on it. He feels like he's at home in the trees. He wanders the mountains like they're his backyard. Inez isn't the only creature here compelled to follow him, she's just the most persistent." He thought back to the crow that had tried to cross state lines with them—the crows that beat their wings from the sidelines while Sir fed on him for the first time—the cicadas that covered the mountains when Sir started to succumb to the weight of his mark—

"That's odd. Low-level devils usually repel nature, like the cub and such. It's not like he's some high-ranking general with familiars. I mean, he's not, right? His mark doesn't say anything. All it does is help to explain why I lost contact with Gaviel and Gargatyl the moment they took off after him." Tariel shook her head with a *tsk*. "There must be something strange about his mastery that corrupts whatever it interacts with. Fucking devils and their fucking monsters."

"Tariel, can you not? He's still my husband."

"Yeah, how could I possibly miss that? It's not like his mark is this big black stamp on your chest or anything."

"Thanks." Ero rose, catching himself with his hands against the floor at first, but Tariel's healing had done the job. He was fine. A noise in his skull, like a head rush with needles instead of blood vessels, was all that remained. There was no structure or meaning to the sound, just a jumbled, static-like snowstorm that didn't make any sense.

"Ugh." He brought his hands to his temples. "What is this? Sir..."

"Wow. Fine then, have it your way," Tariel said, standing. "You clearly don't give a shit about anything else. I'm already exhausted. I won't interfere anymore. I just hope you know what the hell it is that you're doing. Don't make a martyr of yourself for a devil who will only use you up until there's nothing left of you to use. *We* will always be part of you. You're already loved, Ero. Remember that."

Ero didn't answer. He couldn't stand it when the other angels saw right through him as if reading his expression and seeing his heart. But he couldn't exactly blame her, either; no matter how much he tried to hide it, he felt disconnected from all other angels on some level. Even his closest friends and family couldn't cross the final distance. Only the human, Lios, had never gotten close.

Sighing, Tariel stretched her wings and prepared to go. "Good luck, Ero."

"I appreciate the help."

She shook her head, disappointed, then returned home.

Finally alone and healed to boot, Ero stretched his wings and left the house, too, disappearing out the hole where the front door used to be. He had at least one blessing now. He could afford to eschew the rest.

Chapter 14

SIR

S IR'S HEART THUNDERED IN his chest. A heavy, primal rhythm matchin' the intensity of the chase.

He'd tried everything from outpacin' to outmaneuverin' the Archangels. Through fields, woodlands, and the high expanse of the skies. No matter where he went, though, Gaviel and Gargatyl were a relentless force on his ass, a show of power that damn near scorched the air. Their auras pulsed with a palpable energy that mirrored the unwaverin' strength they'd displayed back at the Alexander house.

Sir bit back a smirk. Their strength and skill were exhilaratin' and nerve-wrackin' by the same token. The mix coursed through his veins like the wildest fire. Acutely aware of the weight of every moment and the gravity of the impendin' second battle that hung in the air, but not afraid of it.

Where'd fear get him? If he couldn't escape the Archangels, he'd just have to find a way to end the chase.

Ero's words slid into his head: *Most ghosts have a weapon, or two, or three.*

Slowly, he called a second punch dagger to nest in his free hand. Same size, cobalt color, and titanium tip as the first. Twins.

The Archangels were gainin' on him quicker by the second. The air 'round him charged up with energy and tension. His fingers twitched at his sides, and his muscles coiled tight like springs, ready to drive right back into action. Wouldn't be long.

"If you think you're doing something noble or righteous by refusing to Rise, know that whatever your reasons are, they're wrong," said Gaviel, gettin' closer. Closer.

"Surrender now," said Gargatyl.

"Nah, don't think I will." Sir turned on a dime to bare his fangs. "Think I seen enough angels for a lifetime."

"Have it your way!"

Gaviel made the first move. She surged ahead with supernatural speed, disappeared in a blur as she closed the gap between them. Her sword and circlet flashed in front of Sir. She brought them down with the force of a thunderbolt.

Sir's reflexes kicked into overdrive. His punch daggers rose up to meet her. Steel clashed against steel, the echoin' like a battle cry across the landscape. The sheer force of the impact sent tremors racin' through his arms, too, threatenin' to unbalance him, but Sir held his ground. His jaw cemented into a grimace as he pushed back against the unyieldin' force. Gaviel's attacks were as relentless, insistent, and pressin' as ever. They almost overwhelmed him every time they landed.

And beside her, Gargatyl. The gleamin' staff, the iron defense. Movements fierce and swift, each swing of the staff was executed with grace and power. "Now you'll learn," he said, his voice low and sharp as his weapon.

"Not so sure 'bout that." Sir's heart beat, steady. He met Gargatyl's strikes head-on, too.

The clash of the weapons echoed through him—raw strength behind Gaviel and Gargatyl's attacks, each hit pushin' him to his limits. Nothin' at all like fightin' Ero, who smiled wide all the while. Every swing of their sword and staff, every thrust, sweep, and figure eight testified to their heightened skill and experience.

Still, Sir refused to cave, matchin' might for might, as best as he knew how.

So...

These were Archangels.

Ero'd said it a thousand times already. He was The Last Angel. And yet there were always *other* angels in the back of his mind or tip of his tongue. Were all of them Archangels like Gaviel and Gargatyl? Were some... worse?

The minutes stretched on. Eons of sword-shing and bright light blurred into a whirlwind. Sir's breath started comin' harder, his body a growin' chorus of internal aches and strains he'd never really felt before. Different from his need, but similar in the way it made his fangs ache.

His mind raced all over as he worked to keep up with the fight. Couldn't hold out for too much longer against their combined power like this. Knew that much. He needed to find a way to turn the tide, to break through their goddamned defenses.

"C'mon..." he hissed under his breath. "Don't need the fuckin' Angel. Get it together. Go."

Right—never needed Ero before. Sure as hell didn't need him now.

With a pained shove, Sir launched his counter. He blocked Gaviel's strikes with his daggers flyin' in complex patterns. At the same time, he ducked under Gargatyl's powerful staff swing and kicked him square in the middle.

Gargatyl staggered back, momentarily off balance, and Sir found his golden opportunity.

To get Gaviel. The primary offensive.

"Ha!"

He spun back 'round, and his dagger sliced through the air in a straight line right at her.

Gaviel's face froze in shock as the blade found its mark, cuttin' a deep gash into her eye. A cry left her as she stumbled back and clutched at the leakin' wound. "Goddamned fucking devil! You impaled my fucking eye!"

"Die already!" Gargatyl launched a quick counter of his own.

"If I could...!"

Sir kept pressin' his narrow advantage, weaved and dodged, his movements less fluid, less precise, as he avoided Gargatyl's staff. Fought against every attack with a renewed sense of determination, though. His own hits were flashes of bloody knuckles and dagger steel that seemed to move on their own, they were so in sync.

But it still wasn't enough yet.

The Archangels were damn near dauntless, and their injuries only seemed to fuel them, sealin' up faster than they did on Ero. He could see the fire in both their faces and the unyieldin' resolve that burned inside; even Gaviel, still bleedin' and seethin' with spite as she clutched her damaged eye.

Sir needed more than an upper hand. He needed a way out.

A distraction, a moment of confusion that'd allow him to at least slip their grasp.

And then he saw it—a break in Gargatyl's guard, a split-second openin' that could be his last chance.

Without a second thought, Sir faked another attack on Gaviel, divertin' their attention to her for a crucial moment.

"Weak bastard," Gaviel hissed.

"Uh huh."

Then he lunged, his dagger aimed for Gargatyl's side instead. Tended to leave his center unguarded. Sir's dagger sunk deep in his ribs. At the same time, Sir dug his teeth in, too, deep and quick, right in Gargatyl's throat. Drew out a fresh mix of blood and curses.

"You... motherfucker...!" Gargatyl choked on his last words. His grip on his crystal-crowned staff slacked off. It clattered to the ground.

Thunk—

Sir didn't waste another second. A single bite, and he ripped Gargatyl's neck open, sent him sprawlin' to the ground, too. Shallow breaths came in ragged through the gapin' wound in his torn throat.

Meanwhile, life flooded Sir's cells. Warmth, light, love, power. A fraction of Gargatyl's wisdom and strength subsumed into him.

Somehow it was different than usual. Not different like Vincent'd been different, but different because he enjoyed it less.

He'd just filled up on Ero, damnit. Now that was ruined.

"Demon!" Gaviel's uninjured eye ignited with malice as she watched Gargatyl fall. She rushed forward with twice the ire, her attacks becomin' even more forceful. "Disgrace! *Devil*! How dare you touch an Angel of the Right Hand with those disgusting vampire fangs?"

Sir smiled with his teeth drippin' blood. "Do it all the time. You ain't hear your angel beg for it?"

"Shut your goddamned fucking trap!"

Sir's blood was pumpin' with new adrenaline, his instincts re-sharpened and refocused. Gargatyl's rich, energizin' blood scoured his veins as it filled and healed him. Another difference between the blood of an Archangel and Ero's blood—his wounds zipped up in half the time. He started wardin' off Gaviel's strikes with sharper accuracy, his new twin daggers an easy extension of himself.

This was familiar territory—him, full of ethereal blood, takin' an angel one on one, even an angel as strong and persistent as the Archangel Gaviel.

"You monster," she hollered, eye streamin' fresh red blood. "You're not worth the grace and mercy you've been given!"

"Fuck off already. Sick and tired of the words you angels always use," Sir growled.

With a burst of stacked up strength, he got in a last, furious strike that sent Gaviel reelin'. She stumbled back, her wings flarin' out for balance as she struggled, eventually capsizin'.

Now.

Sir disappeared.

Seized his chance, turned, and sprinted far and fast into the closest woods. The only protection he could think of.

He didn't look back as he took off, the sound of Gaviel's furious shouts fadin' into the background. All he heard were the complaints from his wings as they carried him up, up, and away.

He fell out the sky when he heard it—or at least, swore he heard it: a single, solitary heartbeat.

"Guh!" Sir hit the ground hard and laid there.

Thanks to everything Ero'd taught him, and all the insight gained from his kills, he'd managed to pull through and slip the grasp of the angels, sure enough. But just lyin' there felt like all he could do after everything.

The night sky hung heavy above him in a comfortin' stretch of sentinel darkness. Stars pierced the black expanse like cold, distant eyes, their glimmers muted by blue, grey, and purple clouds, and the crescent moon cast a feeble glow over the canopy without reachin' the ground below.

Sir's labored breaths were a raspin' counterpoint to the night's ominous quiet as he rested in the shadows under the moon. Goddamn, his wounds smarted. His whole body was a battlefield. The nebulous cries of every bruise and gash melded with the memory of the fight with the Archangels. He'd never responded so much to bein' hurt before. Also never fought an angel who was out for blood before, either, so there was that.

Ero didn't count. Ero was always so soft...

Goddamnit.

Where even was that Angel?

Shit. Didn't matter anyway. Didn't need him anymore.

Sir got up and staggered on despite the weight of his injuries. He'd just have to ignore the pain like he used to. His problems were bigger than his pain.

The woods were a livin' abyss 'round him, old, strong oak trees reachin' out with limbs that seemed to grasp at him in the dark, helpin' him along. The earth underfoot was marshy and murky, the ground uneven and littered with broken branches and lightnin'-struck tree trunks. As he marched on, stride unsteady, his mind collapsed into a one-way train to focus on the pain.

Images darted back and forth across his mind—flashes of brutality, the taste of otherworldly blood, and the feelin' of Damascus steel tearin' through his skin. Tasted the bitter tang of his own desperation, layered with the metallic bite of the other angels' injuries.

Every other angel's injuries.

Gaviel, Gargatyl, Tariel, Ero, Vasariah, her siblings as she ripped them limb from limb...

"What in the hell," Sir sighed.

As the night wore on, exhaustion came down on him, chokin' off the last vestiges of his strength. The oaks couldn't support him anymore. He finally stumbled and fell to his knees.

Fine. Here. He'd meditate here. Heal, stay on alert, but bolster up. Here.

Not sleep. Not yet. He wasn't done with them angels any more than they were done with him.

Closin' his eyes, he let the distant hum of cicadas and riverwater wash over him. The air smelled faintly of sugary fruit and decay—a strange mix of life and death that mirrored his own tangled emotions.

"Did I really hear that heart beat...?" he found himself wonderin'. The one that took him out the sky.

Without Ero's eyes always there to give him a glimpse at the truth—without anyone there at all—he had no way to find his answer. Gargatyl's blood ain't say much, either. Like Ero's at the beginnin', most of the secrets in Gargatyl's blood were expertly hidden.

Gradually, Sir lifted his gaze to the sky where stars hung like eyes glarin' back at him.

"Stars," he mumbled, without thinkin'.

And just like that, sheltered in the distant understory, he suddenly recognized this place.

A star'd fallen here once—the angel with a taste for blood.

Vasariah of the Euphrates.

A whisper of wind stirred the tall grasses all 'round Sir, almost like an acknowledgment. Encouragin'. Rememberin', too.

It looked different, even felt different, to his vastly improved senses, but there was no mistakin' it. This was the same open, billowin' field of wildflowers. Bluebonnets, pinkladies, tickseeds, and winecups stretched far as the eye could see, here on the far side of the old live oaks. The scent of rottin' flowers rose. Incense smoke and ozone.

This was Vasariah's restin' place.

Sir bit the inside of his cheek. Vasariah's grave—'cause that's what a restin' place was, *Ero*—had exactly zero significance to him the first time he'd visited. He hadn't known who or what Vasariah was, her legacy, or even her name. All he'd known was that she awakened a devastatin' vortex in him that led him to kill. Now, even though her body'd already disappeared long ago, he closed his eyes again and saw her restin' place with better under-standin'. *Start small*, Ero'd told him. *It'll come naturally sooner than you realize. Just concentrate.* There. So, so easy. An eerie glow reflected off every small flower petal and lush tower of grass. In the heart of this soft ethereal light lay Vasariah's empty grave.

How could he not've seen any of this obvious shine before?

Sir's fingers dug into the dirt, grass, and herbs on either side of him, and their eerie glow seemed to seep into his skin. "Vasariah," he murmured, his voice a rasp that echoed in the stillness.

Such an ancient angel'd been here for so long, cursed to die without restin', and rest without dyin'. And Sir'd devoured as much of her as she'd allowed. It'd established a connection, a des-olate communion between them, that transcended the realms of the livin', the dead, the damned, and beyond.

Maybe he was more tied to the angels than he even realized, through no one's fault but his own.

Hours passed, the warm air clingin' to Sir's body as he meditat-ed on top of Vasariah's restin' place. His thoughts were a labyrinth, ruminatin' over each and every step he'd taken leadin' him inex-orably to this point. Soon, though, the first tendrils of dawn started to scar the horizon, and a small, ecstatic light galloped across his senses, shatterin' his concentration.

"Inez?!"

She bounced straight over to him like he was some kinda bea-con and then crashed into his lap, exhausted.

How insane of her to follow him all the way out here.

"In your condition…"

Already unconscious, Inez didn't respond. She must've run all night.

"Sleep," he said, strokin' her lil ear. It twitched as he let it go.

Didn't really trust himself to do nothin' more than close up some of her nicks and scrapes, though. Without Ero's expertise to guide him here, her chances of survival under Sir's power would amount to zilch. Might've been the one thing he actually could need Ero for. Fragile, mortal things like Inez couldn't bear Sir's towerin' strength. He couldn't control it well enough yet. He'd never struggled with it before, when trainin' with Ero, but knew he shouldn't try on Inez. Not if he wanted her to live.

He calmed her down and stroked her fur pensively. Her breaths evened out, and with her patchin' up, her aura started to shine through. Simple, clear, and straight-forward—like pure crystal.

Exceptin' a flash of red light.

Ero's mark.

The same light that'd saved Sir from followin' Vasariah down into damnation.

Even back then, Sir'd seen it clear as day: a ring of blood. Now he knew for sure that was Ero's voice he'd heard, too. Vasariah'd captured him like she meant to take back all the life Sir'd stolen from her, but instead, after hearin' Ero's voice, he gained more.

Flashes of sun-gold. Memories of fallen angels at the end of the world. Torn up flesh and red-lined teeth...

Enough. Sir had to focus on patchin' himself up. His body still throbbed with pain now and again, but the healin' came, bit by bit. Just so long as he rested.

Gently, Inez shuffled over onto her back 'til she was nestled firmly between his legs.

Sir's breath caught in his throat as he felt the soft press of her fur. The tension inside him started unravelin', revealin' the threads of warmth and comfort keepin' him all tied together. "Glad you're okay, princess."

Inez comin' back was such a balm—a reminder that he might be alone, but he still had her. A friend. For some reason, time and again, she kept seekin' him out. He kinda had to look out for her.

You even adopted Inez after you protected her. I can see why you were chosen to Rise...

Sir reached out a tremblin' hand, his fingers brushin' against Inez's coat. She responded with a low, rumblin' purr—a sound that seemed to vibrate with her trademark understandin'. Inez was always curious, and clever, and quick to find him. His thoughts drifted—

To Ero.

Again.

An ache in his chest that refused to go away, even as all his other wounds sealed up: the constant reminder of Ero's absence.

How could Inez've found Sir before Ero did? They hadn't got too much of a chance to find their path forward together yet, but Sir, almost stupidly, thought it was still possible. Shit.

He could never think straight when it came to Ero. Ever.

As if sensin' his irritation, Inez snuggled down harder. Her body pressed against his legs, her warmth a stark contrast to the early-mornin' chill hangin' in the air.

"Fine..." Sir closed his eyes, his breathin' slowin' as he threw aside any expectations he had for the future. They'd all been tenuous to begin with. It helped to remember that.

But even with the reminder, his mind churned with thoughts of what he'd lost.

Ero Ero Ero.

Always fuckin' Ero. Gold as the sun.

Goddamn, but he'd spent so much time tryin' to get Ero out his hair, and right when it seemed like he could get used to it... this shit happened. Should've known better than to expect Ero to follow him as easily as he was expected to follow Ero. The pain was a weight he didn't expect, didn't know what to do with, and couldn't heal on his own. He didn't know he cared so damn much. Wasn't s'posed to.

Inez croaked and whined in complaint.

"Sorry, princess," he shushed her, "you can head on back to sleep."

Inez...

The idea whispered through his thoughts like a seductive promise—do it. *Transmogrify* her. Like Ero'd done to him.

Before, Sir couldn't survive the life that lay ahead for him in the state Ero'd found him in, so Ero'd fortified him accordingly. Changed him. He could do the same for Inez—give her his strength, his agency, his intellect. Between his blood, energy, and mastery, he could do just 'bout anything.

He stared at her sleepy, crystalline face. "Fuck it. C'mon."

He had the power to change her, alter her form and ensure that she'd never have to leave his side again. A temptation that clawed at the edges of his mind, a path he knew he shouldn't tread without more insight. But in return, Inez'd enjoy a long, cozy, secure life of leisure beside him.

As his familiar.

He gazed down at Inez, his fingers tracin' the contours of her dark rosettes. Sir's decision held so much weight; it'd alter the fabric of her existence and test his mind as much as the Archangels tested his body. And if he accomplished it, he'd certainly be further from grace for it.

Not that that kind of thing'd ever really matter again if Ero didn't come back 'round.

Either way, didn't matter. Didn't need him. Didn't want it.

As the last brushstrokes of dawn finished brightenin' the horizon, Sir made his choice to kill Inez.

A strand of strong, yellow sunlight cast Inez's fur in a golden silhouette. The large dark patterns on her skin shone through her ultrablack coat, and the air was charged with an immeasurable spark. The woods held their breath, waitin' for the outcome of the surgery right 'longside Sir.

His heart thudded in his chest as he gazed down at Inez nestled in the circle of ancient symbols he'd traced onto the ground. They were the images that came to mind when he focused on his intent, so he executed them to the best of his ability, etchin' every inch of the incantation circle in his mind with his twin daggers.

He extended a hand over Inez, fingers tremblin' slightly.

Nothin' to it, really. Just a fusion and splicin' of spirits that held the potential to destroy as much as it accomplished. He'd probably done more with less in the last week.

"See ya soon, princess."

Drawin' on his well of energy, Sir felt it surge in him, a potent force that pulsed like a spare heartbeat. He couldn't afford to hesitate right now—for Inez's sake. All his doubts 'bout bein' able to handle her without crushin' her shrank to the back of his mind. With a whispered breath, he channeled his energy down into the symbols etched on the ground and used it to bind his will, amplify it. The symbols glowed a faint silver-blue, respondin' to the mark of his mastery. His heart beat so loudly...

Inez stirred, her too-green eyes poppin' open with a mix of apprehension and an instinctual understandin'. Her bright mortal spirit, a shimmerin' thread of life force, swirled up 'round her.

This was the origin of her energy, the essence that brought her to life. Sir carefully and swiftly dissolved it.

Inez yowled. Her aura emptied of all her vitality, leavin' her limp and unresponsive on the carved ground with no trace of her usual crystal shine.

"Sorry, baby," Sir said, then marched on with his procedure.

The transmogrification.

Couldn't give her a new spiritual life without endin' her material one first.

Closin' his eyes, he delved into the depths of his own bein', touchin' the immortal spirit that pulsed inside him; the quiet, silent blaze behind his aura, mark, and mastery.

It was a sinister strength, the Left Hand of Destruction, or whatever Ero liked to call it.

And it was the force Sir'd use to replace Inez's mortal spirit. To sustain her aura with his own, and mark her.

At first, their energies resisted one another, pushin' back like opposin' tides. It was nothin' at all like markin' Ero. Ero'd been a welcomin' livewire. Sweet, wet, hot, open—

By contrast, Inez was dead, and her spirit resisted.

Sir's cheeks warmed with sweat while he operated, his brow stitched in concentration. He'd mastered countless spells in moments, executed thousands of techniques, but this went beyond anything he'd done up 'til now. It wasn't 'bout bein' the fastest, loudest, or strongest—it was more 'bout impact.

Precision and restraint.

Inez growled, both low and desperate, deep in her throat. Her body twitched, caught between her natural instincts and the forces actin' on her.

Sir gritted his teeth. "Keep fightin', princess."

Tendrils of ash-grey energy curled 'round his outstretched hand as he shuffled into the circle with Inez and cradled her close.

The last of her aura flickered, its radiance dimmin' as the dark energy of Sir's essence whipped 'round it. The air tensed, too, as if the whole world waited with bated breath for Inez to accept him.

As beads of blood welled from Sir's ears and nose, somethin' finally gave way.

Inez's tide of energy broke apart, and he dove in to cover the empty shores left behind. Like a vacuum, her depleted self siphoned vital energy from him once he rushed to fill her empty corners. Energy really was like blood, a life force that fueled everything it touched, and here, he was pourin' it out in streams, bleedin' it into the soil of Inez's new spiritual presence. Sweat instantly soaked his hairline. He fought to keep ahold of her.

Eventually, though, the procedure became less taxin'. As she filled back out, so did he. His strength fueled her, and hers cycled back into him, in a steady stream that kept him upright. Then the incantation symbols glowed with a half-light, and Inez's lil body convulsed as if she'd been struck by lightnin'.

"Princess?"

Exhausted but alert, Sir bolted upright without takin' his hands off her side. The constant outpourin' of energy left him a bit hollow, like her spirit was a dam that he could only feed so much energy at a time. But as he looked at her against the sheer from the incantation circles below, a spark of somethin' unfamiliar stirred in him.

A connection that defied his understandin' of power.

He'd thought of himself as strong before he'd ever devoured Vasariah. And then Sgt. Esmeralda, and then Alexander, and then the long thread of Texas Rangers and other State Troopers who'd come lookin' for his warrant. And then Ero... and then, and then, and then...

Each time, his power increased.

This time was different. This time, it was like his power *expanded*.

Sir looked at Inez. She met his gaze with an unspoken intellect, her eyes gleamin' with a wisdom deeper than her own. If he looked hard enough, long enough, he could see so far into her that all he could see was a reflection of himself.

"So sick, princess..." With more awe than Sir'd ever regarded anything in his life, he reached out and gently scratched behind Inez's ears. "How you feelin'?"

She gently purred into his hand, just like the lil cub who'd sought him out in the first place. Her fat lil paws flexed as she rolled over onto her back, stretchin' hard enough to bare her talons. Sharp and deadly as her teeth.

"Welcome back."

Right when he finished, Inez tensed up. Her eyes went wide, her purr shifted to a suspicious rumble, and she leapt from his lap with her tail on high alert. She stared dead into the trees.

"What is it?"

Sir asked, but he already knew—his senses flared with overwhelm.

They'd been found.

And not by the Archangels.

"Hey, punk! You're already fucked. Don't try to resist," a State Trooper called from behind a bunch of river birches.

Literal fuck. How'd this shit keep happenin'?

Again, soon as he formed the question, Sir answered himself in the next breath. Ero just had to go and spare that last officer on the task force he'd taken out back in Georgia. This was exactly why he wanted to get every last one at the time of. HPD ain't have shit better to do than tackle a big murder mystery like the one Sir'd left behind. Only Ero could distract him away from completin' a kill like that.

He hissed as he took a quick assessment of the teams surroundin' them now. His power'd expanded, sure enough, but he was still exhausted from the operation, and healin' Inez, and himself. A fine, cold sweat replaced the heat in his face.

Inez crouched low in the underbrush, her sleek black fur meldin' seamlessly with the shadows of the dense woodlands. The clicks and clatters of the Texas Rangers' equipment drew her attention. They had Sir cornered, and her new, protective instincts spiked.

He decided to test them.

"Go 'head," he whispered to her.

With a barely contained growl, Inez rushed forward, her powerful muscles propellin' her through the undergrowth. Her footfalls were fluid and silent as she disappeared into the tall grass.

The State Troopers'd formed a semi-circle 'round Sir, their flashlight beams bright even in the morning. Sir stood hunched and weary, leanin' heavily on his knuckles.

"Don't fuckin' move, you! There's nowhere to even go," a faceless Captain announced. A Ranger on a second team.

Inez eased her way into the midst of the Troopers and Rangers, her lithe form movin' like a shadow. Her claws extended, and her sharp fangs bared.

"Sh-shit!" someone shouted.

A swift and powerful swipe of her paw. Inez knocked the closest State Trooper off balance, sendin' their flashlight clatterin' to the ground.

"What in tarnation?!"

Another State Trooper raised their rifle, but Inez pounced on them before they could fire off a shot.

"Contact! Contact! It's the cat!" The Rangers laid down a blanket of cover fire.

Chaos erupted in the clearin' as State Troopers scrambled to fend Inez off. She darted back and forth, her compact form a blur of slashin' claws and snappin' jaws as she zigzagged between both teams. All her strikes landed with a chillin', deadly precision, leavin' police crumpled on the ground, drenched in bright red blood. The hot tang of iron thickened the air, and the sounds of pained groans cut right through.

Sir's heart thudded as he watched. He wouldn't let them hurt Inez. So far, she fought cleverly, skillfully, but he still had to protect her from stray bullets and any idiots who caught a wild hair. He'd just taken her from the natural world and turned her into this force of destruction. It was his responsibility to control what he'd unleashed in her. A burden he'd gladly bear.

"Hold!" The Captain of the Texas Rangers raised her free hand to hush up the last of her team. Cpt. Vala Sanchez, by the looks of it, her eyes wide behind her helmet visor as they took in the scattered bodies in the clearin'. Half of them were her own subordinates. Suddenly, she aimed her weapon at Inez from a distance. "What in the hell is that thing? We don't have a lick of intel on this. How is it killing my troops?"

Inez planted her paw on her last victim's chest and turned 'round, easily tearin' their throat out at the same time. Thick streams of blood dripped from her maw as she locked eyes with Sir across the field.

He'd only met Inez the other day, but she'd sought him out, placed her trust in him, endured pain with him, and even accepted his eternal mark. She was his familiar; a part of him, a reflection of his own energy.

Without another thought, Sir stepped forward, between her and the remainin' few Rangers. "Her name's Inez."

He was talkin' to three targets—Cpt. Sanchez and her last two cops—but kept his eyes only on her.

Cpt. Sanchez paused, her weapon silent. She seemed to catch Sir's answer better than the other two. They both aimed their rifles in Inez's direction.

"Shot's clear!"

"No, don't—!" Cpt. Sanchez called.

Sir cut her off. He gripped the handle of his silver-blue dagger and flung it, sendin' her sprawlin' to the ground and blastin' her body armor apart. Her heart stopped on the spot.

Before she even hit the dirt, Inez took care of the other two.

"Good girl," Sir said as she trotted back over to him. "But you can't do it alone. Next time, lemme help out some."

Chapter 15

ERO

ERO WOULD NEVER BE able to catch up with two Archangels under normal circumstances. He was just an Angel, the lowest of the low—so low that others sometimes dismissed him as human. Yet, he was stronger than other Angels. Some said he was too strong. And for what?

For this. For Sir.

It was always for Sir.

He flew with an unmatched intensity to find the Archangels before they could arrest Sir. If anyone was going to have to take Sir in, he'd have to find a way to make sure he was the one who did it. His wings sliced through the turbulent air as he tracked the Archangels through the outskirts of Houston. Finally, when he found them, streaks of light and shadow wove through the sky, painting a surreal panorama of war around them.

Gargatyl, despite countless deep injuries, still exuded an imposing presence. His wings unfurled, resembling metal plates, and his eyes blazed with an abject gleam. A bright red scar cut clear across his neck.

Gaviel, in somewhat better shape, hovered beside him, offering her support to help heal the worst of his damage. She kept one gashed eye closed as she did.

Wow. Sir had gotten further than expected. Ero bit back a proud grin.

"So you caught up with us," Gaviel said with a sneer.

Ero hardened his voice. "Please leave now, Knights. Tariel went home already. You two can follow right behind if you want."

Gaviel stepped toward him, her voice resonating like a thunderclap. It stunted Ero's. "We know Tariel went back. She's *our* commander. We knew it the second she left. You don't have to deliver the news like a bird. Still. As much as it's her right to give you that grace, it's our right to arrest that goddamned fiend and be rid of his influence once and for all. That's how it should've been from the very beginning."

"This is ridiculous." Gargatyl spat at the ground. "That thing has caused so much suffering since your mission began. He's known as the Ghost Killer by the people here, for fuck's sake. We're going to put an end to it, now. Don't worry your pretty little head over it anymore, *Angel*."

Ero took a breath.

It really was fine if he was the only one who saw the potential for grace and mercy in Sir. He had never been under any illusions that their marriage would solve half his problems back home. But wasn't it so much worse not to even try?

"You shouldn't call me that anymore," he said. "Sir says it better."

He closed his radiant wings around him in a shield of light and charged straight for the Archangels.

Gaviel and Gargatyl hesitated for a moment, disbelieving and alarmed, before leaping into their senses. Their combined powers deflected Ero away, and he rolled into a spin to keep up his barrier against the dual blasts of energy.

"What the hell is wrong with you? Just stand the fuck down already!" Gaviel said.

Ero called his halberd into his hand. A faint glow emanated from the shaft. Gripping it tight, he dissolved his barrier and struck with the weapon, cutting right through their mastery with his own.

"I'm not just an *Angel*. I am the Last Angel. The *only* Angel! You'll never understand what that's like. You, Tariel, everyone, you were all created together. You were made for each other, you chose each other, and you're stronger for it. Me? I was made alone! I was made to be strong, all alone! And I can do anything, all on my *own*!"

"Enough, or I'll shut you up! Don't make me hurt you, Angel. We got no beef with you beyond this devil."

"Really? Are you sure you don't want me out of the picture so that your perfect commander can finally be free of the stain that is me?"

"Be quiet," Gargatyl barked. He and Gaviel redoubled their power, creating twin torrents of mastery that converged on Ero.

Ero ached all over, feeling bolts and sparks of their existential energy that he couldn't fully deflect with his shield or halberd. The weight of their attack was starting to bury him, even as he braced himself and fired back. "If I want to save a bloodhungry devil from knowing the same pain that I've known for my whole life, then I'm gonna fucking do it! No one can stop me, not even Archangels."

Hot blood leaked from his nose. He braced himself, taking a large brunt of the onslaught, his body pulsating with tides of warm light. His strength wavered under the relentless assault, but he held steady, his stand a testament to the inner workings of his heart.

Ero's plan unfolded as the air thickened with so many battling forces of mastery. All he needed was for Sir to escape, far and fast, wherever he was.

His wings stretched out wide, their radiant glow dimming and dull, but still strong.

Gargatyl stopped attacking and reformed his staff out of a beam of light. He twirled it into an offensive stance with fluid grace. Next, Gaviel followed, reforming her shimmering sword.

They faced off against Ero from across the field together, weapons ready, both offensive.

"Where have I sensed emotions like these before, Gargatyl?" Gaviel asked. The circlet around her sword threw a bright gleam across the sunny grass.

"I don't know, but I don't trust them." His strong wings stretched out ominously, Gargatyl took the first step, his staff whistling through the air as he swung it towards Ero. The staff crackled with his mastery, and Ero could feel the sheer force behind the blow.

He swiftly raised his halberd to block. A burst of golden light erupted at the point of impact and sent shockwaves cascading throughout the woods. Underneath, the halberd held steady.

"You don't trust me any less now than you ever did before," he continued, through gnashed teeth. "Admit it. Y'all all think I'll just wander my way into Falling from grace, like I'm the damned Angel of the Apocalypse herself. I always knew it, I just hoped it wasn't true. I think Sir helped me see that."

"Well, good for you. But that's exactly why we have to keep you close to us, A— *Ero*. We want to keep you safe, Ero. Why else would you fight so hard for the devil you serve? It's not that you love him more than us, or that you trust him more than us, or anything else. It's simple corruption. We tried to fortify you against it the best that we could. Your guardians are our leaders. You're not a soldier, but you're better trained than half of the Host. You even have the eclipse matrix, which hasn't been used since the War, for crying out loud, Angel." Gaviel paused as the name slipped out, but didn't bother to correct herself this time. "And yet, it's been two minutes since you left home, and we can't even beg you to come back."

"I'm just fighting for him because I'm supposed to."

"Give me a fucking break. Is that all you heard?" Gaviel snapped. In a blur of motion, she lunged with her radiant sword again. The blade sliced through the air, aiming for Ero's side.

Ero pivoted just in time to narrowly avoid the attack. He could feel the blade's energy brush past him, leaving a painful stroke under his ribs. It was the same spot Sir had pierced with his hand a short while ago—to eat his spleen.

Come on. Clear head. He couldn't afford to be on the defensive for too long. Gathering his strength, Ero thrust his halberd forward and shot a laser of searing light toward Gaviel in a feint he'd seen Sir use back at the house.

But Gaviel was quick to learn from past mistakes, spinning away from the deadly trajectory with a flourish. "Not this time!"

"Ha—?"

"Your naivete is showing, man. It's adorable of you to think that loving him makes any difference. It's our job to love the loveless, and you were even made to love him specifically. That's no excuse to abandon your true heart. If you can't save him, it's also your job not to follow him down into damnation."

"And if you don't stop what you're doing soon, that's exactly what will happen," Gargatyl added somberly.

"See, that's what I mean. You don't care about what happens to me. You just don't want another Angel to Fall."

"Of course we don't. You said so yourself—you are the Last Angel. And as the Last Angel, you should think of Cerviel, and Ireul, and everything else that awaits you back home, already. That devil is not your only reason for living. It never has been!"

"Gav," Gargatyl said, trying to reach for her as if to stop her.

"He knows it, doesn't he?" she asked, then turned back to Ero. "Otherwise you wouldn't be on this silly suicide mission to pursue the love of a devil who will eat you alive someday. You're just hiding behind him."

Ero could only smile. Flashes of his spleen disappearing into Sir's mouth strobed through his mind with the words *It'll hurt* and *You hide*.

"You might just be right."

Gaviel did have a point. The mission was grand, and it had been the fuel for Ero's raison d'être, but as far as Sir was concerned, he was supposed to be the first stepping stone. A show of power. A demonstration that Ero could be useful and *trusted*.

Goddamnit it all. What would Cerviel say about all this mess? Ireul? Would they understand this muddy path he'd tread?

Cerviel, maybe. She often knew Ero in ways that he sometimes didn't even know for himself. Ireul, on the other hand...

"Damn you." Gargatyl took advantage of Ero's distraction to strike again. He flicked his staff to the side, unleashing a torrent of power that swirled around it like a cyclone.

Ero had no choice but to leap back. His wings flared to propel him away from its destructive aura. "Hey, not nice!"

As he soared up over the leafy canopy, he channeled his own mastery, infusing his halberd with fierce resolve. He descended on Gargatyl from the sky like a comet, and his halberd struck in a brilliant arc.

Gargatyl raised his staff to block, and the collision sent sparks of energy scattering in all directions. "You still can't see reason... All for this devil..."

"That's just the thing. I stopped seeing reason way before I met Sir. I didn't realize it yet because I was too busy hanging around all of y'all." Ero pushed forward with force and determination, driving Gargatyl back with each successive blow and creating more erratic displays of light against the grass and trees.

Meanwhile, Gaviel started to circle around the fray, her sword raised and ready. She moved slower now, but with more precision, as she calculated the openings in Ero's defenses. With a lightning-quick strike, she aimed for Ero's exposed back, but Ero caught her. He twirled his halberd and intercepted her sword with a resounding clash.

He certainly felt the strain of the battle, but he couldn't yield. Not yet. His determination was unwavering, fueled by his pounding heart and bleeding wounds.

"Armor!" With a low cry, Ero summoned up his battle armor. A blinding burst of divine light sent shockwaves rippling through everyone.

Gaviel and Gargatyl stumbled back, their celestial weapons faltering in their grip.

"What the—?"

"That armor...!"

Ero grinned. "Only you soldiers of the Host Empyrean walk around in your elaborate battle fits all the time. Did you really expect that Cerviel wouldn't assign me one—the lowly Armiger-of-Heaven?"

He didn't give them a chance to respond. He channeled his mastery into an intense beam of light that emanated from the marks on his armor to the tip of his halberd. The concentrated beam struck Gargatyl, enveloping him in a cascade of bolstered power.

"Gargatyl! Always saving your ass!" Gaviel shouted. She rushed to help him, but Ero's power surged over his armor again, forming a barrier of pale light that kept her at bay.

Gaviel and Gargatyl struggled against the overwhelming force of Ero's mastery. Their forms flickered and wavered as they fought to maintain their footing.

"What do you think you are doing, Angel?" Gaviel roared.

With a final, resolute effort, Ero extended his wings wide, their radiant glow intensifying. "I'm doing my damn job," he said, plainly. He channeled the last surge of his energy into a brilliant burst that engulfed Gaviel and Gargatyl at last.

The earth trembled as a blinding explosion of light erupted, whipping the trees into a roaring frenzy. The intense brilliance whirled like a tornado and tore through the woods like one, too. When the radiance finally dimmed and the tumultuous winds settled, Gaviel and Gargatyl were laid out. They weren't defeated, but they were temporarily incapacitated, and that was a start. Ero's own show of force.

His wings drooped with exhaustion, and he gazed into the distance, hoping that he was buying Sir time to take care of himself. The real fight hadn't even started yet, but Ero was determined to stand between Sir and the other angels, even if it meant taking up arms against his own kind, apparently.

He wasn't like Vasariah. He wasn't evil or corruptible. He was just the only one who cared about Sir. He had to do this.

"Besides," he said to himself, "I was made for this."

His breaths started to come heavier as he surveyed the state of his battle armor. He'd trained with it plenty—enough to think of as an extension of himself, like his wings, or his hands—but it still ached like an underused muscle pushed too far.

"Nghhh..." Gaviel and Gargatyl started slowly regaining their composure.

Through sheer force of will, Ero rekindled his inner reservoir of mastery. His flickering wings flared once more and cast a ragged halo around him. "If I have to keep fighting you, I will. I'll do it as long as it takes."

"As long as it takes to what?" Gaviel groaned. "To keep us from tracking down your husband and... taking him out once and for all?"

She and Gargatyl began to rise, their forms starting to pulse with residual energy. Their eyes blazed with focus, and they exchanged a resolute glance. It was clear they wouldn't be defeated here any time soon.

"We're done playing games with you, Angel. Don't dig yourself in any deeper than you already have. This is your last warning," Gargatyl said.

"Werk." Ero's halberd gleamed with renewed radiance as he crashed down on them again.

Gaviel and Gargatyl met him head-on, their weapons humming from the strength restored in them, too.

The clash of mastery sent echoes through the woods, sending out dazzling collisions of starlike power. Ero's halberd and Gaviel's sword met in a burst of light, while Gargatyl's staff weaved around with incredible speed, seeking an opening in Ero's defenses. They had switched up tactics again.

Always forceful, Gaviel unleashed a barrage of energy strikes from her sword. Ero deflected the attacks with his own weapon.

Gargatyl sensed an opportunity and launched a barrage of dazzling energy orbs at Ero. The orbs whizzed through the air like homing beacons. Ero shielded himself from impact with his armored-up wings.

Gaviel's turn again. With a powerful swing of her sword, she unleashed a colossal wave of energy that threatened to overwhelm Ero.

Ero's wings flexed open, setting off Gargatyl's orbs in a cascade that exploded all around him. "Arghh!" Burned and bruised, he summoned the last of his strength to create a shimmering barrier around himself.

The tag-team assault crashed against Ero's barrier, creating a blinding explosion of energy that sent tremors through the smallest yellow leaves. Ero gritted his teeth as he struggled to maintain the barrier against the relentless onslaught.

"Stay down!" Gargatyl finally closed the distance between them with his astonishing speed. His staff pierced through the barrier, finding its mark without an ounce of hesitation.

Ero cried out as the staff struck him, its ethereal mark burning through his skin and muscles. His halberd wavered, and he staggered backward, depleted.

Gaviel and Gargatyl pressed their advantage in a final, coordinated assault. Their weapons blazed with ferocious power as they closed in on Ero.

"Obey, Angel!"

Sure.

Ero lived to obey.

A brilliant surge of celestial light erupted from out of his body. It was a reflexive force seal, a burst of divine energy that enveloped everything in blinding radiance, fueled by the ire from his wounds.

The explosion of light sent Gaviel and Gargatyl hurtling backward, their weapons flung far from their grasps. Ero almost laughed at the sight, but then coughed up a bubble of blood, and saw total black.

He couldn't send a pair of Archangels back home against their will—but he could at least send them away from here. Anywhere away from here. Apex Earth, Chronos Earth, straight to hell for all Ero cared. It didn't matter as long as they weren't in this world right now. The woods fell silent except for the wind.

Bolting upright as soon as he came to, he wiped the blood from his nose and sped off before he even took a breath.

He needed to get to Sir. The best he could do for himself was concentrate on healing while he flew.

"What was with those Archangels?" he murmured as he did.

Had they planned to pound him into the ground then drag both him *and* Sir to justice?

It wouldn't be the first time he'd been underestimated by higher-ranking angels, and it sure as hell probably wouldn't be the last.

Even if he had another Armiger-class angel to compare himself to, he would outdo them by miles. He may have been merely an Angel, but he was no mere Angel. Just like Gaviel pointed out, he was stronger, faster, more resilient, better trained, and quicker to heal. He'd been created by the highest angel in his sphere, outfitted from birth with ancient combat technology, and mercilessly trained to surpass all of his predecessors—and their weaknesses. Whenever others underestimated him, he never really understood why.

Blood laced the air soon enough. Ero ground to a halt near a small contingent of harried State Troopers who were pulled onto the side of a nearby freeway. Their cruisers, lights strobing red-blue, red-blue, cast an anxious glow over the asphalt. One trooper leaned against the hood of his car, wiping sweat from his brow under his helmet, while the Officer-in-Charge barked orders into a handheld radio.

"You haven't heard back from Cpt. Sanchez yet, have you, sergeant?" the Officer-in-Charge asked the State Trooper in the shiny black helmet. Blake and Wang.

The same Blake from the Georgia mountains. Ero recognized her instantly.

Her pale green aura stood strong around her like the leaves of a young forest. There was no trace of the terror and rage that had clung to her before, being the lone survivor of Sir's attack the other day after he summoned his mark.

They're like flies, Sir had said, later. *Can't ignore them, or else they'll just keep comin' back.*

"Not since we lost contact with Zulu after they found that monster," Sgt. Wang answered her.

Officer Blake checked her wristwatch. "She told us not to follow if it's been longer than 30..."

"I'd reckon it's been about double that, ma'am. Should we go on ahead and send for backup? Some of these survivors won't last too much longer if we wait it out hoping for the best case scenario."

"Yes, of course, see if you can't get in touch with EMS. I keep trying, but no one will put me through. They should've been here by now," she said, gloved fingertips pressed to her forehead. Her radio crackled, as if to tease, then went dead silent again. "Ugh. Front load the critical cases when they finally arrive. I'll stay on comms for a bit before I haul ass in there myself. We really can't afford to lose any more people to this travesty than we already have."

"Yes, ma'am," Sgt. Wang said. "Take care out there." He clicked his visor closed, turning sharply away from the trees on the periphery, and took off obediently, without ever once looking back.

Alone, Officer Blake deflated, and her shoulders sank beneath her Kevlar. "Damn it, Sanchez. What've you gotten yourself into this time?"

Ero swooped in next to her on silent wings. He probably needed to stay the course—to find Sir and steal him away somewhere no ghost or man could find him—but Lios flashed at the front of his mind, keeping him anchored until he couldn't resist the chance to redress something he had ruined. He had left Lios to her fate in an attempt to be perfect. He would not leave Officer Blake to hers.

"Excuse me, ma'am? I don't mean to interrupt, but can I bother you for a minute?"

Officer Blake jumped about a foot in the air at the sound of his voice. All the slack in her body snapped taut, and she reflexively grasped at her sidearm. "You—!"

Ero tried his best to look harmless. For humans, like Officer Blake, he was hardly the easiest sight to take in, and it really must've been like seeing a ghost for her. She couldn't keep her jaw closed.

"Please, don't be afraid," he said, his voice measured and calm. "I'm just here to help. Like last time, remember? Forget about me. I overheard you mention that your missing Cpt. Sanchez came across the Ghost Killer and went dark. Can you tell me more about the situation? I promise—I'll handle it."

Officer Blake started to breathe easier as she took in Ero's overwhelming sincerity, her aura recognizing his, replaced with warmth. Trust.

He remembered Lios again for a moment—the way her face suddenly softened when her aura embraced his own. Humans were so warm and receptive, so much easier to connect with. He would miss them when he went back home.

The few State Troopers who'd gathered at the edge of the woods thinned out as distant sirens drifted across Ero's senses. Everyone here would be safe soon enough. He had to concentrate on the people who *hadn't* made it out of the woods yet.

Officer Blake sighed, long and hard suddenly, as though Ero were a close friend she could vent her deepest worries to. Magic at work. "Well... well, about ten hours ago, we finally tracked down and cornered that damned bounty that keeps wreaking havoc on our forces. Cpt. Sanchez spearheaded the Zulu offensive line almost an hour ago. I'm afraid to say it, but... I think they've left us. It's a reality we were all prepared for, given the last encounter, but still. We got all the best defenses, state-of-the-art training, and the latest tech behind us, but even with all that, no matter what we do, we can't seem to go after this guy without suffering massive casualties. It still makes no sense to me that I made it out alive. Cpt. Sanchez was one of our best. What are we supposed to do if she was taken out, too? It's like some sorta horror flick."

Ero's brow furrowed in concern. Officer Blake was right—everyone who hadn't escaped the woods was dead or would be soon. Their blood and guts splattered many of the sycamores in the distance. Cpt. Sanchez, and anyone else who took it upon themselves to get in Sir's way, all met the same violent ends.

His heart sank as he fully absorbed the enormity of the situation. It was clear the Archangels' interference had caused turmoil not just for him and Sir, but for the innocent people caught in the crossfire, too. If they cared so much about making sure the balance of reality remained intact, maybe Gaviel and Gargatyl should've thought twice about the lives they were giving up to that end. They really weren't much different from Sir, by the look of things on the ground. These people wouldn't be able to tell the difference between a devil and an angel if one emerged from the desecrated trees.

"You don't have to do this anymore, you know," Ero said. "Why do you keep trying to track him down when it's so dangerous?"

"...What?"

"I'm sorry. Just hear me out. You're back here because it's your job, right? But you had a chance to get out. You're forty-two and love every part of life except for the fact that you have to risk it every day by going after a dangerous person because the state pays you to. Why not do something else? Anything else? Be selfish, and enjoy your day? I saved you so you wouldn't have to die like this."

Officer Blake opened her mouth, but someone interrupted her, bolting over out of the woods like a bullet from a gun. They crashed into Officer Blake and clung close with frantic, bloody hands, and peered out from fractures in their helmet with a striking blue eye.

"Ma'am, run! You gotta fuckin' run! I-I don't think I can do this! There are these fuckin' zombie things rising up from the dead back there! I can't believe I'm still alive...!"

Quelle surprise. Ero eyed Officer Blake meaningfully, but she ignored him.

"Zombies? What are you talking about, Trooper?" Officer Blake asked with amazing calm.

"I'm talking about goddamned *zombies*, man. The Ghost annihilated everyone on the front line. He had this... this demonic hellcat with him that just eviscerated our ranks. It was chaos from the start. I ran as fast as my legs would take me. Then—then after they went down, they all got right back up, like they weren't deader than a doornail a second before, one by one. I sure ain't stickin' around to see what else was about to happen! I'm telling you, *run!*"

Ero turned to study the Trooper, looking into his heart and mind. Lt. Glaser, a 37-year-old single father. He was a basic, compassionate, responsible person. His emotions flew around everywhere, overflowing like a river that flooded Ero's senses. They were so strong—like memories instead of pure feelings.

Memories of the Ghost covered in blood—of *Sir* covered in blood—with Inez right next to him, every inch as bloody.

A bone-deep chill came over Ero.

What did Sir do to Inez?

What did Sir do to those people?

"Okay, okay, take a breath. All right?" said Officer Blake. "Good. Take another. There ya go. It's okay. You don't have to return to duty. A casevac should be following behind this here medevac soon. Make sure you get cleared by psych and operations whenever you get back into town, but once you do, go ahead and take some time off. Stay in contact with the rear detachment. You'll be fine, I promise."

Lt. Glaser hiccupped with fear, hands still trembling where he clutched Officer Blake's shoulders. "You won't come, too, ma'am? Captain and the others... Everyone is gone." His single visible eye flicked around the quiet highway. "Let's leave together. No one can face that thing alone and live. We can petition the state to drop this warrant if we pursue it enough. Come with me."

"Petition the state to drop a warrant? Who are you fooling? This is still Texas, mama. You don't think anyone would've done that before if it was that simple?" Officer Blake shook her head as she raised a hand to Lt. Glaser's on her shoulder. "You have my permission, lieutenant. You can go—enjoy your leave already. But I can't leave here with you or anyone else," she said, turning to eye Ero. "It's my job, and someone has to do it. I can, so it should be me."

Lt. Glaser's eye shut as he resigned to leaving alone. A loudspeaker announced the arrival of the non-critical casevac. Without another protest, his hands fell from Officer Blake's shoulders, and he took off in the direction of certain rescue.

Silence stretched out between Officer Blake and Ero, who narrowly resisted grabbing his chest in pain. He'd wanted to avoid feeling responsible for the deaths and lives of so many people, but the worldview of humanity was just too narrow to focus on anything beyond their own small, certain, finite reality. Some would run away from the world, while others tossed themselves into the flames. He couldn't save every single one.

The only way to put a stop to all of this was to deal with Sir.

In whatever way he could.

"Is there anything else I can do for you? I'm fixin' to go after my captain here soon," Officer Blake said, full of fearless defiance.

Even though Ero wanted to cry, all he did in the end was nod. "Thank you for your help today. Seriously. You don't know how much I thank you. Everything'll be okay. I promise."

Officer Blake nodded back, a bit blank. She had no idea what to say to such an earnest, open-ended declaration, even though she had just issued a similar one.

That was okay. She didn't need to know anything.

No one needed to. It wasn't like Ero had signed up to save the world in order to be recognized. He hadn't signed up at all. He'd been tasked with it—created for it. All that was left for him to do now was just *do*. There was no turning back now. Sir was waiting.

With his back ramrod-straight, Ero took off again, his powerful wings carrying him swiftly into the sky.

Chapter 16

SIR

SIR STOOD IN THE middle of Vasariah's once-peaceful grave, now decorated with bits of blood and gore. The returnin' winds whipped 'round the severed body parts of a dozen or so Rangers and Troopers in the clearin'.

He really couldn't help but be impressed. Inez's intelligence had always been clear, but now, as a familiar, her talents revealed themselves in even more incredible ways.

And not just her.

Sir, too, was left changed by the procedure.

He couldn't put his finger on it exactly, but after transmogrifyin' her, somethin' 'bout the composition of his mastery seemed different. Quieter, yet louder. Darker, yet brighter. Even without bein' able to explain it, the feelin' was undeniable—he'd grown stronger somehow from makin' Inez immortal.

Ero would be proud. Sir'd come a long way from his clueless days.

But damn... *would* Ero, really? He'd probably hate how far Sir had steeped himself in so-called malice to get to this point. This newfound strength was both a blessin' and a burden. The more he embraced his darkness, the further away he slipped from Ero. He could feel the weight of that growin' chasm every time he glanced back at the memories of their progress to a stalemate.

Sir always secretly knew it—sooner or later, he'd have to leave Ero, even though Ero made it more and more impossible by the hour. Time came to face facts. They weren't meant to go very far together. Even if they wanted the same things, their paths pulled them too far apart. They could play house, conspire, and even commit to a consensus, but at the end of the day, if Sir couldn't be an angel, he couldn't be with Ero.

And Sir had no desire to be an angel.

Risin' was a joke from jump. He straight up didn't want to do it, didn't see the worth. Why give up everything he was, everything he'd built, just to fit in a mold someone else had made for him?

Maybe this was just how it had to be.

In the end, he just wanted to be left alone, after all. He'd finally broken away from Alexander and was lookin' forward to spendin' the rest of his days outsmartin' and probably livin' off various State Troopers. If there was anyone he needed to trust, it was himself. Wasn't like he was aimin' to manipulate cosmic forces, or enforce his will on the world, or somethin'. He had to eat, that was it.

The deeper Sir delved into his own barely beatin' heart, the more it came clear that his hope of keepin' Ero on his own terms were pipe dreams at best. With every step further into his nature, the chasm widened between them. The strain of their different ambitions weighed heavy on the relationship, pullin' it taut like a bowstring stretched beyond its limit.

I'm here to marry you. To save you. To make you an angel. You won't have to wander alone anymore...

But before I can save you, I have to cleanse you of all the years you spent corrupt...

I chose this role...

And yet, Vincent's sharp memories of the past—and the words of the Archangels—seemed to say otherwise. Angels were low-rankin', distrusted, disgraced, and all but extinct with the exception of the Last Angel, Ero. He was made to be perfect, but treated like anything but. What choice had he ever had?

Sir suddenly wanted to prove the angels wrong. Wanted to show them how smart, and strong, and talented Ero was. How fuckin' chaotic, and conninvin', and competent...

"Shit," he muttered, confusion and frustration edgin' into his voice. "Never should've married that Angel."

Never should've caught feelings, never should've got involved. If he had to die tryin' to run from Ero, he should've just done it. The more he thought 'bout it, the more Sir realized he hadn't taken anything seriously. He'd been... havin' fun, after that sunrise at Bulls Bay. Playin' along, learnin' everything he could, and standin' right next to Ero like it was natural.

Just as back then, Sir still ain't understand why Ero was so fixated on Risin', as if it was the only possible path for them to tread. Wouldn't even consider anything he hadn't been prescribed beforehand. Refused to meet in the middle.

You're like me, Angel—closer to the earth, closer to humans, than other ghosts. We could stay right where we're at. I don't Rise. You don't Fall...

And Ero just froze.

When it came down to it, even if he felt the same way, Ero wouldn't renounce who he was to be with Sir. Only Sir was bein' asked to do that. And Ero was only doin' what he'd been made to do.

Love the devil, if need be.

Fuck the devil, if need be.

Kill the devil, if need be.

Just get it done, *Angel*.

"Yes," he probably said. With that short-fanged smile.

Sir let out a long, deep groan. "Fine. Kinda figure he don't feel nothin', anyway. Fuckin' psycho angels."

The thought still gnawed at him, though, a deep-rooted insecurity that lingered in the back of his mind for longer than he realized.

It shouldn't've mattered. It shouldn't've been a problem. And yet...

He hated bein' rejected. Again.

Sir'd spent so much of his life trapped in the Alexander house, constantly bein' tolerated, or outright abused, but never once accepted. That twisted bastard'd been a poor excuse for a guardian in the end. Clingin' to Sir to fulfill his own needs, then icin' Sir out whenever Sgt. Esmeralda came back into the picture. And now even Ero was caught out weavin' the same empty damn promises of *love and trust*.

What in the hell.

Sir couldn't sit here chewin' on all these pointless thoughts anymore. He had his wits, Inez at his side, and a bone to pick with the higher echelons of the so-called Sanctuary. One way or another, he was gonna have to get them out his hair. Back to square one. Die tryin'.

Just then, a pair of bodies in the trees started to stand.

"The fuck're you?" he grumbled. This had to be the longest day in human history, and it'd only started a couple hours ago.

Inez snarled and snapped to defense mode, her tail tall and stiff.

The dead State Troopers pulled themselves together with rickety limbs, dragged into coordination by invisible strings, their weapons hefted in bloody hands.

"How is it you can't recognize us?" Gaviel's voice came from one of the corpses. "Amateur ass vampire...!"

Fuckin' A. The Archangels.

"You bozos're worse than the state cops."

Inez's hackles raised, and her snarl deepened to a low growl, her talons piercin' into the dirt and grass.

"I hope you saved your strength," Gaviel said as she marched forward. "This is only a minor inconvenience for us—but lucky, at the same time. Like this, we can work on freeing ourselves from Ero's force seal and then get back to Lesser Earth more easily. Thanks for guiding us here with the aura blackout, by the way. You may not stand out on your own, but anyone could follow the trail of silent gore you leave behind you."

"You two are a goddamned match made in heaven," Gargatyl said. Walked beside her with the same imposin' power. "I still can't believe Ero managed to force seal us."

"Yeah, well, it happened. Cerviel trained him well," Gaviel said.

Sir suppressed a small grin. That Angel was so damn good.

The Archangel Troopers radiated with misplaced power and purpose, their idle eyes fixed firmly on Sir. Gaviel's pale and Gargatyl's green auras bled out from the dead police's open wounds as they ambled into the overgrown clearin'.

Then Gaviel emptied the remainder of her rifle magazine. "Now, surrender!"

"I was kiddin', man!" Sir dipped out the way and tossed up a shield the same time he fired his dagger at her.

Gargatyl swooped in to block it, but Inez forced herself between them. "This animal—!" he growled.

Gaviel tore the dagger from her shoulder. "That thing's not an animal. Not anymore. He damned her! Trying to make himself a familiar, and it's more like he made a monster! Pathetic."

Maybe. Inez wasn't perfect, but she *was* Sir's familiar. He'd brought her back to life with his own mastery.

"What does Ero see worth saving in this guy? If it was me, I would've eliminated him the second I met him. He's trash," Gargatyl said.

"Thanks, I agree." Sir launched at them in the clearin'.

He clutched his punch dagger, its tip flickerin' with the remnants of mastery he'd recouped. His energy was still somewhat tapped from the transformation that'd created the new Inez, but his resolve remained. Inez paced beside him, her inky coat ripplin' with tension. Her feral eyes locked onto the approachin' Archangel Troopers, and her instincts were honed for takin' more blood. A low growl. She readied herself to pounce.

"Your efforts are admirable, I'll give you that," Gargatyl said.

"But ultimately pointless!" Gaviel shouted.

Together, they charged, their footsteps creatin' an ominous rhythm in the muted daylight. With a sudden, explosive force, they crashed right into Sir.

The battle re-erupted in a storm of steel and energy. Sir bounced back and launched his daggers with every ounce of his strength, castin' protective barriers to shield Inez and himself. Inez lunged with both claws and fangs to slash the Archangel Troopers with her lil fury.

Gaviel and Gargatyl fought back with nearly all of their supernatural strength and speed. Like they weren't doin' all this remotely from another plane of reality. Their strikes were precise and unerrin', and their weapons hit with the same otherworldly precision. Sir got pushed back, time and time again.

Inez kept on, though, ferocious as she darted from one Archangel Trooper to the other, her fangs findin' purchase, and her claws tearin' straight through body armor.

"Gahh!" Gaviel yelled.

"Enough! Get outta here!" Sir called to Inez. He could break through the rest of their defenses on his own. *Go! Now! God-damnit!*

Inez refused. She swung her bloody paws again, and Gaviel sliced her wide open before Sir could yank her away. She crashed against his chest with a wet splat. Her blood rained down his clothes, turnin' him slick.

"Oh, fuck, kiddo," Sir gasped quietly.

Inez's blood soakin' into his hands. For a minute, Sir couldn't breathe. He'd brought her back to life, given her strength—but was it enough? Was *he* enough? Or did he just drag her down with him, like everything else he tried to make his own?

Inez chuffed, soft and low. The wound started slowly closin'. Sir breathed again.

"I wouldn't call her a monster *or* a familiar," Gaviel said. "Just a failure. You can't control her, and you can't protect her. The problem, as always, is you."

You ruin everything. You keep ruining everything...

Sir could only nod. Inez lay bleedin' in his arms right now, after all. He crushed her close. Too close. She groaned.

"Hey, y'all two!" he said, lookin' up. "Gaviel and Gargatyl, is it? What'd y'all do with that angel of mine? His mark's all over you."

Angels loved bumpin' their gums more than fightin'. They both paused for a moment, the ethereal glow in their eyes flickerin' in consideration. Weighin' options, tryin' to decide if a devil was worth talkin' to.

Whatever bought Inez all the time he could give her to mend.

Gargatyl answered first, but he couldn't entirely mask the distaste in his voice. "The Last Angel Ero has escaped our custody for now. Don't you worry about him. He'll live and pay for his insubordination soon enough."

"His fate is in his own hands, at this point. It's interesting to see you so concerned about him. Didn't you just abandon him back there to save your own ass?"

Haha. Abandon Ero? Sir'd wished for nothin' else the past few days. By the look of things lately, he wouldn't need to worry 'bout that anymore.

Inez was already honed in on the Archangel Troopers, ready to spring back into action any second, but Sir clutched her even closer to keep her still. She wasn't done healin' yet. Crazy kid.

"And?" he said, pettin' her quiet.

"And?" Gargatyl echoed. "Do you hear this, Gaviel? 'And?' This is how love and mercy gets repaid by those who don't deserve it: pure malice and evil."

Always with this "evil" junk. Wasn't Sir just misguided or whatever Ero'd said?

Gentle. Empty. Lonely...

"We should've known better than to expect anything less of this whole ordeal," Gaviel said. "What a disaster. The angel goes on a mission to balance the world and falls in love with the devil instead. The devil sacrifices him anyway. How's that for a happy ending? Hahaha!" She cackled, and her aura poured from the State Trooper's thick protective clothes like floating blood as she did. "I don't think so. Your time corrupting our only Angel is over. We're not going to let you have him. Ero's actions have consequences, but they'll be dealt with fairly, by his family. You, however..."

"You're barely a ghost, much less an angel. There's no need for you to concern yourself with heavenly things anymore. We'll send you home where devils like you belong."

As if she could shield him from the words, Inez curved herself into Sir's chest, and pulled her lips into a droolin' snarl directed at the Archangel Troopers. She was almost done healin'. Almost.

"Send me home...?" Sir said back.

An idea he'd spent his fair share considerin'—home.

Not many places, people, and other things'd been home to him over the years. If he had any, he didn't even remember and had no way of knowin'.

The only one that ever mattered was the one he'd found after devourin' the fallen star Vasariah. The one that'd embraced him through everything—before consciousness, through awakenin', and past enlightenment.

The one he'd told to Ero.

"What d'you mean 'send me home'?" Sir flashed his fanged smile. "I *am* home. This is where I belong. The whole world—*this* world that y'all sent your only angel to save—is my home! Inez, let's show them what I mean."

With a flicker of movement, he unleashed his mastery, and silver shadows erupted 'round him. Always been better with actions than words. They pulsed with his heartbeat, slow and flickerin' like flames caught in a distant storm. More stable than ever before. He got the sudden urge to show off to Ero—look, see how calm and controlled he'd become, how far from chaos.

Gaviel and Gargatyl reacted with the precision of their rank. Gargatyl summoned an energy barrier, formin' a shield 'round them both, while Gaviel drew her glowin' sword to strike.

The rest of the fight was quick and dirty.

Sir hurled his daggers at the barrier, each one detonatin' on impact with a burst of his spite. The shield held, but it flickered under his continuous attacks.

Gaviel was the first to close the distance between them with her amazin' speed. Her sword and circlet sliced into the air, searchin' out blind spots in Sir's defenses. Sir dodged away, narrowly avoidin' the blade's deadly arcs, before Inez leapt in the fray with her bloody teeth bared. The searin' heat of the sword as it flew bruised him and left a trail of acrid light behind. Inez struck back with a surge of new energy from Sir, and her claws suddenly snagged skin and feathers, steel and light.

The edge of Gargatyl's wing.

"Yes," Sir hissed.

"No!" Gaviel and Gargatyl gasped together.

"No, Inez, don't!" Ero echoed, his voice crashin' through the sycamores.

Everyone stopped to stare.

Sir's heart stopped, period. He hated how much relief flooded through him at the sight of Ero droppin' into the clearin'. But he still held his breath.

His angel finally came back.

Chapter 17

ERO

JUST AS INEZ LATCHED onto Gargatyl's wing, the sky had darkened, and the air crackled with dense swaths of mastery before Ero landed like a lightning strike.

"I'm sorry, Inez, but please," he said, and hauled her away from the chaos and carnage. She landed a couple dozen feet away, snoring even before she rolled to a soft, sleepy stop.

Oh, Inez...

What had Sir done to her to make her capable of aiming for an angel's wing like that?

She slept soundly, her tiny body twitching as if she were still mid-fight. Ero crouched beside her and brushed a wound quickly stitching shut on her exposed side. He couldn't help but marvel at what Sir had turned her into—terrible and exceptional all at once.

"Sir..." Ero started. He found him right away.

Sir was standing with a strange, easy, but unpolished composure, his brown skin glowing faintly under thick streaks of blood. His cloud-colored fox eyes held the same haunting magnetism that always drew Ero in. They were hard to find behind the mess of his long, half-gathered hair, but the fangs peeked through clearly, like starlight on a cloudless night.

"...Angel," he said.

"Angel?!" Gaviel barked.

Ero ignored her. There was so much he wanted to tell Sir. There was so much he wanted to ask. But he couldn't voice any of it in front of the Archangels. That much was clear.

"I..." he tried again, star-crossed. His armor glinted under the dim daylight, and he almost stepped into the shade as if to hide it.

"How dare you show your face to us after that fucking stunt you pulled back there?" Gaviel demanded.

Ero finally looked her way. Even though she and Gargatyl were using human corpses as hosts for their spiritual energy, in a kind of twisted angelic possession, he recognized them immediately. Sir (and, he guessed, Inez) had really done some damage here. Ero had to bite back another satisfied smirk.

Gargatyl let out a sharp sigh through his teeth. "Never mind that! I'm sick and tired of dealing with all this shit. That cat almost ripped off my wing. Gaviel, I'm detaining the devil. Can you handle the Angel?"

"Oh, can't I," Gaviel said, and recharged her shining sword as she stood back to back with Gargatyl. Its incredible light sizzled through the State Trooper's heavy gloves, but she continued as if it barely bothered her. "You'll learn better than to take the Spheres' compassion for granted again, Ero. I'm actually surprised at you more than anything. Why will you use your full strength to resist *us* but not *him*? And if you say it's because you love him one more time, I swear to fuck, I'll put an end to you where you're standing. Be for real!"

Sir went still as she spoke. He turned his gaze away for the first time since Ero found them and wiped the blood from his mouth as if to get rid of a sour taste.

Ero lowered his eyes, too, but he didn't miss a beat otherwise. "I can't be more real than I already am, Gaviel. Don't ask questions that you already know the answers to if you don't want to hear them, I guess. I don't know what else to tell you."

"Don't know what to tell me? Tell me why you're going against everything you've ever stood for—for this heartless vampire who would rather drag you down to hell than have anything to do with the divine? He's poison. He poisoned you. You weren't supposed to love him, you were supposed to deal with him."

He shrugged. "I can love him if you want to. I am who I am because he is who he is. And he's my husband. That decision was made for me a long time ago. By Cerviel, and Ireul, and those above them, all of whom are above *y'all*. I'm just doing what I'm supposed to and what I was made for. That's it."

No. That wasn't it, exactly. But that was all anybody else needed to know.

He looked to Sir again, hoping to find his gaze.

They met straight away.

Every time Ero lied, Sir saw through it. That was why he sometimes hid his face from Sir—to keep his secrets as safe as they could be from someone who looked through him like Sir did. The angels thought they knew Ero's heart. They saw the surface. Only Sir ever peered deeper inside.

"You know it's true," Ero finished.

He was doing precisely what he wanted to do.

Gargatyl scoffed, his temper rising a bit more, while Gaviel hefted the tip of her sword to Ero. "It's pretty clear that your loyalty is blinding you, Angel. This devil as he stands in front of us is as much a blight on cosmic order as he's always been, and you don't seem to particularly care whether that changes. Well, guess what? I don't particularly care that he's your husband, either. You can find another partner if you really feel the need, but this one is no good. He's outright refused every step of the way. He's just a stain that we can—and should—erase. You think you're doing the right thing by going against us to stick by him, but all you're really doing is betraying your *real* purpose, your *real* duty, that you claim to care so much about fulfilling."

"Maybe you're right. Who am I to say? But until the very angels that sent me here show up to take me back, I'm not going anywhere. So keep dragging me, or my love, or my loyalty, or whatever else you want—it's not changing anything. Not tonight."

"Enough of this sentimental nonsense," Gargatyl said. "You're an Angel, Ero. It's about time you start acting like one!"

"You really think being an angel is about blind obedience? Is that really all it takes for you? Killing, living, loving, and working all for someone else's sake? Do you even know whose sake? At least I do. Cerviel taught me better. I'm not trying to choose a different path, I'm just trying to go about it another way. Hopefully, a way that ends better than the last time Angels were sent to Earth. Now, Sir is mine to deal with, so I'll deal with him, and I was given the ability to protect him, so that's what I'ma do."

He shifted subtly into a defensive stance, his armored-up wings gleaming threateningly under the leaf-shaded sunlight. He had pictured this moment once—or something similar, at least. Himself, proverbially standing against all the authorities in the Sanctuary, beside Sir. It was a lot funnier back then.

"Please, test me on this. I fucking dare you," he said.

"Challenge accepted," Gaviel growled.

She tightened her grip on her sword and lunged at Ero with all her disdain, but Ero narrowly dodged aside. She moved with less of her trademark precision in her current body. Meanwhile, Ero's armor cut through the air as it moved with him, streamlined and deadly.

"How could you Archangels have brought yourselves to commit something like possession? Just so you can bring Sir in?" Ero scoffed. "Unthinkable."

"Enough!" Gargatyl said as he joined the fight. "Ero! I won't hear any reprimands from you. Arrest the devil right now, or else you're going in the pen next."

Then, and only then, did Sir join, too.

He stepped in almost instantly to block Gargatyl from Ero's blindside. In less than a moment, the woods ignited with the clashes of mastery. As seamless as a chaotic dance, he fit right into the fray.

The fight this time was so much easier. Though they were technically outnumbered, Ero and Sir's unique strengths and familiarity with each other kept them afloat as they continued to hold their own against the Archangel Troopers.

"Hey, Sir!" Ero called with an adrenalinized smile. "We fight well together."

"Sure," Sir said. "The fuck's with all this armor?"

Ero deflected a staff strike from Gargatyl meant for Sir's chest. "It's the battle gear of the Armigers-of-Heaven—the uniform I'm supposed to wear when I fight. It's enhanced to combat ghosts, especially devils. I'm sorry you have to see me like this, but it's helping me take on Gaviel and Gargatyl right now. Still, you can't be having a good time."

"What d'you mean? Havin' the time of my life," Sir said, and aimed his punch dagger at Gaviel's swordhand, plunging in deep.

Ero's eyes locked onto Sir's again. Despite the melee surrounding them, their need for words evaporated in the heat of the fight. They had been here together plenty of times before for different reasons and similar ones—but they weren't usually on the same side. They were always fighting each other. It was a small moment like so many other small moments that Ero had seen and clung to for the past few days.

They were the same. Hearts in a hundred broken pieces.

For the first time, for just a second, Ero saw almost as much of Sir as Sir always saw of him. The way that Sir would look into his eyes and absolutely know, as if Sir was seeing through Ero, or past him, wasn't just coincidence. It was deeper. It was sturdier. It was insight gained by divination—like sangromancy.

Except sangromancy belonged to the Left Hand of Destruction. It made sense if Sir could use it. Something like this, an immaterial use of mastery, divinations performed with the mind, was an unmistakable mark of the Right. Ero knew dozens of diviners with similar powers back home.

It must've been the effect of the eclipse matrix, the same reason Ero could fall in love with his devil without Falling from grace. That was the only reason he could think of.

"Sir—I—" Ero started, pausing as he searched for what to say.

"You might want to pay attention to me instead," Gaviel said. She swooped in from behind Ero faster than he could follow for a second. He took a hit, then took her advice.

Ero focused on the fight, but in the middle of his mind, he reached for Sir. He stretched as much as he could, trying to buckle the constant shield on his mind and sneak Sir inside it.

Sir, he called. *Can you hear me?*

...Angel?! Remarkably, Sir barely stuttered in his battle rhythm as he replied. His eyes found Ero in the battle for just a moment before Gargatyl dove in between them again.

Your one and only, Ero said with a heart-filled smile. *Gaviel and Gargatyl are trying to keep us apart.*

Can't imagine why.

Do you really have the energy to spare for sarcasm right now? Listen to me, Sir. You can see the truth when you look into my eyes, right?

Sir was quiet for a while as he countered Gargatyl's staff a few more times. *Not emotionally, but really* see. *Yeah. Like a shit movie. Why?*

Because that's a form of mastery called oculomancy from the Right Hand of Protection. If it's true that you can use it, even a little bit, then we can keep going forward in the same direction as always. It's a good sign you'll be able to Rise.

Ero's efforts were paying off. Despite everything, Sir's eclipse matrix was taking, expanding his access to powers beyond the malicious Left Hand of Destruction.

Goddamn, Angel. Maybe I'm just some kinda fuckin' freak, Sir hissed. He sucked in a quick breath to calm himself down.

I'm telling you—we can do this, Sir. All you have to do is make the same choice I always hoped you would. Choose mercy, and choose me. The Archangels won't have a reason to fight after that. The rest will be easy. Ero winked just before he gripped his halberd with both hands and cut a deep gash into Gaviel's arm.

With their human hosts, the Archangel Troopers hardly even cried out when they got wounded. Instead, Gaviel and Gargatyl shared a glance, and suddenly exchanged arms.

"Careful, Gaviel!"

"Yeah! You, too!"

Their weapons dissolved into particles of light that reformed in the other's hand, burning brighter. Gaviel grasped and spun the crystalline staff, cutting at Ero even as her aura rushed to replace Gargatyl's. In her impatience, the weapon backfired on her, making her scream as she dropped it and cradled her burned palms.

"Oh, no! Gav!" Gargatyl doubled back to her side. "Didn't I just warn you not to get too hasty? Our weapons are full up to the brim with our own marks right now. Not to mention we're in these human bodies. Give it a second to restructure. We've been fighting longer and harder than I thought. Here. There's no need to rush and hurt yourself. We'll deal with these punks soon enough."

Gaviel growled again, accepting healing energy from him. None of the wounds on the corpse she wore faded as she healed. "That's just it. We should be done with them already. Both of them. Why the hell haven't we been able to overpower them yet? In fact, we're getting shoved into a corner here."

"Yeah, no need to state the obvious. I wasn't really expecting the devil to create a familiar while we were fighting Ero earlier. Come on, let's get you up. Just take your own sword. We don't need to switch anything up for these goons. Look, you're barely even worn." Gargatyl offered a weak smile that immediately belied his promises.

Ero drifted over shoulder to shoulder with Sir, halberd in hand. His armor didn't made a sound. "So what do you think, Sir? Do you still think we're alike?" he asked, watching the Archangels closely. *We're alike enough to speak in each other's minds. Do you think we're alike enough to use the same schools of power?*

Sir bristled. "Not that much."

Ero laughed a little bit and slowly turned to face Sir, then stabbed his halberd into the ground to restore it with more power and light. Sir squinted against it.

"I came back because I don't want to lose you," Ero finally said, shrugging. "I had to come back. I already knew it wouldn't make anything perfect, or even better. But if I let them take you..."

Sir raised his chin. "Then you can't bring me in yourself."

Ero pressed his lips together.

Even now, Sir could find it in himself to masticate another uncomfortable truth into an ugly lie.

He had to see past the black and white of it, didn't he?

A barrage of intense blasts suddenly slammed against Ero's barrier, and Sir sped off to deflect the rest while Ero repaired his shield. They returned their focus to the fight for a while before Ero called out again.

You're not wrong. I have to be the one to arrest you. But there's more to it than that, and you know it. I know you do.

The fuck I'm s'posed to know, Angel? Sir bit back. *You still gonna try to arrest me, it's just that you feel bad 'bout it now? 'Cause you love me? Is that it?*

I told you, I'm always gonna love you. That's never gonna change for me, said Ero.

"Then tell me why!" Sir jammed his blade into Gargatyl's chest, and plunged it in deep a few more times for good measure before he pointed the gory dagger right at Ero. "That dog don't goddamn hunt."

Gaviel roared as she rushed to recover the body Gargatyl had been possessing. It flopped in her grasp. "Nooo! You god-forsaken piece of shit worthless ass devil!"

Sir was forced back by a shock from her aura. Ero teleported across the field to catch him.

"Sit this out," Ero said, clutching his weight close for the first time in forever. "Trust me, Sir. I'll be right back."

Sir leaned against a nearby tree with a glare as shady as the leaves above. At least he'd put his bloody dagger away.

Ero took it as his answer and snuck a kiss before he left to deal with Gaviel.

She spit a couple more curses at him when she couldn't get Gargatyl to revive in the cold body he once occupied. Ero spread his wings to their full width and drove the shining tip of his halberd through her midsection.

"Ha... you fucking... Angel... Not... bad..." she muttered as a mix of blood and aura bubbled out of her mouth. Finally, the body went limp.

The woods were silent for about a second. The trees shifted silently. They were surrounded by people, but not one of them issued even a breath. Corpse silence.

"Well?" Sir said.

Ero turned slowly. Sir really did look like he belonged wherever he stood, under the loom of the black willows, or next to ocean shore. His pale eyes almost gleamed in the shade.

"Well what?" Ero asked.

"Don't shit change. Already told you once, I refuse. What else's left after that? Want me to hack up your spleen?" Sir said.

Ero folded his wings demurely behind him. If Sir really thought he could get away with rejecting Ero now, he had another thing coming. It was far too late for talk like that.

"What's left, huh? If you insist on refusing to Rise, what's left is a program running in your body that will force seal you, over and over, again and again, until you aren't able to see, think, breathe, sense, or feel anything. I know because I'm the one who installed it in you. It's a copy of my own. I think it's the other reason you can use that oculomancy of yours so well."

Sir's face went blank. "What the fuck? You mean... my... mark?"

Ero shook his head. "Not your mark. But similar in that it's another connection to your mastery—a conduit that grants you access to all powers beyond the standard Right or Left Hands. It's called the eclipse matrix. It's ancient ghost tech developed in the highest heaven during the Great War, after the first angels to become devils Fell for their pride. If you think me force sealing you once was unpleasant, just wait until your eclipse matrix senses an irreparable shear in the balance of your mastery. It can take a lot, because it was designed to, but it's not limitless. You'll succumb sooner or later if you keep pushing it."

As Ero talked, Sir stood there staring into his eyes, just doing what he did best, and sussing out the truth. Ero couldn't believe he never realized what Sir was doing before today. It was just so strange—almost impossible—for a devil to use Right Hand mastery. Then again, Sir was nothing if not strange-almost-impossible from the outset.

"Huh," he finally said. "So it's useless for me to resist now. That's what it boils down to?"

Ero sighed a bit, pain as heavy in his voice as it was in his heart. "I wouldn't say it's useless to resist, but it's not like I think you'll get very far if you do, either. I'm sorry, Sir. I didn't think I'd ever need to tell you something like this. I didn't think it'd be an issue. If I did my job right, it wouldn't. *Damn it.*"

"S'enough, Angel," Sir said, resigned. "Not fixin' to happen. Think you know that. You known a while. S'too late to Rise." His shoulders slumped, his voice flattened as he spoke, but behind his pale eyes, something flickered—a faint, stubborn ember.

"That's right." Gaviel landed at the speed of sound, half a second after they heard her voice. "It is too late for you."

Chapter 18

ERO

RIGHT AWAY, ERO RE-ENERGIZED his armor and spread his wings threateningly. Sir recoiled away from him, the sound of cicada wings rapidly rising for a moment.

Another second later, Gargatyl descended, too, dropping right next to Gaviel.

They had regained their original bodies from whatever dimension Ero had thrown them to earlier. After looking at their eyes through the skulls of dead humans, Ero was bizarrely relieved to see their Knights-of-Heaven armor. He would never dream of possessing someone—even a corpse—in order to win a fight.

Seeing the Archangels back in their full glory should've been terrifying, but all Ero felt was exhaustion. And then there was Sir, standing tall like he'd been born to outmatch them. His potential had outpaced even Ero's wildest expectations. They were so ready. If only they got the chance to prove it.

"Y'all are persistent," he said, halberd gleaming in his hand.

Gaviel lifted her chin. Her eyes flashed as though she was too proud to spit out her next words. "The same could be said of you two."

"Fuck're y'all doin' here?" Sir asked, low and flat.

"We have nothing to say to you! Damn you," Gargatyl said.

Ero would've expected Sir to be rearing up for another round, but he was studying the Archangels closely. Ero did the same. There was something different about them now than the last time he'd seen them in their true forms. A touch less threatening, maybe. Ero couldn't tell just yet.

"Don't take it personally, Gar. He clearly has no idea who he's been dealing with, or else he would've made like a good devil and accepted the gift that was given to him days ago. As for you, Ero," Gaviel said, eyeing him hard, "I came because I have a proposal."

Sir straightened out his shoulders and waited. Ero arched his eyebrow.

"That's curious. Did you get new orders while you were away, by any chance? Did Tariel say you can finally piss off? Or maybe y'all realized I might actually be stronger than you despite that I'm just an Angel."

Neither of the Archangels had an answer to that. Ero was satisfied to take that as their effective admission to defeat, but Sir had other plans. He quickly called up a force seal—succinct, vicious, impossible—and anchored the Archangels to the ground in front of them.

"Now, stay," he said, his voice rough, and spat in the dirt as though dismissing the enormity of what he'd just done.

Ero stumbled back, his breath caught somewhere between a gasp and a shout. "Sir?!"

His eyes darted to the two Archangels—Gargatyl's shoulders straining under invisible weight, Gaviel rigid and seething, and the glow of their power flickering like a flame in a windstorm.

"How did you manage to force seal a pair of Archangels?"

Gargatyl tried to break free, but he only broke out in a beaded sweat. "Goddamnit, Gav, that's why I said this would never work. He's too far fucking gone."

"Just shut up!" Gaviel concentrated on Ero, her nostrils flared. "Angel, this is your last chance. We're not the rogues here, you are. If you just do your damn job, everything else can be forgiven. You know he can't hold us forever, even in our current state."

Ero's gaze flicked to Sir again, searching him for any clues—any cracks in the facade of certainty. True enough, the Archangels wouldn't remain bound long. Their auras still roiled and flexed, seething beneath the invisible cage Sir had thrown over them.

But as a threat... they had all but passed the torch right back to Ero.

They didn't have to chase Sir anymore. If they weren't fit for the job, the perfect angel was standing right there.

It was amazing that they could expect Ero to fall in line after everything that had happened—and they were right.

"I..."

Ero swallowed hard, his pulse pounding as the weight of expectation settled on his shoulders. But even as Gaviel's words hissed in his ears, his mind refused to let go of the scene before him—the near-impossible made real.

Sir, standing there like a thundercloud, his power still hanging in the air. He had managed to force seal *two Archangels*.

How the hell had he done it?

Somehow, the best Ero could come up with was "I don't know what you mean."

The Archangels erupted.

"Oh, for the love of—!"

"God, give me strength—"

But neither of them got the chance to finish before Sir took a step forward.

"C'mon. Let's go," he said simply.

The sun was starting to fall, and the dull shine of twilight made his shape that much eerier. He was covered in the disappearing blood, guts, and bones of the Archangels and Texas State Troopers. Ero shuddered. It was a sight from both his best and worst dreams.

"I don't think I can fight you, Sir. We don't have to listen to them."

"Yes, you do. Yes, you can." He leveled Ero with a steel glare. His voice was calm, but his power raged in the air around him, a storm barely held in check. Ero couldn't tell if he was witnessing a defense or a declaration of war—couldn't tell, either, if there was a difference anymore. "You will. Else the Archangels'll do it for you. Day ends one way or another. Just fight me, Angel."

Only a few days ago, these words would've made Ero smirk and throw his hair nonchalantly over his shoulder. *Sure, let's do it. Yes, yes, yes.*

Now, he was cold down to his bones, the tissues and cartilage in his throat icing out his withered protest.

They tread through the woods, leaf litter rustling beneath their feet, the echoes of their recent clash lingering in the air like a charged current. They had been here before, too—so many times that it was almost cozy, familiar. If he closed his eyes, Ero could imagine that he was just teaching Sir another principle of mastery, or the world, or reality. There was no way this could all be real. He still saw a way out. Somehow. If *he* wasn't enough, there had to be *something* Sir wanted from the Rise.

Although, for the first time, Ero bit his lip as he considered what Sir had said earlier. What if they met in the middle? It wasn't as though Sir was asking him to plunge to the deepest, darkest corner of hell, or anything. If they stayed, though—if they made this place a home—they would be hunted by everyone. The angels would never let them rest. The humans of the world would stay on top of them, too. Who even knew what the devils would do if they ever found out about Sir? Every day would be a waking nightmare.

The tension in the air was thick. Ero almost choked on the unease hanging around them like an invisible fog.

"Look, Sir," he began, attempting a last line of communication.

"No," Sir said, quick and cold, with a rising scowl. "We done talked about it as much as we possibly could. I am not Risin'. I refuse to be an angel. So let's just do what we should, now. No one to interfere. Just you and me, sugar."

Slowly, he shifted into a battle stance right in the middle of a clearing between the sea of swaying, paper-bark sycamores.

Ero subtly reinforced his armor. It felt too heavy, too hot, too tight. "I hope you know what you're doing, Sir. I won't be able to take it easy on you if you're serious."

Sir didn't respond. As usual.

Force seals had taken care of him pretty effectively in the past. No matter how strong or sinister he'd become, Sir could still be restrained. He was still subject to authority. He could force seal the Archangels, fine. It didn't cost him *nothing*. Ero was sure that with a clear enough shot, if he landed the right one, he could be done with all of this mess as soon as possible. He'd arrest Sir and move on, whatever that looked like. He couldn't exactly afford to think ahead any further. Sir wasn't giving him a choice. It wasn't as though he had much of one to begin with, either. This was, somehow, always where he knew he'd end up.

They started out at that clearing in the woods, the wind cooling his feverish skin, and facing off on equal ground. Sir vanished first.

Ero searched the trees and palmed a handful of dense half-formed shapelessness that barely even manifested at all. His intent was still too fuzzy to generate a real force seal yet.

"C'mon, Angel! Don't start borin' me now," Sir called out. His silhouette flickered through the leaves, and he sent a flurry of strikes down.

Ero stumbled out of the way and sent up his own attack in the same breath. As he rolled, his wings spread out and lifted him into the canopy where Sir had been hiding.

Except... there was no Sir. Only blood that dripped on crackling leaves a few feet away.

Ero aimed at it, further into the canopy, but he still couldn't get himself to actually form and activate anything he recognized. Why couldn't he get any of his mastery to fully bloom? He slowed to a standstill, concentrating. It was almost impossible with Sir's words echoing in his head, pulling at every thread of doubt he'd tried so hard to bury.

And then he felt something brush his cheek. Ero dove through sidelining trees before the aftershock could set in. Behind him, the ground roared and imploded and sent thousands of shredded leaves up into the understory as Sir's attack lomped into it. It was pure assaultive energy, sharp as a dagger, a weapon unto itself. He didn't recognize it, either.

If he couldn't analyze, he needed a different advantage. Ero rose up to clear the trees and scan the earth below. He fired a few random force seals into the sycamores, relieved when the last ones finally took on proper form.

Sir was right. Ero could fight him.

Suddenly, he appeared, as if invoked—a foot ahead, all dilated pupils in his freakish eyes, with fangs bared. Ero braced himself. Sir ran into him in midair and trapped Ero's arms by his sides before biting into his shoulder.

Ero groaned in pain. It was so dizzying and familiar that he hardly realized they were hurtling back to the ground.

"Shit...!"

Sir threw his weight aside at the last moment, powerdriving Ero into the dirt. Ero's eclipse matrix pulled snug around him just before he cratered like a comet.

Debris and dust scattered in every direction. Ero's crater was deep and jagged, glowing faintly from the intense energy of his impact. He flexed his neck until it cracked, twice, then did a quick self-survey. A shockwave of force had pushed back any nearby trees. Somehow, only a few of the closest ones smoldered or were splintered, despite the air thick with damp earth and ozone.

Ero was kidding himself if he thought Sir was taking this as seriously as he claimed to. He'd spared the Texas live oaks.

"What the fuck," Ero hissed absently. He shook out a shiver.

He was still patching up his shoulders when Sir's voice struck out from faraway. "Well, what you holdin' back for? If you meant everything that you said, then you'd fight me like you mean it."

"Just shut up! You have no idea what you're talking about," Ero said, firing back randomly. None hit.

He took a measured breath then and let go of some caution. The barrier around him surged, amplifying the intensity of their clash. The woods responded, half-burned and twisted branches swaying with a whirlwind energy. The fabric of reality seemed to warp as the power unleashed in their battle reverberated through the humid air.

Sir finally showed his face, appearing from the shadows of leaves with a macabre smirk. "See your head's in the game now."

Ero's only response was a wave of energy, an unspoken acknowledgement the gloves were off. Their mastery intertwined in a collision of bluish shadows.

"Good," Sir said.

His strikes immediately became more direct, fueled by a determination to break through Ero's defenses, but Ero met every single one. There were a few he had to take on the nose. He quickly lost the luxury of taking it easy once Sir's momentum picked up. But he could do this. He was built for it.

And then Inez leapt up from behind with a low growl.

She had her claws extended and fangs ready—the same lunging move that Ero had interrupted before when she had been aiming for Gargatyl's wings.

"Inez?!" He turned and found her in an instant. Her eyes, gleaming with intelligence and determination, locked onto Ero, signaling her warning a second before her small, vicious jaws clamped shut.

Ero hesitated, momentarily taken aback by the intensity of Inez's ferociousness.

Then her claws raked across his neck and shoulders, leaving deep gouges in the armor of his wing joints. Ero recoiled, taken aback by the attack and momentarily stunned by the unexpected impact.

"Not my wings!" he roared. Almost out of instinct, he lashed out blindly, and his halberd stabbed through the air—straight toward Inez.

Time seemed to slow as the axe-head connected, the force of the blow sending her crumpling to the ground. Blood stained the woodland floor as Ero froze, and horror dawned in his eyes.

What had he done?

"Inez..." His voice was a broken whisper, the reality of the situation sinking in. Her clever eyes were shut tight.

Sir's reaction was instant and savage. A roar tore from his throat as he delivered a brutal kick to Ero's chest, sending him crashing into a nearby tree. "Motherfucker!"

"Wait, Sir! Stop!"

"Sure, like you did!"

Before Ero could say anything else, Sir returned to pin him in place, hand closed around the base of one of his wings. With a sickening crack, he twisted and pulled, tearing the armor from the socket joints. The rest of the uniform dissolved away, too. Ero's scream of agony split the air, a sound that echoed with the pain like being exposed down to his bare bones.

Without armor, his golden wings were soaked in blood. Sir stopped with his hand poised to rip the wing right off Ero's body, but a pool of red dripped from the armor on the ground just at his feet. He breathed quick, and deep, their bodies pressed so close together that Ero could feel the thunderous beat of his heart. His nose, lips, and temple leaked dark blood, too.

"Sir," Ero said sternly, "I'm sorry about Inez. But she will live because you damned her to live. If you rip my wings off, I won't. Please..."

He fell to his knees, clutching at the ruddy feathers that slumped along the ground on either side of him.

"I never wanted to fight you in the first place. I thought I could bring myself to do what I should've done all along, but I mean it when I say I can't. I love the person I was made for, and that's you. You can't make me hate you, and you can't make me kill you. But if all of that's really no problem for you, then I deserve whatever happens to me because it means I haven't done anything right. If that's really what you want to do, then do it. Because I'm not fighting anymore. It's not worth it. *I refuse.*"

Chapter 19

SIR

"I REFUSE" WAS S'POSED to be Sir's line. Ero'd been the one houndin' him to do this, do that, jump high, lay low, and everything in between. What the fuck Ero think he was refusin'?

"Can't make you hate me," Sir said slowly, "but you can make me love you? That it?"

"You never have to love me," Ero barely managed to get out.

"And yet!" Sir snapped. "Inez—sleep."

Even without turnin' to face her, Inez obeyed straight away. She dozed right off. He couldn't stand the feelin' of her bleedin' out over his shoulder while he was dealin' with Ero—also bleedin' out—right in front of him. Now, Inez could focus on healin', and Sir could focus on Ero.

Fuck. What was Sir even s'posed to do with Ero now?

He wasn't strong enough to fight forever, and if the only way to stop Ero was to kill him, it was still all up to Ero in the end. Sir probably could kill Ero, if Ero didn't resist—or couldn't resist, what with his shattered wings—but it'd be so fuckin' risky to hinge all that on a maybe. What would Sir even do if he managed to take Ero out anyway? He'd still have to finish off those two Archangels over there and who knew how many others after that. It'd never end. He'd end up butchered by Ero's family.

"Angel," he said, fallin' to kneel beside Ero. He fought to keep his face straight. "Look me in the eye and tell me you really think I could live up to your 'simple' standards. 'Don't prey, don't lie,' but s'what I do best, sugar. Y'know what you signin' up for, and you said yourself you could love anyone. You'd be better off if it wasn't me. I'ma keep on as I am, no matter where I am, and if you stay with me, there's only gonna be more preyin' and lyin'. Tell me you can take that."

"*Yes!*" Ero shook his head suddenly, as if stabbed by a painful reminder. "You don't believe it, but *yes*. You just can't keep doing everything your own way. We've already tried, time and again, and look at where that's gotten us. Yes, Sir. I can take it. I see the pieces of you, even the ones you've buried. Maybe it's selfish of me, but I *want* you to Rise. *I* think you deserve it. If I—if I let you break my wing—"

"Shut up," Sir said, cold and even, like snow-covered stone. He'd had just 'bout enough of Ero's self-effacin' bullshit. "You goddamned martyr. Wouldn't you Fall? Isn't that what you just said? Why d'you give yourself away like that? Someone like me, I'll take it."

"I was—" Ero started.

"Made for you," Sir finished.

Should've known better.

They only had each other to blame: a devil with a desire for angels' blood and an angel with a thirst for devils' desire.

Sir still couldn't help blamin' these goddamned motherfuckin' angels that Ero called "home," too, though. He couldn't imagine callin' not a one of them kin, but regardless of what Sir did, Ero'd have to return to all of them. It was either gonna be with Sir in tow or not—either with Sir's help or without it. The closest that Sir'd ever get to the freedom that he chased was gonna be in marryin' his angel and doin' whatever he wanted with him.

"Wasn't a choice from the start, was it?" Sir picked Ero's hand up off the ground and set his thumb against the artery there. Pressed hard until a bullet of blood appeared. "I'm just s'posed to fall in love with you, smile, and say yes, like you do."

Ero kept his eyes hid behind the bloody curls of his hair. "I'm not saying I think it's easy for you, but at this point, it's probably the thing you need most."

"Yeah, those angels you work for made sure of that, didn't they? Makin' me marry you, and then sittin' me with that goddamned eclipse matrix waitin' to force seal me to high heaven," Sir snapped again. He sighed and sat back as he tried to collect himself. Few things bothered him more than how easy he lost his temper with Ero—how easy he could lash out, like his wings had when he'd killed Alexander.

And that was the crux of the matter, wasn't it. Sir lived off blood and bones; killin' completed him. But here he had this unkillable angel who gave him all that and more. He had no need to take Ero's head or finish rippin' off his wings. All bein' equal, no, it wouldn't be easy to Rise and dedicate himself to a life that sounded like the exact opposite of everything he'd ever known. At the same time, though, he'd tried runnin' from it, tried fightin' it, tried fakin' it, tried everything outside acceptin' it. Maybe, for however long it lasted, it was worth it to distrust his instincts for once.

To obey, like an angel.

"God-motherfuckin'-damnit," he seethed. "You want the rust and dust I call a life, you can take it, but don't you run away later once you realize it ain't for shit."

"I won't." So sure. Always so sure. The red of Ero's eyes peeked out from under his hair. "I've always known who I was marrying. And I know you. I will never run from you."

All Sir's resolve crumbled any time Ero tried to drag the commitment out of him like this. Under other circumstances—literally *any* other circumstances—Sir could see himself fallin' for Ero easily, pushin' him 'round 'til he cried just for fun, and givin' in to those jewel-toned eyes every day. Thing was, Sir resented authorities that got in the way of the one thing he wanted in this world: to eat. When he ate, he was strong. When he ate, he rid himself of ignorance. When he ate, it was the only time he knew who he was. Ero'd never be enough to replace that. No one could. *Nothin'* could. Sir was a black hole.

Wasn't a heaven real or false that'd take him for love alone, not even his own.

"You don't run."

"Damn skippy. I chase," Ero started again, sluggishly foldin' out his defeated kneel to crawl closer. With his blood-soaked wings trailin' behind him like broken limbs, he was the picture of pain and persistence, a devoted horror show, that Sir could look at like this forever. "I chase you, and chase you, and chase you, until you can't run away from me anymore."

Sir had to physically swallow down the urge to do somethin' horrible. "No shit. S'what pisses me off 'bout you. I'm all yours," he said, eyebrow lifted.

That same, deranged smile from the first day they met resurfaced on Ero's face. This time, it was covered in blood. What a magnificent monster in Sir's lap.

"And I'm yours," Ero said, "but I won't let you do what you want forever. No one will. You were never meant to be here in the first place—you just don't remember where you're *supposed* to be. You're meant to grow, and change, and find yourself, and yes, love, if you want to. And I want to do them with you, even though you piss me off, too. I'll make it all worth your while. It'll be my lifelong challenge—and pleasure—even if I have to fight you every step of the way. Because, Sir, if you're not gonna kill me, then..." Still with that wide, wild smile, Ero tilted a small kiss onto the end of Sir's nose, and whispered, "You're coming home with me."

When all spelled out like that, it set Sir's teeth on edge. He latched onto Ero's hair by the root and yanked to expose his throat. Elsewise, Sir'd probably give in to the urge to knock Ero right onto his injured wings. The smell of blood saturated his senses. He could barely hold still anymore. "This works," he said, "I'ma need a word with the angels who made you. They sent you to slaughter."

Ero's voice got suspiciously quiet. "If you're so sure you won't Rise, then that won't be a problem, anyway."

"Shut up, now, Angel," Sir said and flashed his canines. "You don't deserve me. Remember that."

But then, who did? No devil. No angel. No one. Least of all, him.

"Yes, I do." Ero's breath hitched as Sir's hand traced over the line of his waist, fingers brushin' the bruised skin.

Sir's touch was deliberate, tracin' up toward Ero's chest, and pushin' his clothes out the way at the same time. He had no clue if it was plain hunger, vicious desperation, or somethin' else altogether, but he needed Ero's full attention right now. The way that Ero stayed on his mind, he wanted to engrave himself across Ero's heart, too; in revenge. He eyed the center of warmth and blood under Ero's skin.

Ero's breath caught again when he noticed. His heart beat hard beneath Sir's palm.

"Breathe deep," Sir said, softer than he'd ever spoken to anyone. "Need your blood a last time."

He needed to eat even less than when he took Ero's spleen, but if they were gonna have a hope in hell of Risin' together, Sir did need to eat.

Ero met his gaze, dark and intense, and nodded once. "Then you Rise."

Sir ain't have a choice anymore—if he ever did.

"Yeah," he said.

He leaned in. His lips brushed against Ero's skin, trailin' down to the hollow of his throat, then lower down 'til Ero's breath started comin' in shorter, shallow gasps. His heart pounded so loud—like a livin' thing screamin' for help. Like the clickin' cicadas buzzin' in the oak trees. Sir kissed Ero's chest as if to calm it down. He had a lot to thank this stubborn, frustratin' heart for. More than he'd probably ever wanna say. Maybe that's all that love was. Maybe that's all that angels lived for. The warmth of Ero's skin under his lips was a lifeline, groundin' Sir in moments of chaos. His thoughts were always tangled with the intensity of their connection. Maybe it was only ever these simple, raw connections that give meanin' to anything. Maybe that was it. The world outside seemed so vague and faraway, cicada cries reduced to a lil hum as he focused on the warmth of Ero's skin and the steady rhythm of his heartbeat. If this was all there ever was, if this fleetin' peace was all they'd ever manage to grab hold of...

Sir shifted his mouth, exposin' his teeth, and sank them right into Ero's heart. Quick, but quiet.

Ero's body arched into him, a sharp gasp rushin' past his lips as Sir drank straight from his heart. The taste of Ero's incredible blood always washed Sir's senses, his favorite reality and the best high. He couldn't stop himself from takin' more, drawin' deeper, 'til Ero's strength flamed out, and they started fallin' together.

Sir never let go even as his eyes snapped open. He snuck his arms under Ero's back and crushed him close to shield his ruined wings. Ero's body relaxed then, infusin' Sir with a raw power that was as intoxicatin' as it was overwhelmin'. As he drank, the rush of energy poured into Sir like a cascadin' waterfall or a pedestal of power that made him feel alive for the first time, every single time.

Finally, it was done. Sir shifted away, his head spinnin' from the effort. Ero laid under him, his breathin' unsteady but strong, and Sir finally folded, really folded, layin' his head on Ero's chest. From where he lay, he spotted Inez in the shade of some southern magnolias, sprinkled with their fat white flowers—not a speck of blood in sight anymore.

She was okay.

Ero was okay.

The rest would Rise with them. A crow gently landed at Sir's side. Watchful while he surrendered.

It was quiet for a long while before he heard it again—that faint, warm voice, sayin', *Wake up*.

And a glarin' red ring of light that, just like every time before, peered through the darkness to reach him.

For a long time, that's all there was.

In the quiet between his thoughts, Sir could still feel that same thread pullin', hangin' on like it didn't know how to let go. Ero's presence—even if only barely—tugged at him from the edges of his mind.

Sir... can you still hear me? Wake up.

It wasn't loud as before. It slipped in soft, like a whisper at the back of his head. Sir didn't answer right away, but the bond between them still hummed, steady as ever.

Yeah, Angel. Hear you. His thoughts moved slow, like they were sloggin' through syrup. *Them Archangels—*

They're not going anywhere, Ero's voice floated back, calm as ever, like he wasn't rattled at all. *Gargatyl's seeing about my wings. He has experience with the effects of your— You know what? Don't worry about all that, Sir. Just rest for now. I've got you.*

Ugh, them words just reeked of trust. They weighed heavy on
Sir, sittin' awkward in his head, too thick, too full. He wasn't built
for this surrender. But Ero was close, holdin' on in ways no one
else ever had or even could. His perfect, awful angel.

Rest...

Sir pressed the thought back, solid like a rock. Just rest.

It was short, that exchange, quiet like it didn't need no more
than what it was. Ero's presence stuck 'round a lil longer, fadin'
slow but stayin' right there in the back of Sir's mind. Even after
it dimmed, Sir could still feel him. Always could. Light from a
sun-like star in the sky.

———————————

Inez licked him awake right before nightfall. The soft, wet nudge
of her tongue on his face pulled Sir out the depths of his coma. The
master bedroom he sat in was dim, the shadows lengthenin' as dusk
started settlin' over the Alexander house. He recognized the place
instantly, even without the large bed that dominated the middle
of the room, the heavy, dusty drapes that never let in any natural
light, and the crooked stacks of broken trinkets that added to the
oppressive atmosphere always hangin' 'round in here. He'd never
forget how this room used to look. He'd shared it with Alexander
for the better part of a decade. He never wanted to sleep here ever
again.

Sir sat up to find himself fresh and clean. All the mess from yes-
terday'd been meticulously dealt with—the blood, the debris, and
the lingerin' traces of their confrontation were all gone. Must've

been Ero. That guy'd do anything to get Sir into heaven. Or maybe he just hadn't wanted to leave Sir alone with the Archangels.

That was probably it—'cause Ero suddenly appeared from the other side of the door like a phantom, his big, golden smile pasted perfectly in place. He looked freshly cleaned up from their earlier battle, too—his wings wrapped tight in bandages, his blood-streaked hair now back to its rose gold glory, and his clothes free of the grime and blood that'd marred them both. Despite the toll of the battle, he radiated a relaxed confidence as he grinned at Sir in greetin'.

"Hey, there, cowboy," Ero said, dazzlin'.

Sir almost shivered. Every time Ero reminded him that he'd let the angel this far under his skin, it'd probably always make him shiver. On the off chance he managed to Rise, he had no clue how he was gonna survive the days ahead.

Inez sat down at Sir's side as he sat up, full of tender touches. He scooped her up and carried her from the floor.

"Are you ready to go?" Ero asked smoothly. His grin dimmed to a smirk as he watched Inez's face for a bit. She blinked at him.

Sir got to his feet. He didn't know what to say. Never did, maybe never would. Ero really did deserve so much better than both the angels and the devils'd given him.

"C'mere first," Sir said before he knew it. He watched himself stretch a hand out for Ero and tuck him in tight against his chest. The whole scene played out as if he was standin' a few inches to the left of it. It wasn't 'til Ero roped both arms 'round Sir, too—takin' just as much as he gave—that Sir snapped back to himself. He hugged Ero closer. Squeezed him.

Like a light summer shower, Ero broke into laughter right next to Sir's ear. "I'm here, I'm here," he said. "I'm not going anywhere, Sir. You couldn't get rid of me no matter how hard you tried. Now come on. Gaviel and Gargatyl are waiting on us downstairs."

The Archangels. Always watchin'. Always waitin'. Ero might've called them allies, but Sir saw them for what they were—executioners in disguise.

Just beyond the walls of the room, he sensed them standin' stock-still in the livin' room below. Earlier, they'd returned subdued to force Ero's hand after losin' possession of the State Troopers, and now, here everyone was, all the pieces in place. Sir was definitely gonna be keepin' a close eye on them from here on out.

"Seriously, Sir," Ero went on when Sir refused to release him. He stroked his fingers along the side of Sir's face 'til he could cup Sir's jaw in his hand. "They won't wait too long."

As always, nothin' definitive 'bout Ero's aura, tone, or demeanor changed, but Sir knew better than to push it. Elsewise, he'd end up in the same horribly blood-stained nightmare he'd just barely escaped.

"How your wings, Angel?" he asked as he suddenly remembered. He'd almost ripped them clean off, goddamn.

Inez seemed to take that as her cue to trot on downstairs. Sir almost went and snatched her back, the lil coward. Ero dropped his hand, fixed his gaze on her 'til she disappeared 'round the corner, but didn't seem to wanna answer.

Sir bit his lip, worried it, his fingers findin' the scars that stretched across Ero's back with eerie ease. Angry raised scars that hadn't faded. Before he could open his mouth 'bout it, Ero shrunk away and stopped him.

"It's fine. I married a devil. I can take it."

Finally, Sir let out a long sigh and turned to brush his lips against Ero's cheek before lettin' go. "Let's hop to."

Ero covered his face with his hand while they left the room and met the Archangels downstairs. He just tipped his head in a lil nod toward them and started leadin' the way outside. Both the Archangels followed without sayin' squat. It was a different kinda silence from before, though, when it'd been remonstrative and boisterous. Now, they seemed still, too; composed, collected, and pointed in their withdrawal from Sir and Ero. If this was a preview of the life he was fixin' to fall into...

Houston stretched across the horizon outside. At dusk, the Alexander house loomed behind Sir like a relic caught between worlds. The red sun draped the place in a somber, dark gold hue, makin' it glow as it cast long shadows across the tangled vines in the yard. Tall, leanin' sweetgum and bald cypress trees 'round the perimeter seemed to sigh as the day dimmed, and the air grew thick with the scent of the cool, ethereal light that hung just outta reach of dusk. They walked a good, long while north-northeast, with Ero up front and Sir at the six. Inez kept watch over Gaviel and Gargatyl without a single complaint the whole while. Sir'd have to do somethin' nice for her later.

They crossed Houston in moments. City lights flickered in the haze of the downtown skyline wrapped in towerin' transparent wood and green canopies. In a breath, they were gone. Ghosts in the shrinkin' daylight. They passed through as if the city couldn't hold them, untouched by the urban sprawl, followin' the contours of the woods and bayous. The roar of life faded as they left it behind, the air turnin' quiet.

After another moment, Lake Houston came into view—vast, dark, and fed by the far-reachin' San Jacinto nearby. They followed it silently, dodgin' well-maintained park spaces for quieter corners hidden by the kudzu. A runnin' mumble issued from the current of the water, and as they came up on the murky edges of the river, Sir couldn't help but sense a crack in his post-coma calm. The blue hour set jewels atop every lil ripple. He followed Ero down the verdant path that meandered toward the lakeshore with the distant hum of cicadas blendin' into the soft rustlin' of the tall grass and water oaks. The smell of damp earth, bluebonnets, and spider lilies stained the humid air.

Ero beckoned Sir up from the back. "In you go. Last step before you Rise."

With a mischievous glint, Sir met him. "Come on with me, Angel."

Ero hesitated, flickin' a glance toward the Archangels a few feet away, then nodded. "Why not? It'll probably be a while before we get a chance to relax once we're home."

A new home. Sir tried not to think 'bout it too hard. It seemed like they still had such a long way to go before that'd ever be true.

He waded with Ero into the large, deep river. The embrace of the water felt like a cleansin' ritual in itself, a natural sanctuary that needed no recitations or incantation circles. It was a balm to his busy thoughts right now.

"Water represents life," Ero said, takin' Sir's hand and holdin' him close under the water. "In your case, it represents new life, sealed with a promise from your heart—your marriage into the divine. Here, hold onto my hand. I'll be with you every step of the way."

Sir didn't take those words lightly. He'd been convinced before that Ero was fakin' every line just to get what he wanted, but he knew better now. Even if Ero talked a big game, he always, always backed it up. Hat *and* cattle.

Sir kept their eyes locked and gripped Ero's hand hard; his wordless answer. For the first time, he felt the weight of his surrender. True surrender. The last piece of himself he'd kept untouched. But Ero's hand was steady, unshakin'. Sir wouldn't let go.

"Come on," Ero said, his grin wide and fearless, "we're going under. One, two."

As they submerged, soft drags washin' away the remnants of his worries, Sir's cracked calm reformed underwater. He'd lost fair and square. Least he could do was accept the consequences. And if the consequences were a lifetime or more of marriage to Ero... well, then... he could do a whole helluva lot worse.

Ero must've been thinkin' somethin' similar 'cause he wrapped his arm 'round Sir's back and pulled him into a soft kiss under the gentle waves. With their lips laced together, they let the moment stretch out for a bit, savorin' the quiet and the closeness without the worry of pryin' eyes.

Back on the surface, Sir wiped his face clean. "Please tell me that's it. No more fuckin' steps."

Ero glanced back at the Archangels who had the pissiest expressions on their faces. But he'd bought their patience with his damned loyalty—they'd watch without intereferin', so long as Ero stuck to it.

"Well, it's been witnessed that you made your vow. You promised yourself to me, and I promised myself to you. You're clear of all blood that's not mine. You're baptized. Now, you can Rise."

This was the hard part. Lettin' go of what came easy. What came natural. Tryin' to be good.

"G'luck, Angel," Sir said.

Ero broadcasted another insane grin. "Thanks, *husband*."

"Any day, now," Gaviel said, her tone damn near piti-ful—none of her usual bite. Must've killed her to break her silence.

Inez clicked her teeth at her, hackles raised.

Ero's eyes almost glowed with impatience. "It'd be my plea-sure. Sir?"

Preparin' for the final ritual, he retrieved a handful of herbs and oils from a random spot in the air. With deliberate care, he rubbed them all over Sir's hair, skin, and clothes, the mixture of scents and textures creatin' an aromatic veil that stuck to Sir like a new aura. Rosemary and frankincense. Basil, geranium, juniper. Lemongrass. Cedar. Rose, at the end. After he was done, they took another dunk to rinse all the herbs and oils away.

Sir climbed out and lit a smoke with a snap. The softpack Vincent left behind. "You not turnin' me into a sacrifice, too, are you?"

Ero chuckled, even as he concentrated on tracin' an intricate incantation circle onto the surface of the ground. The lines lit up stark white against the leaf litter. "Haha. There are no sacrifices here, Sir. Just preparations for what's to come. A lot's gone wrong since we met. I wanna foolproof this ritual as much as possible. The circle's to boost my intent. You'll stand in the middle to draw the focus to yourself." A beat. "Like you did with Inez. You know."

Yeah—Sir did know. He'd had to kill Inez and use that circle in order to bring her back to immortal life.

"That's kinda fucked up, by the way," Ero kept on. "I didn't expect you of all people to curse the princess like that. She wasn't dead or dying, and it's cruel to force the spirit from a host the way you did. She could've died. I'm surprised she didn't."

"Yeah, well, and now, she never will."

"Yes. You are right about that." Noddin' carefully, Ero straightened up, took Sir by the shoulders, and directed him to stand dead center of the incantation circle. "Now, pray," he said.

Sir smirked. "S'all you, Angel. My part's done, recall?"

Ero chuckled again, his tension easin' some. "Trust me, I don't need any more help from you. What do I always tell you about myself?"

"Made for this," Sir repeated the old reprise.

Silence fell, and their grins faded. They really only had Ero's determination to rely on from here on out. If he thought he could overcome all the malice and viciousness pumpin' through Sir's blood, they had to try. The angels'd carefully paved this path for them to trek and blocked off all possible exits. They'd made Ero for this.

"It's time to Rise, Sir. I hope you're ready, for real this time." Ero's eyes locked onto Sir's, an unspoken challenge and reassurance in his gaze. The same one that'd always been there.

Sir walked over, smoke still burnin' in hand. Ready as he'd ever be.

"Yes."

Glossary

Angel—*a divine ghost of the Empyrean realm.*

Aura—*a visible energy that fills and surrounds all living things. In someone who has harnessed and mastered their spirit, the aura is an extension of their mastery, offering protection, amplification, and a means of identification, or mark.*

Bridges of Chaos—*the interstitial dimension between realms, characterized by darkness, vertigo, and voidness. It is required traveling to traverse from one realm to another.*

Devil—*a demonic ghost of the Infernal realm.*

Eclipse matrix—*an ancient and powerful ethereal implant from the era of the Great Ghost War. It grants its bearer access to both the Left and Right Hands, allowing them to seamlessly wield the energies of the Empyrean and Infernal. Serves as a conduit for harmonizing and balancing the dual forces within the user, providing access to a unique fusion of abilities that transcend the conventional boundaries of angelic and devilish powers. A relic of a brutal conflict, it stands as a testament to the origins of these opposing forces, offering the potential for unparalleled strength in the user's mastery.*

Effigy of Evil—*the title given to Sir by the angels before his true name is known.*

Empyrean/Empyrium—*the state of, belonging to, or related to the Nine Spheres of Sanctuary.*

The End of the First World—*an event in the Endless Cycle that describes the destruction of the First World, or the first apocalypse. It was disrupted by an Angel who annihilated all other Angels.*

Endless Cycle—*refers to the recurring pattern wherein the First World became the present world through a series of destruction.*

Familiar—*the spiritually linked entity bound to a user of mastery, who usually provides assistance, companionship, guardianship, protection, and more to the master.*

Force seal—*a potent technique to arrest dangerous ghosts that encases the target in a metaphysical vice. A formidable enchantment capable of subduing even the most powerful ghosts by severing their connection to the fundamental forces that empower them. Can only be performed by angels with Right Hand mastery.*

Ghost—*an unliving entity, either human or non-human, which populates the material and immaterial realms. Angels, devils, monsters, etc. are non-human ghosts.*

Ghost Killer—*the moniker for Sir used by Texas State Troopers and other authorities who are tasked with his arrest.*

Great Ghost War—*the war in heaven that caused the first Angels to Fall.*

Infernal/Infernum—*the state of, belonging to, or related to the Nine Circles of Slaughter.*

The Last Angel—*the title given to Ero as the only Angel to exist since the End of the First World.*

Last evil of Lesser Earth—*the title given to Sir as the "Ghost Killer" known to kill humans indiscriminately.*

The Left Hand of Destruction—*the demonic mastery of devils which favors physical and elemental forces (i.e., pyrokinesis, sangromancy, etc.). This reflects their connection to the primal, darker aspects of existence.*

Lesser Earth—*the present-day world, 7138 CE, population 5 billion.*

Mark—*a symbol that shows up on ghosts who have harnessed and channeled their mastery to a significant degree. Serves as both a badge of their mastery's prowess and a representation of their unique abilities and affinities. Also acts as a conduit for the individual's mastery, helping them focus their abilities more effectively.*

Mastery—*the energetic life force, or spirit, harvested and fine-tuned to become an extension of an individual's consciousness. Naturally aligns with either the Right Hand (for angels) or the Left Hand (for devils), respectively.*

Nine Empyrean Spheres of Sanctuary—*the realm of divine ghosts.*

Nine Infernal Circles of Slaughter—*the realm of evil ghosts.*

Oculomancer—*a practitioner of oculomancy, the divination of information from others' eyes.*

Pyromancer—*a practitioner of pyromancy, or pyrokinesis, the control of fire and flame.*

The Right Hand of Protection—*the divine mastery of angels which leans towards manipulating energy with their thoughts (i.e., telekinesis, healing, etc.). This mental manipulation approach reflects their deepest desire for consensus, balance, and order.*

Sangromancer—*a practitioner of sangromancy, the divination of information from others' blood.*

Transmogrification—*the process by which a mortal being is transformed into an immortal familiar.*

Universe—*the human world, the material realm, used interchangeably.*

About the Author

T. Light Sylvan is a Houston native who has been captivating readers since 2012 with their thought-provoking speculative works. They now publish a variety of fiction under Alien/Robot Press which explores stories with themes of identity, self-discovery, and of course, love and hell. They are currently pursuing a degree in Creative Writing and Film Studies.

More Releases

Insubordinate: A Short Story of The Last Angel

*

The Devil's in Texas continues in *Gulf Coast Angels: Book 2 of The Last Angel* (coming 2026). Turn the page for a sneak peek at the synopsis.

Subscribe to the official Alien/Robot newsletter at tlightsylvan.substack.com.

For more information about *The Devil's in Texas* and other works from The Last Angel series, visit tlightsylvan.com.

Gulf Coast Angels

BOOK 2 OF THE LAST ANGEL

Ero Hartsend has failed.

The ritual that was supposed to transform Sir—earthbound devil and his new husband—into an angel has imploded, leaving Ero to pick up the pieces of everything he's ever known coming apart overnight.

Stripped bare by the torment from ruining the ritual and clinging to a second chance no one granted him, Ero struggles to regain the trust he's lost, especially Sir's and the angels back home.

His path forward couldn't be bleaker, and the weight of the expectations placed on him only deepens the self-doubt that botched his mission in the first place.

As Ero flails, trying to mend the rift between himself and his old home, he finds himself in the sights of a devil yet again. But this one has no love for him, like Sir. He is older, more powerful in stranger ways, and he does not travel alone.

Worst of all, he doesn't want anything to do with Ero.

No. The devils have been on the hunt—for Sir.

Ero once burned heaven to save Sir. He would do the same to hell in a heartbeat.

If only the angels would allow him.

Sneak Preview

Note: The following is an unedited excerpt from a rough draft of the upcoming novel. It is not final.

"Sir!"

Ero followed faint blood trails straight into a big billowing cloud of richly dark blood. Such blood could never belong to an angel.

Sir lay a few feet into the discolored currents, at the center. His wings were half-folded behind him in a relaxed cruciform, and his eyes were closed so he looked like he was coasting peacefully along the surface.

But they were way at the bottom of the San Jacinto. And he didn't respond to Ero at all.

Ero swam towards him, a mixture of relief and sorrow fighting in his veins as he reached his husband. He didn't even think about it, he just threw himself at Sir under the water.

I'm here. Sir, wake up. I'm here! *"I'm here! Wake up! Sir, please, you have to hear me!"*

They were both whisked away downstream by the current in a cloud of red. Ero hung on tight and spoke into Sir's endless hair. The burn in his throat and lungs barely even bothered him anymore. "Please wake up, Sir. I fucked up. I don't think I can fly us home. Come on."

He didn't think Sir actually heard him. He was choking on pointless tears.

But slowly, silently, one of Sir's hands shifted to fit around Ero's back.

Ero could've sobbed.

Just as he slipped away, they took off. The last thing he heard was the whoosh of wings and a cool, distant voice, saying, "I heard you. I'm here, Angel. I'm awake."

"You lose your memory or somethin', Angel?" Sir's head tilted aside a bit as he studied Ero's expression later.

"No, just... I've been racking my head since I woke up." Ero shut his eyes as if to hide the chaos inside. A tense, high tone cut through his concentration. He winced.

"You sure about that?"

"I can't seem to think straight. Sorry." He ran his hand into his hair then sank down into the blankets and sheets. "I failed the whole damn ritual. Isn't that just fantastic? You're still a devil, we're on *goddamned Echo Earth, and the Archangels that were watching us are dead—"*

Cutting him short, Sir reached over to reposition Ero across his lap. Ero's thick, curly hair fell back from his face as Sir tipped up his chin until they locked eyes.

"What d'you mean, dead?"

"I mean, I found them first before I found you, at the bottom of the river. There was so much blood in the water, I could taste it in the back of my throat. I was bleeding, too. So were you." It still didn't make sense. He wished he could forget the whole experience. What he wouldn't give to admit defeat already. The pain was a constant reminder that he'd failed his only purpose.

"Nightmare," Sir said.

Ero paused. "Nightmare." He'd suffered a Nightmare.

But that was impossible. He was The Last Angel. He was stronger than some lowlife Nightmare. No way could such a weak insentient monster force its way past his divine barriers.

"Either way, wasn't real, what you saw. Maybe the ritual did a number on your noggin, but the Archangels can't be dead. We'd be hunted if they was," Sir said seriously. "Let it go. I got you."

Just like that, for some reason, Ero actually felt at ease. Sir's power over him had grown so much while he wasn't paying attention. If it weren't for Sir, Ero had no idea where he'd be right now. He felt so secure in Sir's arms. And Sir was right about the Archangels. Probably.

About the Publisher

Alien/Robot Press is the brainchild of founder T. Light Sylvan's desire to create, discover, and publish meaningful, eclectic stories. It is a small independent publishing print that connects readers to unique and eerie poetry collections, short stories, novels, and more, by multifaceted authors with distinct creative visions from south Texas and beyond.

A SPECULATIVE LIBRARY